For every woman who is taking a second chance on herself.
You don't need permission to shine—but here it is anyway.

CHAPTER 1

My daddy always said he was keeping his mother's house in East Texas in case somebody in the family was ever "down and out." Though my family moved away from the town, Daddy wanted to keep that stake in Robin Creek. I always thought Uncle Sherman, with his gambling habit, or Cousin Gail, with her failed multilevel marketing schemes, would be the first one to desperately need a roof overhead after Daddy died two years ago.

But despite having checked off all the prescribed boxes for optimal success and respectability, turns out it was me who needed the house. Only I wouldn't exactly say I was down *or* out—more like moved-over and reset. And old, and single, and currently broke, but no one could have known about the broke part because I drove up that uneven driveway in my blue Mercedes sedan, rocks kicking up a plume of dust.

Not that it mattered.

Well, yes, it did.

I was sixty, recently divorced, old enough to earn full retirement from teaching but not old enough to withdraw the highest levels yet. By all accounts—and by *all*, I mean my daughter Terri's and my friend Dawn's accounts—I should have stayed in my thirty-year marriage to Eric.

"He's *not* terrible," Dawn had fussed. "Girl, you cryin' with a loaf of bread under your arms."

But now wasn't the time to worry about other people's opinions.

So there I was, pressing the silver button to park my car, boxes and laundry baskets filling every inch possible of the passenger's seat, back seat, and trunk. I'd driven all the way from Austin nonstop, a fact neither my bladder nor my knees appreciated.

My bones needed to unravel slowly from the four-hour drive, but the weight in my midsection said that the moment I stood up, I must beeline it to the bathroom to avoid an accident.

I hadn't had one yet. A blatant bladder malfunction, I mean. And God knows I didn't want my first memory back in town to be peeing on myself. In a little Texas town like Robin Creek, it wouldn't just be *my* memory—it would be *everyone's* memory. I'd already seen the living room curtains fluttering open as I drove down the street. People knew I was there. I could hear the gossip already.

"She did what?"

"Splatted a puddle, right there on the porch!"

"Are you sure?"

"Sure as I'm Black."

Keys in hand and a prayer on my lips, I speed-walked across the gray stepping stones, past the screen, and into the house, my hips rolling side to side, my pelvic muscles defying gravity. I swear, it was one fluid move from the driver's seat to the toilet seat. Thank goodness the layout of the left side of the house had remained as I remembered it. I didn't know what felt better: the whoosh of liquid leaving my system or the relief of making it to the bathroom in time. *Yes!*

You have to celebrate the little victories, you know.

Glancing around, I noticed subtle signs of change in the hall bathroom, the fresh paint masking old memories. The carpet was gone, replaced by laminate flooring designed to resemble hardwood. No one would have been fooled, but I'd picked the faux floors because, according to the contractor, they were more durable.

And then, like clockwork, I began to scold myself. Who was I kidding? The floors looked cheap. Like rental-house floors. If I skimped on *real* wood, I had no business trying to play this game of landlord. Unlike me, folks who flipped houses were rich.

Shoot, I'd barely made it inside the house before I peed on these floors. Then again, it wasn't my fault. Everyone knows teachers have the worst bladders from "holding it" for so long. You can't leave eight-year-olds unsupervised for a second.

As the stream of relief continued to flow from me, I defended myself to my own conscience all the more: *What do you want me to do—drink half my weight in water every day or get myself all dehydrated? You can't have both!*

This was the story of my life. Warring within my own brain. Wanting what I wanted, needing what I needed, but not feeling like I could have both. Water *and* bladder control. Marriage *and* love. Peace *and* people. Something always had to give because, cutting it this close, I was going to make a mess of myself one of these days.

I texted my daughter to let her know I had made it safely. She replied only with a thumbs-up, which I'd expected. She and I hadn't been on the best terms since I made the decision to move away.

Well, at least the toilet in the main unit flushed properly, which had been a concern a few weeks ago. Looked like the construction company I'd used had finally gotten it right. In fact, the entire bathroom looked amazing, now that my biological crisis had passed and I could fully see straight again. Those cabinets had turned out smooth and shiny.

The washroom, with its claw-foot tub and intricate tile work, whispered of practicality mixed with a touch of luxury.

I finished my business, washed my hands, and ventured through the rest of the house to see what had been accomplished despite them not being able to create the second kitchen and separate both sides of the house completely because I'd run out of money. For now.

As I walked the first few steps away from the bathroom, the home's old character returned step by step—a creak here, a groan there. I passed through the living area, where my grandmother's old rocking chair still sat in the corner, the wooden armrest glossy from years of use. This was not the house I'd grown up in, but these walls knew me as a child—wide-eyed, tracing the patterns on the rug, counting the ticks of the old grandfather clock, which was now missing from its nook.

In the newer bathroom, someone had made a sorry attempt at cleaning the mirror, leaving streaks of dust that skewed the reflection staring back at me. It was comforting, actually. This woman staring back wasn't the real me. She had a dusty filter. The *real* me looked way better; I was sure of it.

I rolled a paper towel from off the holder, dampened a square, and wiped to reveal a better view of myself. It had been three years since I'd stood in this bathroom looking at myself, but from this angle, and these extra countrified rays of sunlight... It seemed like time was moving a little faster. My lips, always my most prominent feature, still held their softness and strength, accentuated by a neutral shade of brown with a pop of gold in the center.

Learned that trick on YouTube.

High cheekbones and a broad forehead carried my wide nose in a way that somehow made me look serious all the time. Black don't crack, but it does sag with years, gravity, and stress. Those three factors know no race, color, or creed.

Maybe if I hadn't divorced Eric…

Sweat beaded around my receding hairline, reminding me that the house hadn't been occupied in nearly a week and the air-conditioning had been turned off. At a little under two thousand square feet, it wouldn't take long to reach a comfortable temperature in the house.

I made my way through the primary unit's living room, stepping over an area rug with curled edges.

Continuing on, I crossed into what used to be the main hallway but was now in the renter's unit. The walls on this side had also been painted a neutral grayish-white color. They were bare, but in my mind's eye, I could still see faded photographs of relatives I had not thought about in years. I couldn't help but pause at each one, memories flooding in to welcome me back to Grandma Jewel's house.

This was where I encountered my first problem: The person with hot flashes needs control of the AC. I made a note-to-self about ordering a personal fan to mitigate this oversight.

With the gentle push of a button and a hopeful click of the thermostat, the system hummed to life, a promise of relief soon to come. I continued surveying the house, the air from the vents beginning to stir, inviting the curtains into a lazy dance.

Two thousand square feet was about half the size of our home in Austin. The kids had their side of the house, Eric and I had ours. "Master suite," they called it back then, before folks started waking up to Black history and women's history more. When I'd begun looking at homes in the city, just before I announced my intent to divorce Eric, I noticed they called the main bedroom "primary" now. It's a step in the right direction, if you ask me. There's much to be said about changing a name, which was why I decided to return to my maiden name, Hicks, in the divorce.

Joyce Marietta Hicks. Formerly known as Joyce Jackson through the biggest chunk of my life. My married name had a nice ring to it, I have to say: Mrs. Jackson. Eric and Joyce Jackson; it's proper to say the man's name first, I was taught.

Anyway, when I'd listed the other half of the incomplete duplex for rent, I made sure to call it the "secondary" unit. And at the time, I'd thought it would be completely separate, which was why I could charge a pretty penny, by Robin Creek standards. But now that my new tenant would be sharing my kitchen and the laundry room—at least for now—I'd had to let the previous signee out of the contract, re-advertise in the local paper with the reduced price, and lower my standards to get somebody who wasn't as particular as me.

Gabriella Santos.

I wondered if she was Mexican. And then I wondered why I wondered. Because the same way I appreciate the Realtors changing the name from "master" to "primary," I'd like to think someone would welcome me despite whatever reservations society and/or their entire family had taught them to think about people who looked different from them.

Letting go goes a long way, and it goes both ways.

Besides, I was already well-versed in letting go, seeing as I'd let go of a thirty-year marriage. Living next to Gabriella couldn't be any worse than living parallel to Eric. He and I both being

Black, making vows, and raising kids hadn't made us stick together forever, clearly.

"Yoo-hoo!" a voice rang from the front of the house, along with a gentle rap on the screen door.

Instinctively, I pressed down the front of my cotton skirt and re-fluffed the bottom of my dolman shirt to better camouflage my stomach.

"I see your fancy car!" the visitor announced. Her shadow tilted to the right, along with her body, as she attempted to look inside the house.

Nosy folk gon' be nosy; it's in their blood. The only way to deal with them is to stay polite and keep distance between you and them.

"Morning," I said, pulling the main door closed behind me and stepping onto the porch and into her personal space at the same time, effectively shutting off her view of my newly remodeled home and pushing her back with my midsection.

It's not that I don't like people—I do. It's the small talk that I don't like. And being married to Eric came with wheelbarrows full of shallow banter at dinners and conferences and fundraisers where technically you didn't have to donate. But if you didn't, you wouldn't get a personal invitation to the private luncheon with the headmaster of the exclusive school where you wanted your kids to go. And then your child would be in the lottery *for real* for real, just another number like all the other folks without connections.

That was how it worked in the city, in wife-of-a-city-engineer world. You laughed and smiled and played nice because it was a giant game of chess.

In the country, it wasn't so much a game. It was more a slow, deliberate waltz.

This woman standing on my porch was the mailman. Mail*person*, I should say, and I did recognize her, but I couldn't imagine that the same woman who had brought mail to this house when I was a child still held the same position and same route.

Then again, how many paths to promotion or delivery routes could have been open in Robin Creek?

She squinted, and suddenly I noticed that neither the glasses on her nose nor the wig on her head were sitting quite right. I wanted to help her out, push them up a little. But I knew better.

"You Miss Jewel's grandbaby? Charlie's daughter?"

"Yes, ma'am," I replied softly, enunciating respectfully, the way I'd been taught to show address to my elders. "I used to come here every summer."

She looked me up and down, appraising me, which I understood meant she was also measuring me against all that the Hicks name meant in this town. Fine, upstanding folk. I felt like I'd shrunk five inches at the mention of my grandmother and my father, and with the mailwoman's fake eyelashes—thick as caterpillars—sweeping over me.

I am a grown woman, I chanted to myself until my shoulders drew back and returned me to my actual height. "Yes. I'm Joyce Hicks."

"Li'l Joy?"

A ripple of resentment washed through me. "People used to call me that. But I prefer Joyce. Now."

She gave me a speculative grin, stretching the thin mustache above her red lips. "Come on, Li'l Joy. You ain't in the city no more; you can let all that proper talkin' go now. I'm so glad you're here!"

And then she clobbered me in a cloud of sweat, hair sheen, and sweetness. She meant no harm, and I had to take that into account.

My shoulders relaxed. "Thank you."

"Name's Mary Buford. You remember me?"

I did. But I'd just walked into my new home. Hadn't even gotten a moment to take a drink of water. "No, but I'm sure we'll be seeing each other…tomorrow."

"We sure will. Every day. I figured you'd be coming soon. Saw mail come through with your government name on it. Your husband coming, too?"

"No," I replied even as the question made my gut twitch.

"You a widow?"

"No. Divorced," I said. The word still scraped my throat on its way out. No sign of that announcement getting any easier.

"Well, that's one way to solve problems. Sorry to hear that."

I gave a tiny shake of my head. "Don't be. It's for the best."

Mary sighed. "I suppose it is, sometimes. Menfolk can be triflin'. Anyway, your box got too full, so the rest is waiting in the mailroom. I can bring it all by tomorrow if you'd like."

Such a kind offer, and such an easy acceptance of the d-word (divorce) made me feel worse for wanting her to leave. "Tomorrow is great."

"Okay. Well, here's the stuff everybody's getting today." She pressed a wad of junk mail—coupons and sales flyers—into my hand. "You sure you and your husband can't work it out? Me and my husband divorced and then remarried each other. Cost us a whole lotta money, when we could have stayed married the first time if we'd just 'communicated' better, you know." For some reason, she air-quoted the word *communicated*.

I didn't care enough to ask why. "Thanks for the mail."

Mary took the hint and moved on to another line of inquiry. "You got somebody named Gabriella moving in, too?"

"Yes. She'll be the second occupant."

"Oh." She paused. "Your daughter?"

Here we go again.

"No." I tensed, remembering that Mary Buford delivered more than just the mail around Robin Creek. The way she looked at me, she was wondering way too hard, ready to fill in the blanks with whatever came to mind. Gabriella might be my nurse, my girlfriend, or my drug dealer by the time the rumors finished racing through the streets.

That was when I decided I'd better use Mary Buford to control the narrative if I wanted to get settled in this small town without causing too much stir.

I grasped my hands in front of my skirt. "My new *tenant* moves in tomorrow."

Mary sucked in her chin. "Oh! Look at you, now, taking in tenants. You always were a smart cookie, according to your grandmother. But you know how grandmothers are—they think all their grands are brilliant and can't do no wrong."

Before I had time to wonder if she'd given me a backhanded compliment, she added, "I feel the same way about mine. I just knew all six of 'em were headed to Howard or Harvard."

"Nothing wrong with high hopes," I said, landing on a note that I thought signaled an end to our conversation.

But Mary elaborated, "Well, two of 'em went to junior college, one went to Job Corps, and two—the twins—got hired at the Amazon factory in Dallas and left on the first bus smoking."

"Well, we have our dreams and they have theirs," I said. Then I remembered she'd said there were six and, without thinking, asked, "What's going on with the last one?"

Suddenly, her eyes drooped, and I knew.

"I'm so sorry, Miss Mary." We were definitely past small talk now, and my heart drooped, too.

"Thank you. He came down with leukemia when he was seven. Fought a good fight, though! He made it to eighteen and almost to graduation. They gave us the diploma anyway. Real nice of the school district. Everybody loved Quinton."

I smiled warmly at her, hoping she could feel my empathy. "I'm sure everyone did."

She shook out her arms. "Well, he's in a better place now." She skipped on to the next topic: "So, now, you plan on getting everything all formalized for your tenant? With her own mailbox and all?"

"I...I guess I really hadn't thought about it."

"If you want her to get her own box, you'll need to designate. Maybe 'A' or 'B' for each unit. And the city has to approve before we can make the change on our end."

"Approve of what?"

She laughed. "They gotta figure out some kind of way to get more money out of you, sugar!"

"Sounds about right."

"Don't make me no difference. Just add her to your address so nobody mixes things up, hear?"

"Yes, ma'am."

"Good talking to you, Li'l Joy."

"Same here, Miss Mary."

"And it's good to have you back."

"It is." I had to agree. And somehow, when she called me Li'l Joy that last time, it didn't bother me one bit.

CHAPTER 2

I took all afternoon Tuesday and Wednesday getting myself unpacked and wiping down both sides of the duplex from the dust that had settled into every nook and cranny possible. Construction leaves its signature all over a house.

The primary side—my side—had half the old living room, two bedrooms, and a bathroom all to itself. The secondary side looked almost the same, except it had only one bedroom. That bedroom was a fairly good size, and Gabriella would have the other half of the backyard, plus what used to be a carport, which gave her more outside space.

Now, both sides had fresh flooring and paint and separate entrances, though right now it made no sense because of the shared kitchen at the back. We shared the wall in our living rooms, and that wall swung into an L on both sides. No open concept for us. But behind the short legs of our L's was one kitchen that stretched all the way across. With the lowered rent and the problem we'd run into with the air-conditioning vents and roof issues, it might be several months or years before I was able to finish the project and completely seal off both halves of the duplex.

I was grateful somebody had been willing to share an almost-duplex with me. At the same time, it made me fidgety. *What-ifs* kept peeping around every corner, making me doubt myself again and again. Good thing there was plenty to unpack, set up, and wipe down to keep my mind busy.

A few days later, Mary Buford brought news that the town might soon have its first set of triplets, as far back as anyone could remember. "Everybody's excited."

"Good for them," I said.

She hoisted a giant shopping bag full of mail from the space between her seat and the door. "Here's your old mail."

"Oh. Wow."

"Yeah. Mostly junk, but we can't rightly throw it away without your permission for a while."

"Thank you again. You've been very helpful to me."

"It's what I do." She winked at me.

I ended our visit abruptly with a wave of my hand when I saw my daughter's name on my phone. Mary waved back and went on her way.

Terri was finally returning my calls in between seeing her clients. It's always the clients with her, just like it was always "the office" or "the project" with her father. "Good to see your name on my screen," I said when I answered. She deserved a little passive-aggressiveness.

"Mom. You called, like, three times today."

"Is that the magic number before I get a response?"

"It's not even noon yet."

I just don't believe anyone is so busy that they can't take two minutes to return a call from their mother. We had this same conversation when she went to college. When she got her first job. When she got married. It's ridiculous.

But I didn't say any of those things, because honestly I was too grateful to hear from her. "How's my grandson?" I started on neutral ground.

"He's fine."

Silence.

"Well, I just finished moving all my stuff into Grandma Jewel's house."

Silence.

"And?"

"And I wanted you to know. I'm settled now. I'm okay. This is going to work out for me, I think."

She huffed. "Sounds like I'm not the one who needs convincing."

"Listen, I know you don't understand why I left your father. It was a hard decision. But I'm asking you, my only daughter, for a little support."

"I can't support what I oppose."

"You oppose me?"

"I oppose what you did. You broke up our family, Mom. Now Dad calls me, like, every single day to do something for him. Order food, send thank-you notes. Like I'm his secretary."

"So you *do* understand a part of my problem, then," I twirled her words around.

"No. I'm saying that I did not sign up to be his life partner. You did. And now you've reneged, and now I have to step in where you left off. It's not fair to me or my husband or Elijah. I can't run two households."

"Let your father run his own life," I blurted out. "Tell him to stand out here on his own two feet like you're telling me, right?"

Terri barked, "He didn't ask for this. He's not the one who left."

My whole body thrummed with anger, blood rushing through my system to prepare me for danger. So I took a breath. Tried not to let myself get entangled in this argument with Terri again. She was—and had always been—a daddy's girl. Everyone's entitled to a favorite person. Maybe I'd have to accept this the same way I'd accepted that my marriage was over long before the Big D.

"I just wanted you to know I'm settled in now," I said with new calm. "And don't take on your daddy's life. You've got enough on your hands already." I stopped shy of mentioning her most vulnerable moment, the one that always reminded me that Terri might have her father's bravado, but she'd inherited my tendency to worry.

It happened late one Thursday night, her freshman year in college. She'd called me huffing and puffing, frantic. "Momma, I can't breathe!"

Those three words nearly took me out, too. I told her to hang up and call 9-1-1 while I raced to the campus. Eric was out of town on business, and Eric Jr. was at basketball practice, if I remember correctly.

By the time I arrived, paramedics had correctly assessed her situation as a panic attack.

Terri was holding an oxygen mask to her face, looking into the eyes of the emergency technician who was coaching her back to a normal state while keeping an eye on her blood pressure.

"You've suffered a panic attack. You're coming out of it now."

Later, once the EMTs had left and Terri's freaked-out

roommate excused herself, I sat holding my daughter on the couch, her head resting on my shoulder in a way it hadn't since she was a little girl.

"Mom. My heart felt like it was about to explode. I thought I was dying."

"I'm so sorry that happened to you, Terri. It must have been terrifying."

She wiped a tear away. "I don't understand. Nothing happened. Like, no trigger. It just came out of nowhere."

"Sounds like you're under a lot of stress."

She softened and leaned into me more. "I took an overload of classes this semester. Nineteen hours."

"Nineteen, Terri. Really?" I'd convinced myself to let her handle this whole college thing by herself, especially that second semester. "Why would you do that?"

"I want to graduate early," she confessed. "Get on with my life."

"Sweetheart, there's no prize for finishing early. Take it at a pace that works for you," I told her.

We sat in silence for a minute. Then she asked softly, "Please don't tell Dad about this."

"Your father wouldn't— "

"No." She sat up and looked me in the eye. Her black eyeliner and mascara had smeared all the way into her hairline. "Please."

"Fine. I won't tell him. But I need you to agree to stop overloading yourself," I bargained with her.

She'd sniffled, then whispered, "Okay."

I pushed past layers of box braids and kissed the side of her head. "It's going to be all right, Terri. Everything always works out the way it's supposed to in the end."

Those words, declared back when I used to have more faith, came back to me now. Terri and I were water and oil, but I had to believe we loved each other still. Otherwise, she would have done what all the other people in her generation do—block and unfriend and change the password to the streaming-music app we share.

She sighed. "Well… I hope you enjoy your time in Robin Creek."

She was trying to sound all hard, but I heard the tiniest crack in her voice. I continued, "And you're welcome to visit me. When you're ready."

"Do you have room for me?"

"Yes. Another bedroom. Just enough space for a short visit." It took everything in me not to emphasize the word *short*.

"Did you do a background check on your tenant?"

"Yes, I did."

"Credit check?"

"No. She's already paid the deposit, though."

"I guess. You got a weapon?"

"It's Robin Creek, Terri."

"I'm just sayin'… People do weird things these days. I don't want to see you get hurt."

Well, at least she was concerned for my basic human safety. "Don't worry about me. I'll be fine. Sounds like your daddy's keeping you busy, anyway."

I heard a scratchy speaker call my daughter's name in the background: "Dr. Riley."

"I gotta go, Mom. My next client is here."

"I love you, Terri."

"Love you, too, Mom."

The day of my new roommate's arrival had finally come. And

gone. Wouldn't be too long before the sun set, and there was no sign of Gabriella Santos. Today, this last Thursday in May, was to be her move-in day, according to text messages mostly. People barely talked these days, especially after the pandemic. Which suited me just fine except when what I needed to say couldn't be adequately conveyed by tapping my thumbs across a two-inch keyboard. Who thought of that foolishness, anyway? These optometrists are going to be rich from all these kids who grew up with their eyes glued to a screen, Terri and Eric Jr. included.

It was 7:45 p.m. already.

I sat on the couch with one leg folded underneath me, the other dangling, though I knew it would cause my folded leg to fall asleep. I had an episode of a house-hunting show playing on the screen as I second-guessed myself. *Maybe I got it wrong? Maybe when I said "next" Thursday, she thought next-next Thursday.* People had different definitions of so many things. Another reason why I should have insisted on talking to Gabriella instead of all that texting. Who signs a six-month lease without going inside a house, anyway?

I felt the tension rise higher inside my body, from my hips up through my stomach. *Where is this child? I hope she didn't have an accident.*

When my own children were teens, I had worried myself almost sick when they started driving. So much could go so wrong so quickly. I often wondered how people went about their days so carefree in light of these facts. Maybe you just had to live long enough to fully understand the unseen dangers lurking around every corner.

This living arrangement could go very wrong as well, especially in an unfinished duplex, where we'd still have to share some space. I'd seen enough episodes of *Judge Judy* and *The People's Court* to know that it was hard for friends and family, let alone strangers, to live together in peace. *Do I really need a roommate?*

I ran the figures through my head again. *Yes, I do.*

In my peripheral vision, I noticed the streetlight pop on. Glanced at my phone. *8:12*. No texts from Gabriella. I checked my ringer again to make sure it was on. I even thought about calling the girl—somebody's daughter—again, but decided that might give "obsessive" vibes if I left yet another message.

Concern mixed with another helping of annoyance by 8:30. Now it was almost dark. Was she still coming? And if so, how in the world would she manage to unpack all her stuff in the dark?

I was limping on my half-asleep leg and had begun closing the blinds and pulling the shades for the evening when I heard the rhythmic thump of bass from a car speaker getting closer. Closer. Stopping in the driveway, to my horror and relief, equally. Gabriella was safe. And late. And loud! But at least I didn't hear any cussing words in the music.

Through the slightly parted blinds, I watched as Gabriella's extremely long, curly hair lifted in the wind, almost like one of those "flying dress" pictures. Except she was wearing skinny jeans and a yellow tank top with a picture of a woman popping bubble gum.

My Southern upbringing led me straight to the word *biracial*. After all those classes and trainings on diversity at the school, I somehow still had to check off a box when I met people.

The streetlight caught the girl's face at an angle that made me soften. She had plump baby-face cheeks. Almost a unibrow. Her tawny skin shone in the light, but that crease between her eyebrow gave off "oldest child" aura. If I hadn't read through the application meticulously and known Gabriella's age, I would have guessed the girl was older than her twenty-six years. Maybe time and stress had done a number on her, too.

The engine died, bringing that ear-popping music to a blessed end.

Gabriella gave her car door a thrust, closing it by virtue of her wide hips. Then she paused, looking at the house like it was the Savior.

I knew exactly how she felt.

But somebody had to teach this child a thing or two about manners. You don't tell someone you're coming over in the daytime and show up several hours later, not having called, not responding to texts. It's just plain rude.

I opened my door, then stepped out on the porch to greet her properly, having hoisted my Parent-Teacher Organization smile in place. "Hello, Gabriella. I'm Joyce. It's nice to finally meet you."

She shook my outstretched hand. "Yes, yes, yes, Joyce! So nice to meet you, too!" She tried to lift her voice and be as cheerful as my fake smile, but her words dragged. She must have been tired.

I'd have to take my lecture down a notch. "I was expecting you earlier."

She looked to my right, at the expanse of our porch. "This is nice." Then she walked three steps to her door. The distinct smell of garlic trailed her. "Is this my side?"

For some reason, my breath caught as I watched her face for signs of disappointment. Her cheeks actually seemed to rise higher, though. That made mine climb as well.

I responded, "Yes, indeed."

She pressed her hands together for a few silent claps. "This place is beautiful," she gushed.

"Thank you. My grandmother lived here."

She gave an approving nod. "Mind if I put up some fairy lights on my side?"

"No problem."

I was glad she liked what she saw, but she'd missed the whole part about me waiting up for her for hours. She couldn't just walk in here late when she wanted to without some kind of communication. "Whew! I was wondering exactly what time you'd get here."

Gabriella tilted her head and smiled at me. "Aww… That's so sweet of you to worry about me."

Sweet? Sweet! There is nothing sweet about worrying for a young girl out in the streets of Robin Creek… Well, it *was* Robin Creek. And the streets were far from mean, so I couldn't give it to her like I would have done for my own kids in Austin. "I just thought you'd be here no later than five. The end of the business day, you know."

She poked out her lips and scrunched up her face in confusion. "Is there…a problem?"

I wasn't ready for her to throw a question back at me. "I—I… It's just…it's late, and it's already dark. I tried calling and texting you to see when you'd be here, and I didn't get a response."

Her face unknotted itself. "Oh! Yeah. That. My phone died while I was at work. And I packed my charger in a bag that was, like, at the bottom of everything. So, yeah, I couldn't respond. But I mean, I said I'd be here today, and it is *today* still, right?"

My anxiety took a big gulp. "Well, technically, yes. Today *is* today," I had to agree.

"Then we're good! Up top!" She held up a hand for me to give her a high five.

And I did, before I realized it, because I couldn't come up with a sharp response in time to beat her happy gesture.

"Before I forget, here's the money for next month." She pulled out a wad of cash from her tight jeans pocket and shoved it toward me. "Can I get a receipt? I'm a stickler for good accounting."

That, I could appreciate. Punctual payment and meticulousness. Overly good manners kept me from counting the money out loud, I suppose. "Sure thing. Let me give you a tour, and then I'll get my book."

"Cool."

We entered through her door, and again, Gabriella's face pulled wide with a smile. "Home sweet home."

The neutral walls made the space seem bigger than it was. "This is your great room. Over here to the left, your bedroom and bathroom." I showed her the private space, remembering all those episodes of home-shopping shows I watched. Being sure to point out the positive details. Walk-in closet, natural light she'd get from the two windows in the daytime, the spacious countertop in the bathroom.

Gabriella ran a hand along the granite. "It's even better than the pictures."

"Thank you."

"I can't wait to see the kitchen," she chirped. "It's where I spend most of my time when I'm not working."

"Oh! You love to cook?" I asked.

"I *live* to cook," she said passionately, her eyes nearly twinkling with the correction. "One day I want my own Blaxican restaurant."

"Black who?"

"Black and Mexican. Blaxican. Spanish soul food. And then I'll get married, travel, have kids, and teach them all to cook so they can carry on my legacy."

I hadn't exactly asked for the map of her yellow brick road, but all righty then. I remembered being that young and optimistic. A long time ago. Before decades of reality swarmed in and dreams fizzed out. "That's good" was my solemn reply.

"Out there's your extended patio." I gestured slightly as we passed her back door. Her feet continued to shuffle on behind me, so I didn't bother to open it. She wanted to see the kitchen.

"Voilà!" I announced as I flicked the switch to show the kitchen. It wasn't worthy of a gourmet chef, but she should be able to stir up some fancy meals so long as she owned the right tools.

I twirled around, expecting to see her delightful smile, but instead her lips were as straight as a ruler. "I see." She leaned past me. "Ummm... Is it...open to the other side?"

A zing of fear sprinted from my heart to my feet and back up again. "Yes. I was clear about that in my advertisement."

Gabriella whipped her phone out of her pocket. "The listing said I'd have my own kitchen. *Updated* kitchen."

"That was my original plan," I clarified, "but the contractors said it wasn't possible. So I re-listed."

Undeterred, Gabriella thrust her shaking phone in my face. "See?"

Sure enough, the words: *Enjoy your own bedroom, bathroom, and kitchen in this completely remodeled, updated duplex home.* Somehow she had stumbled on the old ad. Which also meant she must have given me the old rent amount in that yet-uncounted roll of money.

"I'm so sorry. That was the old ad. Looks like there's been a mistake. I don't know how all this works on the internet... I guess the old ad didn't delete everywhere. I'm charging two hundred dollars less because it's gonna be a while before they finish the kitchen."

Gabriella lowered the phone, and her flushed, tight face returned to focus. "How long?"

"I don't know," I answered as honestly as I could, then gulped down the anxiety climbing up my throat. "It was an honest mistake. But if you don't want to stay, I understand. Seems like cooking in your own kitchen is quite important to you."

"It is. Was," she barely could whisper.

Tears began filling her eyes, and I fought the urge to hug her and fuss at her at the same time, as I did to Terri when she got to her college dorm and realized her room was about half the size she'd imagined it would be.

But Terri wasn't a rent-paying tenant like Gabriella, who had been thoroughly deceived by an outdated post. I apologized again.

She took a deep breath, and her pretty face softened a bit. "Mistakes happen."

"Yes. They do. Maybe we can work something out?" I asked.

She crossed her arms and asked point-blank, "Do you cook?"

I felt like I was the one being interviewed now. "Not much. I mean, it's just me, and I don't eat much." Even when it was just Eric and me, we probably threw out more food than we ate. A shame before God, my father would have said.

"What about cleaning?"

"I never go to bed with dishes in the sink," I stated. "Not so much as a fork."

Gabriella tilted her head slightly, her eyes reflecting deep thought. "Golden kitchen rule."

My body buzzed with panic. What if she left? I'd have my first month in the new place with no rent money from a tenant. My plans couldn't fall apart this quickly, could they?

Yes, they could. This could all backfire, just as Eric had said it would. *I'm not trying to scare you, but you're going to find out what a cold, hard world it is out there without me, Joyce. I don't want that for you.*

Maybe he'd been right. If I'd been a woman with a husband, those contractors might not have been so quick to ask for more money, and then I wouldn't be standing there, wringing my fingers behind my back and hoping this young lady wouldn't walk out the door with her cooking aspirations and her rent money in tow.

Gabriella sighed. "I'm already packed up. And I need this fresh start."

I'd been frozen for so long, I felt my eyelids creak when I finally blinked back to life. "Welcome, Gabriella." I thrust her key at her.

She took it. "Gracias. I'll start unpacking."

I nodded, glad we'd come to something reasonable. If it meant I had to live like a hotel resident for a while, fine. Sandwiches and small meals and fast food, fine. Because I could not make a fool of myself in front of my ex-husband and my daughter, and even my own self.

CHAPTER 3

Nothing beats the smell of bacon and eggs in the morning. Unless you're a vegan, I suppose. Seems like everybody's trying to make everything taste like what they really want to eat. A brownie with real, natural cane sugar can't be worse than one made with synthetic chemicals. I'm just saying—if you're gonna eat a brownie, eat a brownie.

Clearly, Gabriella was one of the actual meat-eating cooks, from the aroma that easily strolled down the hallway, under my bedroom door, and into my nostrils like we were old friends catching up with one another.

"Mornin', Li'l Joy!" it greeted me as though my very own grandmother were in the house again. Except there was the distinct smell of cilantro. *Blaxican*.

I washed up and made my way to the kitchen, hoping to at least get a look at what Gabriella had cooked. "Good morning," I said to her.

She looked up from the sink, where suds crawled up her arms as she washed dishes the old-fashioned way. "Good morning."

"Smells good."

"I made enough for two, if you want," she said with a brief smile.

The cheese melting on top of the egg left me no choice. "Thank you. Looks delicious, too. What is it?"

"It's a mix of chilaquiles and cheesy grits—something my grandmothers used to make, in their own ways. One was Black, from Georgia, and the other was Mexican, from Veracruz. I grew up eating both, and this is kinda like a blend of the two worlds. A little homage to both of them."

I took a bite, and the flavors exploded—creamy, sharp cheese with the slight crisp of tortillas, balanced with the rich softness of the eggs. The grits were smooth and buttery, while the spice from the salsa brought the dish to life.

I laughed. "This does taste like one foot in the South and the other across the border."

"Exactly." Gabriella showed all thirty-two teeth. "I love it when people enjoy my food."

"Well, consider yourself thoroughly in love, because you've got a fan in me." All my manners slipped away as I licked the last bits of salsa and cheese. It seemed a waste to allow even one drop of flavor to sit on a napkin.

"Thank you very much. But I'm going to need more space."

"Space?"

"Yes. For my kitchen appliances, pots and pans, you know? I've barely unpacked half of them, and there's no room left."

I looked around at the upper and lower cabinets of the kitchen, noticing a few doors slightly ajar from whatever she'd packed behind them. And I could no longer see my canister set because of the machinery she'd lined up in front of the four cylinders. My lips twisted to the right. "Not sure how we can get more...space. I mean, it is what it is."

"I was thinking maybe an overhead rack." She raised a hand and traced out a long, invisible rectangle above us.

I quelled an outright "no" with a click of my cheeks. What did she think this was, one of those home-remodeling shows?

Gabriella added, "Just until the construction resumes."

Oh. That. Seeing as I had no idea when the construction might resume, I had to consider her vision. "Where… How… Who would install it?" I asked, still coming to grips with the idea that half her rent would probably be spent on this impromptu project.

"I can get my boyfriend to do it," she offered.

Boyfriend? I should have known a beautiful girl like Gabriella would have somebody. Goodness gracious—what did that mean for me? Would they be making noises in the night? Would I have to actually enforce the three-night-stay rule in our lease agreement?

I looked up at the hypothetical rack again, as though it might give me the answers I was looking for. Did I really want to share my space—my *life*—with someone else and her boyfriend at this point in my journey?

"He's good with carpentry. He's also a cook, kind of. So he'd know how to make it work in a kitchen."

My first thought was to ask if he'd leave holes in the ceiling, but given the fact that I'd be demolishing the kitchen whenever it was time for the rack to come down, it didn't seem to matter. "I suppose that would be all right."

Gabriella clapped three times. "Yaaay! This is gonna be great."

Great wasn't the word running through my head, but my daughter's ringtone saved me from having to don yet another disingenuous smile. I set my plate in the sink on my way out. "I'll be back to wash it."

I missed Terri's call but redialed her a few seconds later.

My belly was so full from the breakfast, I swear my bed creaked a little louder as I sat down to talk to her.

"Momma, where were you?"

"I was eating."

She huffed. "You need to keep your phone on you at all times."

"Aren't you the one who always said I worry too much?" I reminded her. "I'm fine, Terri. My housemate and I are just getting to know each other over breakfast, is all. I don't like to watch my phone over a meal."

"Well, I need you."

My heart dropped.

"Actually, Elijah needs you."

"What's going on with my grandson?"

"He needs a place to stay for the summer."

"He *has* a place to stay," I blurted out without thinking.

Terri finally told the whole truth. "What I mean is, he needs someone to watch him while I go to Tennessee to take a seminar to get an endorsement. I just found out they selected me from, like, thousands of applicants. It's an amazing opportunity. But I have to go to Tennessee for seven weeks for the training so I can take the test."

"Seven weeks?"

"Yes. June and July, basically."

"Why can't he stay with Christopher?"

"Mom," she lowered her voice. "You know Christopher can't watch him for seven weeks."

"The hell he can't," I countered. "He's your husband and Elijah's father. He is perfectly capable of watching his own son."

"Chris works every day; sometimes he has to take a long haul in his truck. And besides, if you and Dad were still together, in

Austin, it wouldn't be a problem for the two of you and Chris to shuffle Elijah around, take turns with him. But with you gone..."

Here we go with the attempted guilt trip. "Terri, stick to the subject."

She sighed. "Elijah *wants* to come with you. He's used to spending weeks with you and Dad every summer. But, of course, you took that away from him."

The food in my stomach rumbled with her low blow. "I haven't taken *anything* away from Elijah," I defended myself.

"Yes, you have. You took stability from him. From this whole family, Mom. Can you at least give him seven weeks of it back?" Terri asked-slashed-accused.

"Ma!" I heard Elijah's voice in the background.

"Hold on, I'm talking to your grandmother."

"Hi, Grandma!" His voice sailed straight into my heart.

I yelled back, "Hey, EJ." The nickname was short for Elijah Joe, passed down on his father's side of the family. He was my only grandchild, and I'd spent a great deal of time with him as an infant, with my daughter working toward her MBA and my son-in-law launching his trucking business during Elijah's first three years of life. We had a special bond, so hearing his voice resonated deeply.

"I'm asking her if you can stay with her for a while this summer," she said to him.

She knew full well that if my grandson asked me, "no" wasn't in my vocabulary.

I cringed. She must be desperate for this certificate to bring Elijah into a conversation between adults. "Get him out of the room," I demanded.

Terri clicked her cheek, but a second later she did obey me, and I heard a door close as he left her presence, presumably. "Momma, if you don't watch him, I'll have to wait until the next application season, and there's no guarantee they'll select me again."

Now, if she had started out the conversation straightforward, told me her predicament and asked *nicely* if I would watch Elijah, we wouldn't have to go around all these mountains of half-truth and valleys of guilt to come to an agreement.

But again, she was her father's child.

"I'm sorry, but I'm just getting settled into my new place. Elijah can't stay here the whole summer. I can watch him for some of the time, but you have a father and a whole husband who are perfectly capable of helping out."

"Fine," she said like she was doing *me* the favor.

"You're welcome."

She hesitated before adding, "Thank you. He'll be very excited to hear this news." She was trying to clean it up now. "I'll be sure to pack all of his electronics."

"We've got plenty of fresh air and outdoor activities here," I said. The last thing I planned to do was allow Elijah to stare at a blue screen all day.

"Well, since he turned ten, it's like his brain switched into preteen mode." Her voice clouded with motherly worry, which immediately sparked my maternal instinct to protect my daughter despite everything. "He's speaking his mind more, and it's borderline disrespectful."

"They go through stages," I advised. "And it's good for him to find his voice."

"Yes, I know. It just feels like he's not my baby anymore. Maybe if he's around you, he'll slip back into kid mode again. You see how he acted when I told him I was on the phone with you."

"Can't promise you anything. EJ's growing up."

"I guess I just miss the way he used to drop everything and run to me when I picked him up from day care. You remember the video that went viral?"

A laugh bubbled up from me. Boy, did I ever. Elijah was on the Austin news and on everyone's social media, dropping a little train set at the sight of his mother, belting out the biggest giggles, arms outstretched, running as fast as his eighteen-month-old legs would take him into her embrace.

My grandson was an adorable baby, and unlike other grandmothers, I had the views, likes, and comments to prove it, thank you very much.

Terri joined in my laughter, and I suddenly remembered some of our better moments together. Taking her to get her ears pierced. Building science fair projects. Working together at her neighborhood lemonade stand—though it was another of her unlicensed gigs. She had always been a salesperson. Persuasive. Business-minded. And it made total sense that an organization would pick my baby for special training this summer.

I just wished she wasn't so pushy with me.

"I'll bring him to you the first weekend of June."

Now, I was born *at* night, not *last* night. I knew that putting me first in the rotation was only buying her time until her next attempt to guilt me into keeping him for the remainder of the summer. By then, we'd be into a routine, his clothes would be all mixed up in my laundry, and he probably would make friends in Robin Creek that he wouldn't want to leave. I knew this, and yet I didn't advocate for a different slot, because, to be honest, I simply wasn't up to any more arguing with her.

Ever since I'd decided to leave my husband, a part of me had felt like the family villain. There was only so much I could take feeling like that at once. In addition to picking battles, we have to pick when to fight them. This one could wait until I had my bearings better.

"I'll be ready for him."

CHAPTER 4

Gabriella's breakfast filled me up and got my Friday off to as good a start as I could have, knowing that I only had a few weeks of freedom until my grandson arrived. Not that he was a bother—but he was a child. A responsibility. Something else for me to worry about twenty-four seven.

I'd need some help with him, so I turned to a mother's and babysitter's trusted ally: the local library.

The library in Robin Creek was named after a Southern Confederate colonel named Billy Harvey Sanderford, who reportedly fought valiantly in the Civil War, leading a group of soldiers through a bloody battle that cost him his legs first, then his life six days later when he succumbed to an infection. Though downtown's most visible attraction was the giant county courthouse, with its clock that still gonged every hour, the statue of Billy Harvey Sanderford standing at parade rest shone in all its Confederate glory only a few feet away from the courthouse steps.

I'd rather not be accosted by such a statue while strolling downtown, but it was a part of history, I knew. And I was in Robin Creek, not the more progressive Lubbock or El Paso suburbs, or even the

Austin city life I was used to. That's the funny thing about moving back to a small town: You gotta mix the past with the present and make what you want out of it all, because the past ain't going nowhere, even if you don't like it.

The sun warmed my left side as I followed the loop around the square until I found a good parking spot at the northeast corner, which put me catty-corner from the library itself. It was late May, and afternoon temperatures could reach as high as the mid-eighties in that part of West Texas. I'd packed a bottle of water in my large straw tote, along with a hat in case I needed it.

The dress I wore swayed across the tops of my knees as I closed the door to my vehicle. *Is this dress too short?* I'd found it online, so I couldn't try it on before purchasing. Returning it wasn't worth the postage and hassle. I still owned the dress because I didn't want to be wasteful, but wearing it out in public on my first Robin Creek outing suddenly seemed like the wrong thing to do.

It had been years since I'd walked past these buildings, peeked into these quaint shops, heard the gentle chimes as doors opened and closed. Time had done a number on the hand-painted store signs and awnings, just as it had done a number on my legs. The varicose veins and spots where my pigment had faded seemed to shine brighter in the vibrant sunlight. *Note to self: No more ordering mid-length skirts online.*

Not that anyone in Robin Creek cared, I knew. But this whole situation—starting over by myself in a small town—made me want to do everything possible to protect myself from unnecessary scrutiny. Fit in...as if that were a real thing.

The townspeople offered friendly nods, tipped hats, and mumbled "Good afternoon"s as I made my way to the library. The smell of fresh-baked goods from a bakery mingled with the dusty air.

Old-fashioned lampposts and flowering crepe myrtle lined the street, putting my lingering skirt-distress to rest. This was the country life. Familiarity, kindness, an unhurried pace, and nature all rising up to welcome me back to some of the best days written in my life's book so far.

Summers with Grandma Jewel had always brought a sense of calm, an ease to my life for three months each year. It wasn't just the fact that school was out, because she darn near made up for those lost hours with church time: Sunday school, worship service, accompanying the pastor to his 3:00 p.m. engagements, Wednesday-night Bible study, and Saturday choir rehearsal. Grandma Jewel sang in the choir. In fact, she led almost half the songs with her strong, versatile, melodic voice. So a summer with her meant plenty of church and good food via their endless potlucks.

But those other hours spent visiting her in Robin Creek felt like an extended recess. Neighborhood kids and other visiting grandchildren gathered in fields, backyards, small stores, and the city pool to enjoy life and nature. To race turtles, pick and eat fresh berries, play Marco Polo. Not to mention Grandma Jewel's full-bosomed, powder-scented hugs. Her good cooking, and the stories about how things were when she was my age, and my father's shenanigans, which he often denied.

And this very library I was entering had served as a weekly free-for-all resetting point. A new set of books to read—with Grandma's approval, of course. I'd spent hours searching through the card catalog, my fingertips crawling along the bookshelves until I arrived at the spine I was searching for.

This was what I wanted for Elijah, if only for half the summer. This would keep him from blinding his eyes out by staring at a tiny phone screen.

The library was perfumed by old pages and polished wood. I'd heard of muscle memory, but this smell evoked olfactory memory, if that's a thing, igniting the sense of excitement at this location. Anything is possible in a story.

Despite the plexiglass surrounding the main desk (surely something that had been erected during the pandemic), the woman on the other side bore a smile that transcended all. In fact, it almost seemed like she'd gone out of her way to exude library life, with her silver hair pulled back in a bun and glasses perched on her long, thin nose. "Hello. How may I help you?"

"Hello. I'm new—well, kind of returning to Robin Creek. I'd like to get my library card."

"Wonderful! Welcome back. What brings you home?" She crossed her hands on the desk, waiting patiently and attentively for my response.

I hadn't expected a genuine inquiry or a warm demeanor that welcomed actual conversation. But I should have known from my conversation with Miss Mary. For whatever reason, people make time to connect in Robin Creek.

"Big changes in life," I summarized.

"Well, my name is Eileen. If you need any help in town, you let me know."

I nodded my thanks. "Will do."

"Did you have a card in your previous city?"

"Yes, I did have one in Austin," I replied proudly.

Her eyes widened. "Well, that makes my job mighty easy, then. Do you have that card with you, or can you pull up the account on your phone?"

"Oh. You can use my Austin library card to set me up in Robin Creek?"

"Sure can. And your previous checkout history will follow you, so you'll get book recommendations and notifications based on the authors and types of books you already love. How does that sound?"

So much for fresh starts and small-town brick-and-mortar charm. "Sounds good."

Within minutes, I had a warm, freshly laminated B. H. Sanderford library card in hand.

"Thank you, Eileen. I've got my grandson coming to town soon. I want to make sure he's got books to keep him occupied."

"Oh!" she chirped. "How old is he?"

"Ten."

She smiled broadly. "We've got plenty for his age. Between us and the school and the YMCA, we'll have him begging to go to bed every night."

I laughed. "Now, that's what I'm talkin' about."

"Here." She handed me a bright-green flyer with three columns listing the library's dates, times, and summer events planned for children. At a glance, it looked like a college semester term schedule, it was so full.

"Thank you, thank you, thank you."

"Sure thing. Oh, and, Joyce…" She leaned in close to the barrier.

I mimicked her movement, wondering what might warrant a hushed conversation.

"There's a group of ladies who meet once weekly to talk about books and whatnot."

"A book club?" I asked.

"Not quite. Just some of us…*seasoned* women in the community who like to get together. We do recommend books, but we're not reading one together, per se. Just thought I'd let you know. It's not advertised."

Were the words *lonely divorcée* emblazoned on my forehead?

"With my grandson coming in a few weeks, I'm sure I'll have my hands full."

She waved. "I'm sure you will. But feel free to join us in the future. If you'd like." She winked at me as though we belonged to a secret club for small-town women of a certain age and stage in life.

I thanked her for the standing invitation and tucked the children's information into my bag, pondering her insinuation in my heart. *Maybe I am lonely.* And maybe I'd need some friends in Robin Creek. Gabriella was younger than my children; I couldn't count on her for companionship. Of course, I could find friends at church. But, like Miss Mary, they would all reference me as someone kin to Jewel, which came with a set of holy expectations that I had no intention of living up to, which would, in turn, tarnish her reputation. Also something I didn't want to do. Not that I was intent on living like a questionable woman. It was just...the last thing I wanted. The worst thing possible would be to leave one set of imposed expectations for another. I had my own standards somewhere inside me, and I wanted to find them and live by them for a while.

Somehow, the temperature had climbed by at least five degrees while I was in the library, forcing me to abbreviate my downtown stroll. Two sides of the square instead of four, unless I found another parking spot. I flipped open the hat I'd packed and flattened it against the top of my head. A halo of shade surrounded me just as a breeze picked up the bottom of my skirt.

"Ooh!" escaped my throat as my arms flew to prevent a viral video.

"Hold up! Uh, excuse me!" a male voice called from behind me. I ignored him because… Well, who would be calling for me in the middle of downtown Robin Creek?

"Hello!"

Still gathering the hem of my too-short skirt in my fist, I double-timed it to my car.

That's when I heard "La-ja!"

I froze in place as the voice registered, that unmistakable smushing together of my nickname, Li'l Joy, into his own version: *La-ja*. It always reminded me of the pulsing sound in a horror movie as the killer searches through darkened rooms for his next victim. *La-ja, la-ja, la-ja*.

Then came the footsteps—his footsteps—fast and sure. "I thought that was you! You always had those athletic legs!"

Of course *he* would know. He'd spent so much time trying to touch them decades ago.

I dropped the skirt and turned to face him, because if I didn't, he'd probably wrap me up in a bear hug the way he used to do. I liked it, but not too much. Didn't want to get a reputation, you know.

Before me stood Richard Tatum. All dark-brown six feet of him, with a bald but dent-less head, salt-and-pepper beard, and artificially white teeth twinkling back at me. He was good-looking as a young man, and honestly he looked even better now. He'd taken care of himself, it appeared, which always makes an older man seem smart no matter what he'd actually accomplished—or not—in his lifetime.

It was kind of sweet of him to run after me. Something Eric wouldn't have done.

Richard stood at a respectable distance, smiling broadly. "Why, to what does this entire town owe this pleasure?"

"Hello, Richard."

"Hello, Joyce. You're looking mighty fine."

"Thank you. Time's been good to you as well," I had to admit.

His eyes swept down my body and back up again. "Pretty legs holding up."

"Stop." I found myself responding to his flirty compliment with a smile that refused to contain itself. *What in the world? Am I desperate?* Maybe this was what Eileen had seen in me, too. Desperate, lonely, and divorced.

"You never answered my question. What brings you back here?"

I noticed he hadn't asked about my family, the most proper way to ask about my husband. No, he just stood there asking about me, like he already knew it was perfectly fine to chase me down the street and compliment my legs.

Miss Mary worked fast; I needed to work faster. "I moved back to my grandmother's old house. How's your family, Richard?"

His shrug drew my attention to his embroidered shirt. *Tatum Printing*. His father had owned that business back in the day. "Kids and grandkids all good."

"And Lucielle?" I asked.

"Lucielle and I split up. About five years ago. A few years before my parents died—they went within months of each other."

"I'm sorry to hear that, Richard," I said. Everybody always said that when a couple has been together all their lives and one goes, the other one might die of heartache soon after. A sad but beautiful love story that I always knew wasn't going to happen to me—at least, not the "die of heartache" part.

"Thank you for the condolences."

"You're welcome. You running the business these days?"

"Yep. When my father passed, I sold my dealership in Dallas, sold my house, and relocated back to Robin Creek. Ready to slow down, you know?"

"Yeah. Slowing down is good for the soul," I had to agree.

He dipped his head low. "Listen, you…uh…not married anymore. Right?"

I didn't respond right away.

"I mean, that's what I heard."

"So you already knew why I was back in town, then?"

"No, no, no," he denied a little too adamantly. "That's what I *heard*. But I can't be sure, not until I hear it straight from you."

Lying about my situation didn't seem reasonable. "It's true. I'm divorced. Retired. Starting over."

He whistled and shook his head. "Whoever thought at our age we'd be out here in these single streets again. You been online?"

"Online for what?"

"For matchmaking."

I scrunched up my face. "No, I most certainly have not. I'm not looking for a match—and if I were, I wouldn't be online."

Richard laughed. "I said the same thing. But it's how things happen nowadays. How else are you gonna find somebody when most of the people our age are homebodies?"

"I repeat, I am not *looking* for anybody. And I aspire to become a prolific homebody."

Richard's eyes swept over me again. "It's a crying shame to keep a body like yours at home all the time."

For some reason, his compliment actually tickled me. A little flutter in my chest. Had it been that long since I'd captured a man's full attention?

"Well. Home is where I belong for now. It was good seeing you again."

I tried to step away, but Richard blocked my path as he asked, "You on social media? Can I message you?"

Whatever happened to *Can I have your number?*

I gave him my full profile name.

"I'll send you a friend request," he declared proudly.

This must be what online daters do. "Fine with me."

Richard tipped his head and allowed me to pass. As I slid into my car, I wondered if I'd done it right. Flirting, I mean. The last time I'd flirted, I was a college junior at a fraternity party, batting my lashes at Eric, hoping he wouldn't take my gestures to mean that I was "too easy." My father always told me to make a man "work for it." *It* could be your company, your attention, sex, your hand in marriage. I made Eric work to get all of it, but I'm not sure either of us knew what to do after all that workin' was over.

Maybe that was why I was single again. Back in my father's hometown, semi-flirting with a man I hadn't seen in decades because the one I married thought that after we got married, his work was done.

I tsked. I didn't sign up for a restart, exactly, but it was happening to me. And maybe Richard—with his song-lyric-worthy lines—was as good a person as any to try on my new self with.

CHAPTER 5
Gabriella

I stirred the pot, watching the mixture of onions and garlic sizzle and soften. It was one of those afternoons where the cooking soothed me, kept me grounded. I had the house to myself, which was rare, and I liked it that way—just me and the sound of the spatula scraping the bottom of the cookware.

I heard the front door creak open, and Joyce's familiar voice echoed through the hallway. "Gabriella? I'm back!" Her footsteps followed shortly after.

"Hey!" I called over my shoulder, keeping my focus on the stove as I stirred the onions. I adjusted the heat just slightly, knowing the key to perfect sautéed onions was patience—you had to let them sweat and release their sugars at the right pace. "How was your trip to the store?"

Joyce huffed slightly as she came into the kitchen, setting down a couple of plastic grocery bags on the counter. I noticed the bags and smiled. Most people used the reusable kind now, but Joyce seemed like a person who was more focused on the here and now—people, relationships—than on trends like grocery bags. *How old is she, anyway?*

"It was good," Joyce answered, "but you wouldn't believe how much groceries for one ten-year-old can cost. I practically cleared out the snack aisle."

I turned off the stove, wiping my hands on a towel before walking over to peek into one of the bags. Inside, I spotted an assortment of things: kid-friendly snacks, juice boxes, clementines, and even a couple of those mini cereal boxes I used to love when I was little. "You really went all out for him, huh?" I said, reaching in and pulling out a box of granola bars.

Joyce shrugged, but I could see the pride in her eyes. "He's my grandson. Gotta make sure he's well fed, right?"

"Yeah, but..." I hesitated for a second, unsure if I should say it out loud. "I don't think anyone ever did something like this for me growing up. You know, getting specific food just for me." I glanced at her, feeling a little self-conscious about the admission. "There was always food around, but I can't remember anyone being like, 'I got this just for you, Gabriella.' It's nice that you're doing that for him."

Joyce paused, looking over at me with a soft expression that made me feel seen in a way I wasn't used to. "I'm sorry to hear that," she said quietly. "Every kid should feel like they're important, even in the little things."

I shrugged, trying to shake off the heaviness that had suddenly plunked down on my chest. "It's fine. It was just different when I was growing up, you know? We always had a lot of people living in the house no matter where I stayed, so it was kind of 'Get what you can when you can.'"

Joyce nodded, placing a carton of milk into the fridge. "I understand. When there's a lot of mouths to feed, it can feel like you're just another person at the table."

"Exactly," I said, leaning against the counter. "My family wasn't exactly the plan-ahead type, either. I mean, my cousin Lisa hooked me up with the job at Lorenzo's restaurant, but before that, it was like... I was always trying to figure out where I fit, you know?"

I hadn't planned to go that deep into my past, but the words tumbled out before I could stop them. *It's those triggering mini cereal boxes!* I looked down, embarrassed by how much I'd just shared, but Joyce's voice pulled me back.

"Gabriella, you're making your own space now," she said. "And it sounds like you've come a long way."

As Joyce unpacked the rest of the groceries, I wandered back to the stove, stirring my masterful onions again. "You must be excited for him to come."

She smiled as she arranged juice boxes in the fridge on a shelf low enough for a child. "I am. He's a good kid. Smart, kind... But you know how kids are. He can be a handful."

"Sounds like you'll be in for a fun couple of weeks," I teased, throwing a glance over my shoulder.

"Oh, I'm sure of it." Joyce laughed. "But I wouldn't have it any other way."

I finished stirring the onions and set the pot aside, turning off the heat.

"Want to sit down for a bite?" I asked, motioning toward the table.

"Sure. Smells delicious. What did you make?"

"Just a simple sofrito rice with Cajun grilled chicken and a lime-cilantro crema," I said, waving a hand. "No big deal."

Joyce laughed. "If that's no big deal, I can't wait to see what happens when you really put your mind to it."

The truth was, I *always* put my mind and my heart into cooking, even when it was just me in the kitchen. "It's one of those meals that reminds me of…well, everywhere I've lived."

Joyce raised an eyebrow as she took a seat at the table, waiting for me to serve up the plates. "Everywhere?"

"Yeah," I said with a shrug as I plated the rice, making sure the grilled chicken breasts were nicely arranged on top. "I was kind of all over the place growing up. Mexico with my mom's family, East Texas with my dad, and Robin Creek with my aunt… I even stayed with my great-aunt for a while outside of Victoria, Texas." I slid the plate in front of Joyce, then served myself.

"Wow," she said softly, her voice full of genuine curiosity. "Lots of schools, huh?"

"Lots of schools, lots of teachers. Not so many friends, though, with all the moving around."

I sat down across from her, glancing at the meal I'd put together. The chicken had a nice char, and the seasoning smelled just right, but I wished I'd gotten a little more color on the onions. The rice had turned out fluffy, though, which was a relief.

I stabbed a piece of chicken with my fork, but I didn't take a bite just yet. Instead, I watched Joyce out of the corner of my eye, waiting for her to take her first taste. Every time I cooked for someone, there was that quiet moment of holding my breath, waiting for their reaction, their approval, hoping they'd enjoy it as much as I wanted them to.

Joyce cut into the chicken, and I watched as she slowly chewed, her eyes widening just a little. "Oh, Gabriella," she said, a smile spreading across her face. "This is delicious. I mean it. I could get used to this cooking of yours. My waistline is in jeopardy."

Her appreciation sank into me, and I allowed myself to savor her words before I took my own first bite. The flavors hit my tongue, and I gave a small nod of approval to myself. It wasn't perfect, but it was very good. The chicken was tender, the rice soaked up the sauce just right, and even the onions, despite not having the perfect color, added a nice sweetness.

Joyce smiled back, and for a moment, we just ate in silence. It was a comfortable silence, the kind that felt like we were both reflecting on our own lives without needing to fill the space with words.

As I chewed on another bite, my mind wandered back to those days in Robin Creek when I stayed with my cousin Lisa and Aunt Fran. Even though Lisa and I were close in age, there was a hint of friction between us. Like maybe she'd been promised a new bike, but Aunt Fran told Lisa they couldn't get it because they had to take care of Cousin Gabriella now.

I didn't share that part with Joyce, though. I wasn't ready to talk about the time I spent in foster care after both my parents disappeared for months, either. That memory still stung too much.

"What's Elijah's favorite meal?" I asked.

Joyce chuckled. "That boy will eat anything. But he does like fruit, I'll say."

"Cool." I tucked the information in my memory bank. Elijah was one lucky kid. I didn't think I'd ever get to be a mom; Lorenzo said he didn't want us to have kids. "They're too expensive," he'd fussed, even as he tapped his phone to send his ex-wife money for their child.

Looking at Lisa, I had to agree. She and her husband, Paulo, had three kids, and it wasn't worth it for her to work and send them to day care; they'd lose money. Elijah might be my one shot to try out recipes on young palates.

Joyce finished her plate and leaned back in her chair, sighing with satisfaction. "You know, Gabriella," she started, wiping her mouth with a napkin, "you've got a real talent. This meal"—she gestured to the empty plate in front of her—"is the kind of thing people look forward to. Not just the food, but the thought you put into it."

"Thank you," I replied, feeling the warmth of her compliment. I hadn't realized how much I needed to hear that, especially from someone like Joyce, who seemed so...solid. Steady. The kind of person you could count on even when everything else felt like it was constantly shifting.

She stood up and began clearing the dishes, but I waved her off. "I've got it," I said.

Joyce hesitated for a second, then gave a little nod. "All right, if you insist. But only because I need to get Elijah's room squared away. Next time, we're doing it together."

"Deal," I said, smiling as I carried our plates to the sink.

As I washed the dishes, my thoughts drifted again—this time to the idea of family. Joyce was preparing for her grandson like it was second nature to make a kid feel welcome, to make him feel at home. It made me wonder if I'd ever know that kind of certainty.

"You are one lucky kid, Elijah," I whispered as I loaded the dishwasher. "Lucky, indeed."

CHAPTER 6

Joyce

Two weeks later, I figured Richard had forgotten all about me, because I didn't see anything from him in my social media feed. But then Gabriella showed me how to see notifications differently on my phone, and there he was!

I told her only that I was looking out for a request from an "old friend," but as soon as his picture showed on my screen, she grabbed the phone from me and teased, "Ooh! He's definitely a silver fox. Go 'head, Joyce!"

Gabriella took too much liberty in our relationship, if you ask me. Calling me by my first name, too, when we were more than thirty years apart. But that's how young people do it, I suppose. They've got ingrained freedoms my generation wouldn't have imagined—not if you wanted to be respectable. Not if you wanted to stay out of trouble.

So I didn't fuss at her for snatching my phone to take a look at Richard. She and I were two different people, with different backgrounds and upbringings. Except, if I'm being honest, I would have to agree that Richard was nice-looking. "He was my friend when I was in high school. I came here to visit my grandmother every summer back then."

"Summer flings, huh?" Gabriella gave me my phone, as well as a pestering grin.

"I wouldn't call it that." I threw the phone in my purse.

Gabriella hadn't made anything special that morning, so I'd made a quick bowl of cereal.

"You need somebody, you know?" Gabriella said.

"I do not. I'm rediscovering myself for myself first." I stood to put my bowl in the sink.

She took it, and my spoon, from me.

"I can—"

"I got it, I got it," she insisted. And in moments like that, I appreciated whatever was in her background that gave her such a sweet sense of hospitality, even if she didn't call me "Miss" or say "ma'am."

"Thank you."

"Go. I need you out of here. Today's trial recipe is major. I need to concentrate."

This wasn't the first time she'd kicked me out of our kitchen. I gave her a playful roll of the eyes and left her alone. When she got in her cooking zone, Gabriella could be somewhat fierce, until it came time for taste-testing.

"Just as well. I'm heading to the airport to get Elijah."

She nodded.

"And by the way," I added, "I hope it's not too much of an inconvenience for you, me bringing a kid into the house. A ten-year-old boy, at that. I could pick up a robe or a housecoat for you if that would help." I wasn't trying to be funny, but Gabriella had a few tributes to Daisy from *The Dukes of Hazzard* in her closet. A housecoat would provide a quick and easy cover-up.

Her face crumpled in laughter. "A housecoat? Oh my God! If

I ever own a housecoat, please call my family and stage an intervention, because at *that* point, I have given up on life."

"I beg your pardon." I gave Gabriella two slow blinks and a throat-clear, which caused her to cover her lips with a hand. "I am a proud member of the housecoat club. When and if you are blessed to join the ranks of the retired and relaxed, you will consider yourself blessed to own lounging attire."

She shook her head. "You need somebody to get you out of the house. To get you out of *your* housecoats. Look at you now—wearing a wraparound." She pointed at my denim dress. "This is seriously only a belt away from a housecoat."

A giggle escaped my lips. Gabriella's quick wit reminded me of myself at her age. Thought I knew it all at twenty-six. Thought getting old was the worst thing that could happen to a person, not realizing that the only way to escape getting old is to die young.

I gave her the index finger. "I cannot with you today. Gotta go get the child."

She threw back her mass of curls and sighed. "Fine. I'll keep my sarong on a hook."

"Thank you. He won't be any trouble," I assured her. "Elijah—we call him EJ—is an only child. He knows how to keep himself entertained."

"To someone like me, who grew up in a house full of people, that sounds really sad," she remarked. She rinsed my bowl and spoon, then set them in the dishwasher.

"How many kids?"

"Only four kids. Me, my sister, my brother, and a cousin. But mi tia y mi tio, mi abuelita. I'm sorry. Aunt, uncle, grandmother."

She slipped in and out of Spanish as easily as I did with Southern dialect.

"Must have been nice to always have someone around."

"It was. And it's nice to be here with you, too, Joyce," Gabriella said. The way her eyes rolled to the left, she must have just come to the realization.

Her kind words surprised me. I hadn't given much thought to Gabriella being my roommate beyond the simple inconvenience of the shared kitchen. But she was right. It was nice knowing there was someone else in the house. In case of emergency, if nothing else. "I'm glad to have you here as well."

Before things got too sappy, I slung my purse over my shoulder, said goodbye, and headed out. I thought about Gabriella's words all the way there and wondered if, subconsciously, I had come up with the idea to make Grandma Jewel's house into a duplex because I wanted or needed some form of companionship. Sharing. Love.

Then I remembered the math. Going from two incomes to sole breadwinner changes your perspective.

I barely recognized Elijah when he bounded through the gate. I was looking for a little boy, four or five inches shorter than the young man who came all the way up to my shoulders when I hugged him. "EJ! What is your momma feeding you?"

"Hi, Grandma!" He held on to me tight, and I forgot all my hesitations about keeping him for a few weeks. This boy was golden to me, looking like my son more than his father, with his curly locs, reddish-brown skin, and a small gap between his two front teeth.

"Everything go okay on the flight?"

"Yes, ma'am. I met the pilots!"

"Oooh! What did you think of them?"

"They were all right. They had a lot of equipment and monitors."

"Sounds about right. You hungry?"

I wasn't finished with the two-word question and he was nodding already. A cash register cha-chinged in my head when I thought about my grocery bill for the next few weeks.

After I texted my daughter to let her know her son had made it safely, we waited for his luggage at the rotating bin, where Elijah gave me more highlights from his flight alone. He'd earned a pin with wings and a sticker for his bravery during the flight, and the attendant had given him an extra packet of pretzels because he'd asked so politely.

We grabbed his luggage and returned to my car. He hopped into the front seat, which surprised me for a moment. "You in the front seat now?"

"Grandma, I'm ten."

"That you are, EJ," I agreed.

We buckled up for the forty-five-mile drive from the Lubbock airport to Robin Creek. I had plenty of questions for him about school, teachers, friends, and church—which, I suppose, encompassed the entirety of his life.

He answered. He liked his teachers at the intermediate school, he had friends in every class, and he was a little sad about missing Vacation Bible School at church. "But I'm glad to be with you, Grandma. I miss you since...you know." He fell silent and lowered his head.

The d-word, again, stumbling awkwardly into the conversation with my grandson.

"EJ, you know I still love you, right?"

"Yes, ma'am."

"And I'm always going to be here for you. Any time you want to talk to me, just ask your mother."

He jerked his head. "Could you get me a phone, Grandma? Two of my friends have phones already—Mike and Randall."

He must have thought telling me their names would have more impact. "No, siree. A phone is a big responsibility. And a monthly bill."

The spark left his eyes again. "My mom and dad don't want me on their phones. All I have is a tablet."

I thought, *Poor thang. All he has is a minicomputer that cost several hundred dollars.*

"And I can't even use the tablet every day because of homework and stuff," he continued to plead his case. "If I had a phone, I could call you anytime."

What in the world? EJ had game? "I can't override your parents' decision that you shouldn't have a phone right now. Maybe you could use that tablet to make a presentation letting them know why you need one now that you're ten. But you must have valid reasons." Just that quickly, I slipped into Grandma mode, scheming with this child to get what he wanted from his parents. Mind you, if he were my child, the conversation would have ended abruptly and resolutely a long time ago.

Elijah asked, "What does 'valid reason' mean?"

"It means your reasons are important and true. Like, maybe you need a phone in order to communicate things with your parents. This summer is a perfect scenario. While you're away, you might need to tell them something. You might want to text them 'I miss you' or let them know that you've discovered a new cereal brand that you like."

He nodded. "Yeah. And then when I go to Grandpa's house for the rest of the summer, I could call my mom and dad and even my friends, because it's boring at Grandpa's house."

"Why would you be bored at Grandpa's?" I asked. "You always have a great time at the house."

"Not without you," he stated with a bit of tweenage attitude. "It's not the same."

His declaration felt more like an accusation. I tried resurrecting every good memory I imagine he had with my ex-husband. "Really, EJ? You and Grandpa love going out back, setting up the tent, and eating lunch outside."

"Because you pack the best food."

"What about the time you two went skating? I sat on the benches and watched. Wasn't it fun being out there with him?"

"Only because you were smiling and waving at us. Grandpa fussed the whole time."

Wow. Elijah had a different recollection of his time at "the house" with me and his grandfather. A pound of guilt thunked in my belly because I understood him well now. I'd spent most of my life managing my husband's relationships with the more passive members of our family, including EJ. I reminded my husband to call our children, EJ, and even my sister-in-law on their birthdays to make him seem caring. Muted him and then paraphrased his often-harsh words to soften the impact. I signed his name on sympathy cards. But now, my grandson was dealing with my ex-husband head-on, and he had come to the same conclusion that had taken me thirty years to reach: He didn't want to be around that man.

Instinctively, my first thought was to curb Elijah's thoughts by pointing out his grandfather's decent qualities. He was dependable. Practical. And he was a really solid baker when he put his mind to it. (He only put his mind to it when I cornered him about not doing his fair share.)

"Your grandpa makes the best cinnamon rolls, you know?"

Elijah muttered, "I know. But he only makes them when Breanne is there."

"Breanne," I muttered before thinking. "Who's Breanne?"

Elijah slapped a hand over his mouth. "Oops. Sorry. I'm not supposed to tell you that Grandpa has a girlfriend."

My entire torso tingled as though I was having a hot flash. But that couldn't be because there was no sweat forming on my forehead. *A girlfriend?* I wasn't naive enough to think that my husband would remain single after our divorce. But bringing her around our grandchildren? And using poor Elijah in this maniacal plan to impress Breanne, to fool her into thinking that he was the kind of man who voluntarily woke up early and made cinnamon rolls for his family?

Ridiculous. Yet typical.

I sucked my teeth to contain my anger.

Though tempted, I didn't want to press Elijah for more information, given his slip-up, so I asked an adjacent question. "Who told you not to tell me?"

"My mom."

"*Hmph*. Figures." Terri was still more bitter than Eric about the divorce.

"What figures?" Elijah asked.

"Nothing, honey. Listen, I don't want to know about your grandpa's girlfriend, so let's just act like you never told me that secret, okay?"

"Okay," he happily agreed and opened his backpack, searching for something.

Everybody knows that children can hold secrets as well as they can hold water in their hands. How old was she, anyway? I didn't start seeing Breannes on my class roll sheet until the Britney Spears days.

The cellophane unwrapping around a crispy rice bar brought

my attention back to my grandson. "How about we stop at Mickey D's and get you a kids' meal?"

"I eat the grown-up meals now," he said, looking up at me with all the certainty of a five-star restaurant critic.

No wonder he'd gained a little double chin since I saw him last. "Is that so?"

"Yes, ma'am."

I stopped and got him some adult-size food on the way home. He gobbled it down like a linebacker, and I could only hope that he snatched Eric's hard-earned food money away with the same gusto. *The nerve of him.* Introducing my grandson to another woman at the house! We hadn't been divorced long enough for him to bring someone in to take my place.

Turned out, I should have gotten myself some fast food as well, because, upon entrance to the duplex, it was clear the kitchen would be out of service for a bit. The smoke alarm trilled loudly, causing both Elijah and me to cover our ears as we crossed the threshold.

I read his lips: *What's happening?*

There were no flames, just smoke and Gabriella running around the kitchen in a flurry, opening windows and, presumably, cursing in Spanish. Her hair was now disheveled, and the apron was streaked with flour and sauce stains.

I helped her by propping open the back door with a chair, and Elijah jumped into action by fanning toward the smoke alarm with the coloring book in his backpack, though it didn't help.

It took three minutes or so for the loud noise to stop. By then, Elijah had started coughing.

"Go down the hallway. Your room is the third on the right." I pointed him down my hallway.

Gabriella took another breath and leaned her hip against the dishwasher. "I'm sorry."

"What's going on?"

As the smoke cleared—literally—I could see the inside of my stove. The once-gleaming racks were now blackened with charred bits of whatever had been cooking.

"I think the oven overheated."

"You think?" I snapped at her. This place was all I had. This house was my past, my present, and my future. My *fixed income and alone* future.

"It was an accident," Gabriella said, defense stepping forward in her professional tone. "I was trying a new recipe. I had to use the broiler."

"Did you *utilize* it or *brutalize* it?"

She crossed her arms. "I *utilized* it. Because my new trial recipe, blackened catfish with elote topping, requires that both the fish and the corn be, well, blackened by the broiler."

I shook my head. "That sounds gross together."

"Corn and fish?" she asked.

"*Elote* corn and fish. That's like mayonnaise and fish. Doesn't match."

She squinted at me. "What do you think is in tartar sauce?"

She had me. I sighed. "So. You broke the oven."

"The *oven* overheated. Probably because it's old. And not *updated*."

Irritation rammed through me. Gabriella must have gotten the blame-everything-on-Joyce memo that Terri had sent out to all my contacts, including my own grandson.

"I need to get Elijah settled in his room. And make sure his lungs are clear."

My eyes stung from a combination of the smoke and my hurt feelings. My ex-husband had a girlfriend, my grandson no longer made special memories at “the house,” and my new roommate had almost burned the place down because I’d run out of money to fix it.

And tartar sauce really is mostly mayonnaise.

What else have I been wrong about?

CHAPTER 7

Both my children used to sleep as late as possible. We have an old VHS somewhere of Eric Jr., around five years old, crying because we woke him up at 9:00 a.m. to open Christmas presents. They both despised cleaning on Saturday, too, but they couldn't go anywhere until they'd finished changing their sheets, dusting, and vacuuming their rooms—all tasks that required straightening up as a prerequisite to cleaning with chemicals.

Elijah, then, was a unicorn to me. That very first morning, he was up before me. I heard him shuffling around in his bedroom and the bathroom, brushing his teeth and running water to wash his face.

Gabriella was also skittering around, though this was no surprise. She had to get to her job at a local Mexican restaurant by 10:00 a.m.

I slipped into a final snooze. I wanted to stay in my bedroom at least long enough for her to leave. Following the previous day's oven incident, she'd kept to her side of the duplex and I kept to mine. Elijah distracted me from the roommate tension. He and I played his card games—two of which I'd never even heard of, so of course he beat me. Talked plenty of noise, too. "Boo-yah! Take that, Grandma!"

But I redeemed myself with UNO and whipped him a few times. I'm the kind of person who will make you draw all four of your cards before I slap down my last one, revealing that I already knew I'd beat you before you went through all the trouble.

It humbles a person.

I showed Elijah the summer children's activity flyers I'd collected for Robin Creek. He said the library would be great, and the YMCA, too. "Are there any kids on your street?"

"I've seen a few," I recalled, suddenly regretting the fact that I hadn't made my rounds in the neighborhood since moving in a little more than two weeks ago. "I'll ask Miss Mary, the mail carrier, tomorrow. She knows everybody and their children and their dogs."

We had hot dogs and beans for dinner—using the stove only, of course. Later, we watched a movie, which I fell asleep on.

"Grandma, you're asleep," Elijah said as he elbowed me. "You should go to bed."

"I will. After it's over." The truth was that I hadn't figured out how to put the child restriction on the television, so I couldn't leave him alone with free rein over a remote control. This was the kind of thing Gabriella could help me figure out, but I gathered she and I were still in "cooling off" mode, with our attitudes lingering in the air as much as the burnt-oven-coil smell.

So waking up again to the smell of simmering fruit the next day and hearing Elijah's voice intermixed with Gabriella's—yeah, that was different from either child I'd raised, and definitely different from the silence between her and me the day before.

My hand reached for my trusty robe first, which ushered

the memory of Gabriella's rant about robes and housecoats. Amusement brought a tiny grin to my face. My roommate was an opinionated one. Strong. Didn't let anyone—including me—run over her. I liked that about her. I could have used more of that in me at her age. Maybe even now.

I proudly zipped up my pink fleece housecoat, handled my morning business, and joined the two of them in the kitchen. Elijah wore Gabriella's "Kiss the Cook" apron. I obeyed the instruction, grabbing his cheeks and planting a smack on his forehead. Then I pointed at his apron, and he smiled at me. "Morning, Grandma. We made breakfast. It's waffles, but we're not using syrup."

"Oh?"

His eyebrows jumped with excitement. "We cooked strawberries, raspberries, and blueberries. We added sugar, water, and cornstarch."

"It was easy," Gabriella singsonged as she set a stack of perfectly golden-brown waffles on the table, avoiding eye contact with me.

"Good morning, Gabriella."

Finally, she looked at me. "Good morning."

My mother used to say that there's more to good manners than just words. "Speaking to folks lets us all know we see each other, and it keeps lines of communication open," Momma said. And she was right.

Elijah blurted out, "We also added lemon, to balance out the sugars—right, Gabriella?"

It occurred to me then that I hadn't properly introduced those two yesterday, with the smoke and all.

"It's *Miss* Gabriella to you, EJ."

"Oh, I don't mind—"

"And I want her to call me Elijah."

Those two were bursting with information.

"It it's all the same to you, Gabriella, I'd like for him to practice his manners, respecting his elders, by calling you Miss Gabriella. And EJ...Elijah...that's fine. Do you want me to call you Elijah, too?"

"No. EJ is fine for you."

"Great. Miss Gabriella and Elijah, otherwise known as EJ, the breakfast looks and smells amazing. I can't wait to taste your creation."

A silent puff of forgiveness passed between me and Gabriella as we all sat down to break bread. Elijah blessed the food, and we passed the plates of waffles, chicken sausage, and eggs around first. Then came their masterpiece of mixed-berry syrup, which melted away the last remnants of my attitude with Gabriella. The syrup, still a little warm and thick with fruit chunks, glistened as it poured slowly from the pitcher—deep reds and purples swirling together like stained glass. It clung to the waffles, seeping into every crevice. This girl had some kind of culinary magic in her hands.

Now, my momma could cook, as could Grandma Jewel. They passed down their cooking skills and recipes to me, and I knew them by heart after so many years of repetition. Gabriella had a way of taking what was already delicious and adding her own twist. Such was the case with this syrup. There was a little more warmth and depth to it—something besides the ingredients Elijah had listed.

I swallowed. "There's something in here. Adding richness..."

Gabriella rewarded me with a wink and a smile. She turned toward Elijah, who was beaming with enthusiasm. "Should we tell her?"

He nodded half a second before shouting, "A dash of vanilla!"

"Mexico is one of the original sources of vanilla," she said.

"Mmm, mmm, mmm," I said, swirling another square of my waffle in the sweet crimson sauce. How she'd known to add vanilla was pure genius. "This is so rich, I hope it's paying local taxes."

Gabriella laughed, and Elijah joined her like he actually understood the joke.

She dabbed the corners of her mouth with a napkin and cleared her throat. "Well, I'm glad you like it, because I'm planning to enter it next week in a contest. At Preston's Fine Dining. In Lubbock. They're accepting entrants for the summer Breakfast and Bliss contest. I'm thinking I'll enter my waffles and this syrup."

"You'll definitely win with that combination," I told her.

"But I need that soul food spin, so I'm gonna perfect my honey-pepper bacon. Which means I'll need the oven. With a broiler. Like, soon and very soon."

Her reference to '70s gospel music struck me almost more than her request. "Whatchu know about Andraé Crouch?"

"They sing that song at *every* single funeral on my dad's side of the family. And 'Amazing Grace.'"

"We might need some amazing grace *and* a miracle, too, to get that oven fixed by next week," I told her with a shake of my head.

She reached into her jeans pocket and handed me a slip of yellow paper.

I unfolded it to find three names with phone numbers.

"Handymen near Robin Creek," Gabrilla added. "My boss recommended the first two. The third is my cousin."

Following her previous marks, I refolded the paper and set it next to my napkin. "I'll give them a call."

"Thank you, Ms. Joyce," Gabriella said.

She learned fast, I tell you.

Elijah and I cleaned up after breakfast so Gabriella could head out for work. He asked me at least ten times what I thought of the food.

"It was amazing, EJ. I never knew you could cook like that."

His teeth—way too big for his mouth—shone brightly. "I took a picture of the syrup recipe. I'm going to make it again for my mom and dad."

"Maybe you could make it with Grandpa. He keeps berries and fruits around, you know."

There I went again, trying to smooth things over between family members. And there went Elijah's smile. "No. Only with my parents. And you."

The next dish to pass from the sink to the dishwasher was the large plate that had previously held the waffles. Elijah grabbed his side of the dish, and I didn't let my side go, which forced him to look me in the eye.

"EJ, you know your grandfather and I still love you very much even though we're not together."

He tugged at the plate again, and I released it. The sullen look on his face remained.

"Did you hear me?"

"Yes, ma'am."

"What do you have to say?"

He faced me again. "I don't think Grandpa loves me."

"Why would you say that, EJ?"

"'Cause whenever I'm around, he tells me to be quiet or go to another room. He never calls me, he doesn't come to any of my games." Elijah concluded, with a shrug, "He doesn't *act* like he loves me."

And right then and there, I stopped trying to convince my grandson to override his people-meter. Shoot, if I had any sense, I would have come to that same conclusion about my ex-husband twenty years ago instead of writing him passes because he worked (which he would have to do, married or not), protected us (I guess by virtue of being a male residing in the home), and didn't cheat (to my knowledge).

I swallowed hard. This hurt. But Elijah was telling "his truth," as they called it now. Blood-kin relationship and proper manners aside, this was his experience with his grandfather. And I had to agree: People who act like they don't love you probably don't.

Elijah deserved an offering basket for that sermon.

I rinsed the next juice glass, passed it to him. "I understand."

Two hours later, the second handyman on the list, who'd offered the cheapest estimate and the earliest available slot, showed up with tools in tow.

"You related to Miss Jewel?" he asked. He was old enough to be my uncle, yet still clearly flirting, with his too-wide grin and his too-tight wedding band.

"Yes. She was my grandmother."

"Whoo! You're just as beautiful, sugar."

"Thank you, sir," I replied, because I wanted him to know he was at least ten years older than me and needed to watch it.

"Naw. Don't *sir* me. Just call me Wardell," he said with a wink. "A pretty woman like you ought to know—age is just a number."

He must have meant to open a doorway for dating. I shut it closed. "I was taught to respect my elders."

A flash of disdain crossed his face, but I guess he figured he'd better not get testy with me, seeing as we weren't at some bar. Bottom line: He was at work and I was a customer. I'd called him over to fix a stove, and I don't mix business with whatever it was he wanted to do on the side.

As I sat scrolling through the news on my phone, I wondered for a split second if I had been too harsh with Wardell. It was my nature to second-guess myself, to replay my words and actions to see if I had given the impression that I was remotely interested.

Bump that.

The better question: What on earth made men think that women were supposed to appreciate them for noticing us? By men, of course, I meant Eric Sr. mostly. But even Wardell, who was now waist-deep in the oven, seemed to think that it was perfectly appropriate to dangle his married bait and see if I would bite.

Elijah had run outside with the first child he saw walking down the street. The boy, named Roderick Everson—I remembered his people's last name—had two bicycles. He let Elijah borrow the old one, and they were off. So there I was, inside my home, alone with a man I didn't know. There's an undercurrent of wariness that comes with a scenario like this. Not to mention, he was married.

Am I becoming a feminist? Isn't that what happens to bitter, divorced women?

Am I bitter?

No. I'm not bitter. A bitter woman would have kicked Wardell out for leaning in too closely when he'd introduced himself.

My thumb stopped at a headline: Ex-Wife Sues Second Wife for Intellectual Theft of Signature Lasagna Recipe. Now, *that* woman was bitter.

"Welp," Wardell announced as he stood up straight and wiped blackened hands on his overalls. "You're gonna need a new stove."

"What?" The math teacher in me saw a three-digit figure.

"I can install it, but there's another issue. You'll probably need new wiring."

Four figures.

"Come again?" I asked.

His face was all business now, flat and brown and frowns. "This house is going on a hundred years old. A new stove has different power requirements. An electrician can upgrade the wiring so the new stove won't overload your system. You've got two jobs up ahead."

"Wow," I whispered. "Wasn't expecting all of this." The air in the kitchen suddenly felt thick, as if the history of the house itself was pressing down on me, reminding me of just how old everything around me was. The walls, the floors—had they always been this fragile? Owning an older home came with its problems, though. I'd known this when I planned the move back to Robin Creek. I had hoped that the renovation, which had unearthed and resolved several issues already, meant I had at least a few years before I ran into trouble again. But trouble didn't have the decency to wait until I was dressed and ready before barging in.

"I can remove this oven and install the new one, once the electrician finishes. I'll email you an estimate, and you can let me know when you'd like to get started," Wardell said matter-of-factly. His curt manner made the news sound even worse. "That will be $125 for today's service visit."

"Of course," I said. We settled up through my phone.

"Like I said, let me know when."

"I have to think through a few things," I stalled, trying to calculate how much an electrician cost, wishing I had a friend in the handyman world. My mind raced, flipping through imaginary invoices and numbers that seemed to stack higher and higher, a mountain of expenses I wasn't sure I could climb.

"And next time, don't be so mean, Miss Lady," he quipped.

Startled, I snapped my neck back. "Excuse me?"

"It wouldn't hurt to be nice. You're not in the big city anymore. Smile. Might even lower my price for ya." And out popped his sly grin again.

I turned on my heel and led him to the front door. Once he was safely on the other side of my locked screen door, I yelled to him, wagging my phone, "I'll call you again if I need you."

"Oh, you'll definitely need me. 'Cause I got the best price in town. Ain't that why you called me in the first place?" he chided.

He was right about his fee, but I was willing to take a part-time job if necessary in order to keep from calling him again. I closed the main door without answering his question.

He laughed loudly and shouted, "I'll be waitin'!"

I leaned back against the door and took deep breaths. The nerve of him, lecturing me, offering me a discount if I addressed him pleasantly. What did he think I was, an escort?

Three rapid knocks shook my shoulders. My breath caught. *Wardell?* No way was I letting him back in that house. If he'd forgotten a tool, I'd chuck it to him through an open window.

"Grandma!"

My lungs emptied in a deep sigh at the sweet sound of Elijah's voice. I felt like hugging him, but the sweat on his face and neck and his "boy" smell postponed the move.

"Guess what?! We found turtles and frogs in a pond!"

"I see. You're going to need a shower before we go to the LEGO club at the library."

He raised an arm and turned his nose to sniff the aroma, gauging himself. "My shirt doesn't smell *that* bad."

I laughed. "How bad must it be for you to wash yourself?"

"Ummm...a seven. Right now I'm a five."

"You're a nine," I assured him. "Shower."

He took another whiff. Smiled at me. "Yes, ma'am."

"Boy, you knew all along you were a nine."

With a chuckle, he took off toward the bathroom.

Elijah's return and his silliness pushed the dread about the oven issue away, giving me my sound mind again.

I said a silent prayer that my grandson would never grow up to be like Wardell, or my ex-husband, or any person who thought they were God's gift to other people. But for real, I needed a gift from somewhere to fix the oven. I prayed for that, too.

CHAPTER 8

The LEGO club was more like the LEGO cult. When I tell you these children and their families love those toys, I am not lyin'. Not only did they bring an ungodly amount of LEGO bricks, but they also had clothes and shoes and jewelry encrusted in them. Elijah must have felt like a loser with the one little section of his backpack full of the hard, foot-maiming toys.

Nonetheless, he had found his people. After meeting the leaders of the group and making sure Elijah felt comfortable, I wandered back to the main part of the library to take a gander at books. The nostalgic smell of aged paper and ink inside the ancient library brought me a sense of peace. I was thumbing through a Victoria Christopher Murray book I'd been meaning to read, when Eileen sang out my name.

"Joyce! So good to see you!"

"Yes, hello. I'm here with my grandson. LEGO club."

"Wonderful."

It did my heart good to witness the glint in her eye. Always a pleasure to be welcome.

"We're about to start the group meeting I was telling you about."

"The desperate group?" I'm still not sure how that slipped out, except to say that it was what I'd named it in my mind.

Eileen poked out her lips. "No… That's not us. Though I do feel desperate sometimes, with the rise in inflation."

"Okay," I agreed emphatically, still in disbelief that I'd said what I thought I was only thinking.

"No, this is the group of women who started out as a Silent Book Club chapter, but we talked too much, so we just decided we'd come and talk about life and maybe recommend books to each other. Off the record, we call ourselves 'the Chapter Chatters.'"

The name gave me a laugh, and Eileen led me into the group without protest. The meeting room was cozy, with a scattering of chairs arranged in a loose circle. The walls were lined with bookshelves overflowing with worn paperbacks, their spines faded from years of handling. A framed print of a field of bluebonnets hung by the window, adding a splash of color to the otherwise beige walls.

For a small Texas town, the group was more racially diverse than I'd expected. Two of the women appeared to be of Latina heritage. There were three White women, including Eileen, and there was one other Black woman besides me. All of us had at least a few gray hairs.

"Everyone, this is Joyce."

The group said a collective "Hello," and then, upon Eileen's direction, each woman introduced herself. The only one whose name slipped into my long-term memory was Sonia, because that was my best friend's name back in high school. This Sonia, however, was White and reminded me of Julia Roberts, with huge, floppy, artsy earrings. I admire people who wear statement jewelry; they're braver than the rest of us.

Eileen put me on the spot. "Anything you want to tell us about yourself?"

"Well, ummm…I just moved here. This is my father's hometown. Recently divorced. I'm here in this meeting because my grandson is here, playing with the LEGO club. And I need an electrician and a handyman because my oven broke."

I'd sandwiched the d-word because it wasn't the most important part about me. And I'd included it because I didn't want to endure questions about my marital status or my husband—*What does he do?* People always want to know what your husband does so they can figure out where you are on the income ladder.

"That was random." The lady with the '80s bangs gave a friendly cackle. "But welcome. Half of us here are divorced, so we understand."

"Twice."

"I hold the record. Three times," a brunette—who had overdone it with her lip injections, in my opinion—confessed.

"Oh, and my husband is a handyman," one of the White women noted. "His name's Wardell. I'll give you his number."

The Latina woman whose bun was held in place by chopsticks squinted at me, a silent warning that needed no explanation.

Eileen cleared her throat. "Maybe later, Christine."

Everyone except Christine nodded. Somebody said, "Yes. Later."

Someone else mumbled, "*Much* later."

Christine tsked and said, "Wardell is much improved. We've been to counseling for four months."

"He's still too frisky. He's gonna need more training before we unleash him on the new girl," Sonia said.

Christine rolled her eyes. "I hate y'all."

And then they all laughed, Christine included.

While I'd already reached my drama quota for the day, I appreciated the transparency in the group. Everybody knew there was a problem with Wardell, including his wife, and they were talking through it.

"I met Wardell this morning, already. He did assess the situation and gave a plan of action," I said, hoping to redeem Christine. Her pitiful expression called to me, and I opened my big mouth.

"But did he flirt with you, Joyce?" Sonia asked.

"Right," Christine piped up. "I want to know. Did he? And don't be scared to tell the truth. That's the one rule of Chapter Chatters: Don't lie."

What in the world had I walked into? My lips refused to budge.

"See how long it's taking her to answer?" The woman in red elbowed Christine next to her.

Eileen intervened. "Joyce, you don't have to answer." She turned toward the group again. "Come on, y'all. It's her first meeting."

Christine's eyes pleaded with me, however, for the truth about her husband. Who was I to deny her that information? On the other hand, who was I to break up a marriage? Just because mine had dwindled down to the size of a pea didn't mean I wanted to shrivel someone else's hope.

After a few more seconds of hesitation, I replied, "He was... friendly."

Christine buried her face in her well-manicured hands, and I wished I'd never said anything at all.

The brunette shook her head. "It takes time."

"How much *time* does it take for a man to stop cheating on his wife?" Christine asked—more frustrated than sad, it sounded.

"We cannot answer that ageless question," Eileen stated in the solemn tone of a funeral director.

"Is cheating the reason your marriage ended?"

For some reason, I was happy to answer. "No. We divorced because my husband checked out emotionally a long time ago."

A collective "*Hmph*," arose, with nods of approval. No one asked if we could have worked it out, if he was otherwise a good man. No judgment. This was a room full of women who knew that relationships were hard work, and neither me nor Christine should be judged for deciding to stay or leave. Unlike my daughter, Eric's family, and even a few of my friends.

"How long were you married?"

Eileen said, "Althea, ladies, we're not interviewing Joyce for a position." And yet, Eileen's slightly parted lips said she, too, wanted an answer.

I made note of the other Black woman's name. Althea.

"It's okay," I said. "I—I think maybe I need to talk about it." I knew no one in this room. There was nothing to lose. And a part of me—the part that always tried to make everyone feel better—was happy to get the spotlight off Christine. "We were married for thirty years. It's a silver divorce. Two years ago."

"Oh! So you're still in your A.M. phase."

"What's that, Lupita?"

Lupita—Latina woman with long eyelashes and a chin dimple.

"A.M. means 'anti-man.' I'm Valerie—it's a Valerie-ism. It's the time right after a divorce when you can't stand men. Like, you woke up mad at them. A.M. Get it?" She aimed the question at me.

Valerie—huge brown eyes with bushy brows.

"Yes, I do." And her philosophy made sense. I *was* mad at men, on the whole, even if I didn't want to be. "What about P.M.?"

She shrugged. "I don't know. I've been A.M. for seven years now. And my lady parts are not happy about it."

The room roared with laughter, and I let myself shift into sister mode. Guard down, giggles ready to spill out at any moment. Finally, a safe space.

Eileen's neck reddened. "Does anyone have a book to recommend?"

Althea snorted. "Not one that's better than our discussion."

It took us a minute to reel in our laughter.

Sonia held up a hand. "Seriously, y'all. I've been married since I turned nineteen. I've never wanted anyone except my Paul. He's as good as God made 'em. But there are days when I wonder if we're gonna make it."

"Make it to where?" Christine asked. "There is no destination except death. Isn't that what makes a marriage successful—just staying together until one of us dies? Does it matter if you wanted to kill the other person the whole darn time?"

The one woman whose name I still hadn't learned shook her head. "You can't even say a cuss word, can you?"

Christine sat up straighter. "No, I was taught that cussing is unladylike."

"Well, I don't trust people who *don't* cuss," Sonia blurted out. "It ain't normal!"

"Hell no, it ain't!" Sonia gave Lupita a high five.

"But, real talk, you could probably get away with whooping Wardell a time or two. You've got that over-civilization syndrome. I saw it on a Hulu show. True crime."

"Is that like affluenza?" Lupita asked.

"Kind of. She'd been socialized to be perfect. Somehow, the wife was found not guilty," Sonia informed us, though I couldn't imagine anyone in Texas over the age of forty who hadn't heard about Candy Montgomery. Even if they hadn't heard of her back then, her story was all over the streaming networks.

"We are *not* planning violent acts as we convene on library property," Eileen declared, followed by, "But we do have a book about that case on our shelves."

Sonia pointed. "Give it to Christine."

Christine playfully slapped her hand away.

"She doesn't have to kill him," Lupita pointed out. "She just has to leave him. You know what they say—the minute you leave a man, he suddenly becomes everything you ever wanted him to be."

That explained Eric making breakfast for Elijah. And Breanne.

I liked all the women, probably because I was somewhere in between Christine and Sonia. Primed for perfection, but finding myself in the fallout of reality. Picking up little pieces of me—like debris—since the divorce. My voice, my thoughts, my dreams all scattered about as I held it together for my husband and my children, who hadn't asked to be born. They deserved an intact family, I'd lectured myself for decades.

Really, before the divorce, when perimenopause hit. All of a sudden, I didn't have an over-civilized bone left in my body. My rose-colored glasses fell off, and I understood that my husband didn't love me. He loved what I *did* for him, but not me. Not *Joyce*.

Our meeting concluded with gathering into a group huddle and Eileen reading a quote out loud: "If you can only take one step today, then take one step today."

"Good one," Althea said, her face brimming with the same gratitude that swelled through my heart.

The Chapter Chatters had done me good. When Eileen had first told me about the group, I had no intention of coming.

Sitting around talking to women without actually doing anything productive—lesson planning, grading papers, folding clothes, cleaning the church, braiding hair, something—seemed like a privileged, first-world thing to do. Yet I felt better than I had in a long time, just being heard and meeting women who had already traveled down D-Word Lane, and I had Eileen to thank for that. I did so as the room cleared.

"You're welcome. It's a fun bunch."

"I agree."

"Think you might join us again?" she asked, her voice full of hope.

"I don't know. My grandson's only here for a few weeks. And like I said earlier, there's so much work to do still with my house. By the time I'm finished, I might need a job!" I half joked.

"What kind of work do you do?"

"I'm a retired elementary school teacher."

Eileen perked up. "Well, you're in luck. Christine and Valerie are retired educators, too. They're both well connected with Robin Creek schools. I'm sure they can point you in the right direction. You want me to reach out to them?"

The power of a small town. "I'd appreciate it."

"Sure thing." She stopped pushing the chairs into place and stood in front of me, hands clasped across her stomach like she was giving an Easter speech. "Just remember, Joyce. Even though you've got a lot going on, it's important to make taking care of yourself a priority on your list of things to do."

Her words gave me pause, in a good way. "Thank you, Eileen."

She winked and resumed straightening up the room.

I sat on an old bench right outside the LEGO meeting room, watching as the children put away their toys, digesting

Eileen's words. She was right. I mean, I used to journal. I used to get my nails and hair done regularly, and doing so used to feel like pampering. But then, when my life got super busy around the time my kids were teens, keeping those appointments got hectic. And then when the pandemic hit and I stopped for a while, I really didn't want to go back to the salon. My nails regained their strength, my hair was long enough for a quick ponytail, and I got used to seeing myself without makeup, quite frankly.

It was Eric Sr. who made a remark that it was time I "got back to looking like myself" when the restrictions were lifted. When that happened, I loathed going to the salon. It was Eric-care, marriage maintenance. Definitely not self-care.

I gathered Elijah from his group, and we began the walk around the square to my car. "How was it?"

"Cool. They showed me how to make a robot, with wires and everything. The leader, Mr. James, his son is Michael, and Michael's in the same grade as me. Do you know about electricity conduction?"

"A little," I told him.

"What did you do while I was in class?" he asked.

His interest touched me, made me slow my stride a bit despite the rising heat. "I met a group of ladies. We talked and laughed."

"Sounds boring. But I'm glad you made friends."

"I suppose I did, huh?"

"Yep. Me, too."

We clasped our hands and swung them back and forth as we walked to my car, never mind the fact that my shoulder joints would probably need ointment the next day.

"I'm going to miss you, Grandma."

His statement slowed the momentum in my arms. "What do you mean?"

"When I go to Grandpa's house in a few weeks. He won't take me to the library or let me make berry syrup."

"The cooking is all Gabriella," I said, attempting to deflect.

"You know what I mean," Elijah thwarted me. "I won't have any fun. Just follow the rules, be quiet, and leave him alone. Might as well be in prison."

"EJ, so help me God, you will never see the inside of a prison cell. And..." I felt myself slip into Superwoman mode. My gold crown clinked into place and my red cape flapped in the wind, because I couldn't stand the thought of Elijah being shunned by my ex-husband, though I knew his prediction was 100 percent correct. Children shouldn't have to suffer because of adults. "I'll look online for some things you and your grandfather can do together in the northern Austin area. I'll come up with a suggested schedule—how's that?"

His face fell slack, unconvinced. "I guess."

My wheels were spinning now as I calculated a plan. I could call Eric's longtime administrative assistant, Sherry, and ask her to keep his schedule sparse, giving him more time with Elijah. I could even purchase tickets for a few evening events. My ex-husband did not believe in wasting money or food under any circumstance. Entrapment.

I lost the last of my arm-swinging juice when Richard came bounding out of his office toward me and Elijah.

"Hi, Joyce. I inboxed—" He stopped, noticing Elijah. "Oh. Hello there, young man."

Elijah shook Richard's hand and introduced himself. I was proud of the way EJ looked him in the eyes and spoke so clearly, saying his name as well. Terri and Chris were doing a good job with my grandson.

"Good to meet you, Elijah, but it's hard to believe this woman is your grandmother. She looks far too young."

A silly smirk covered Elijah's face as he registered this man's intentions, I believe.

"I did see your inbox message online, Richard. As you can see, I've been busy with my grandson the past few days. I'll get back to you."

"Looking forward to it, Joyce."

Something about the way Richard said my name—and the way his eyes, full of sincerity and warmth, caught mine this time—sent a shiver all through me. I nodded and continued my short journey with Elijah, who talked about LEGO sets all the way home. I listened, barely, as I processed the fact that Richard Tatum was as desperate as I was. Not bottom-of-the-barrel desperate, where you'll take anybody with a pulse. No. The proper word wasn't *desperate* at all. I don't think we have a word in the English language for what I felt and what I saw in him that day on the square. The definition of the nonexistent word would be: when you miss the familiarity and comfort of having good times with people you know.

The theme song from that '80s sitcom *Cheers* played in my head. It is nice to be in the company of people who go waaay back with you. I missed that about Eric. But that was where the lyrical parallel ended. Eric and I weren't glad to be in each other's company. We functioned well, like a car that gets you from point A to point B. No music, no AC, no air freshener, no conversation along the way. Just be quiet and ride—no complaints if you don't want any problems.

I wondered what had brought Richard's marriage to an end.

Was it fooling around, like Wardell? Did they grow apart, like me and Eric? Was it both? If so, maybe he had learned something, like Lupita said. Maybe we had *both* learned something invaluable that would serve us well in our next relationships, because truth be told, I missed being able to say, "Just fix it and send the invoice," to my appliance-repair person. This fact made me wonder if I'd been with Eric for financial security as much as he'd been with me for domestic security, if that's a thing.

"Grandma!" Eric poked my arm, bringing me back to reality.

"I'm sorry. What do you need?"

"I said thank you for letting me stay with you."

Whether he meant to butter me up or not, it worked. "Glad to have you, EJ."

CHAPTER 9

A few days later, Wardell had sent an email with the estimate for his service, which, even without the electrician's work, took my breath away and almost caused me to lose the specialty Gabriella and Elijah had prepared that day: jalapeño-cheddar corn bread.

I swear, that girl could cook her behind off. But inflation don't play, and I nearly choked when I saw Wardell's numbers on my phone.

"Is it too hot?" Gabriella asked, alarmed by my reaction to the second bite.

"No, no, no. It just went down the wrong way."

Elijah pushed my glass of water closer, and I managed to take a drink and calm everyone's nerves.

I had only been retired and living in my new place for a month, and already I needed a job, like, yesterday.

Roderick came by, and my grandson took off again.

Gabriella slipped away to her side of the house and started playing her music just loud enough for me to catch the beat, but not so loud I could rightfully complain. If we'd had a full separation of the house, I might not have heard it at all.

I'd volunteered to wash dishes, which left me elbow-deep in suds with plenty of time alone to consider how on earth I was going to get this oven repaired.

One of the last arguments Eric and I'd had occurred after I'd filed for divorce. The conversation started around money. This was odd because we rarely argued about money. We both worked. I handled the daily spending wisely, he handled investments, and that was how things flowed when we were a couple.

"I hope you don't expect me to forfeit half of my 401(k)," he had nearly spat as I was clearing out my side of the closet, preparing to donate most of my clothes.

Attempting to sidestep him, I said, "This is why we have lawyers."

And then he entered the sanctum of my side of the walk-in closet, something he had never done before, to say, "I have always made more money than you."

"A perk of being a man, statistically."

He grumbled. I sighed.

Against my will, my eyes filled with tears because, truly, I wanted to stay married. Who in their right mind wants to divorce after three decades? No one. But the fact that a person would divorce after all this time means they put up with a lot of stuff for a very long time, and at some point, it's just enough.

Eric had thrown his hands in the air and left the closet. "This is stupid, Joyce! Two sensible adults have no business divorcing at our age."

I threw the pile of clothes in my arms on the floor and followed him back to the kitchen, where he poured himself a shot of brandy.

"For the record, Eric, I agree with you."

"Then why are you doing this?"

"Because two *sensible adults* would sit down and talk things out, followed by consistent actions toward improvement. You are the one who is *not* willing to grow with the demands of our marriage."

He threw the liquid back in one move. "You are making our marriage a demanding place. It was always easy before now."

"Easy for *you*," I bit back. "It seemed easy because I didn't ask you to participate. It's like... If our house was a huge party, you would have been the one bringing the ice, and I would be left to do everything else."

"I *bought* everything else," he argued.

"Money is not time, though. Or caring. Or love."

He shrugged. "Why can't you just enjoy today? The kids are gone, the house is...decorated, or whatever you did to make it a home. Now all we have to do is ride it out, Joyce. Why are you trying to ruin a good thing?"

"Because, Eric, it's not fair to me. My reward for getting the kids out of the house shouldn't be that now I only have one other person to take care of. It should be that, despite the years we were just going through the motions, we now get to resume our relationship, get reconnected, relearn each other, and decide how we want these final decades to look...together." Though I had explained that to him several times before, I took the time to do it again, hoping against all odds that this time it would sink into his soul, and he would suddenly desire to make the pivot necessary. I added, "I'm asking for a partner. But it looks to me like you want me to carry on as usual: cook, have sex, and leave you alone."

And then he'd stood still for a second, considering my words.

I knew my husband. The blank look on his face said, *And what's wrong with that?*

Hope died. I knew that if I had stayed with him and let the resentment build up even more, it wouldn't be long before my body broke down in response. Like my mother. Probably like her mother, too.

Grandma Jewel used to say that a woman has to have her peace.

It didn't seem fair that walking away from a loveless marriage and a potential heart attack came with the penalty of losing financial security to the point where you can't afford to replace an oven.

Do we really need ovens? How did our ancestors survive without them?

Just as I was pondering those questions, Gabriella stepped back into the kitchen, wringing her hands nervously. "Can I speak to you?"

I shook my hands dry. "What's going on?"

The kitchen had seen better days—an old linoleum floor with worn spots, faded cabinets that had once been white but now bore the stains of decades of meals, and the faint smell of grease that no amount of scrubbing could fully get rid of.

"My eighth- and ninth-grade homemaking teacher, Mrs. Maine, is in the competition. She was mean. Some of our parents asked for conferences with her, and she made up lies about our classroom behavior. She almost kicked me out of her class once for accidentally breaking a mixing bowl. I didn't know teachers could veto you because of a mistake!"

Gabriella's glassy eyes said there was a great deal of pain behind her long-held grudge with Mrs. Maine. "She humiliated me in front of the whole class. She named me 'the kitchen klutz.' I didn't even know what the word *klutz* meant until I took her class. People teased me about it for years. I almost lost my dignity and my confidence after two years in her class. So…ummm…yeah. I really, *really* need to practice my recipes before the competition because even if I don't win, I must score higher than her. She is my personal Mount Everest."

Dang.

It broke my heart to hear Gabriella's story, being a retired teacher. "I'm so sorry you had a bad experience with her. Teachers are people, too."

Gabriella shook her head. "True that. But some teachers shouldn't be around children. She hated us. One time, there was a new girl in class who went off completely on Mrs. Maine. And we started cheering. Then Mrs. Maine told us that we were all ingrates—another new vocabulary word—and the only reason she kept teaching was because her husband's medication was too expensive to afford without insurance benefits."

I tried compassion. "Sounds like she was going through a lot. Naturally, it impacted her attitude."

"Not my problem. If you're in a bad situation, you should strategize. Find a way to get out of it. Don't take out your frustrations on poor, innocent children, right?"

She had a point.

"How soon is the oven getting replaced?"

"When is the competition?"

"Next weekend. But I've already lost practice time since the broiler coil blew out, you know?"

Of course I knew. "I wish I could say it will be ready in time, but I can't. I just got the information from Wardell. How well do you know him, by the way?"

She tipped her head casually. "Not well."

"Good. Anyway, he sent the estimate for removal of the stove, getting a new stove, and reinstallation. But I have to get everything rewired by a certified electrician before he can put a new one in. None of it is cheap."

Gabriella squinted. "You probably needed him to diagnose the situation, but maybe you don't need him to remove an *electric* oven." She walked over to the oven. "All we gotta do is cut the power from the breaker, unscrew it, pull it out, and undo the plug. That'll save a hundred bucks, and probably a day in the process."

She'd animated her speech with simplistic hand gestures, but I couldn't imagine doing it ourselves. "Sounds like a job for a professional."

"I've done this more than once. In one of my culinary classes. We learned *everything* about the kitchen."

I shook my head. "I don't mess around with home repair. Kitchens, toilets, garage doors—none of it."

"Of course you don't. You've been married almost all your life. *And* you didn't have YouTube growing up."

In one smooth move, she grabbed her phone and opened up YouTube. She input the make and model of my stove, and voilà, up popped three different videos showing how to uninstall. By the time we'd finished watching the third one, she and the DIY fanatics had me nearly convinced that we could save ourselves some time and money.

With an enthusiastic chirp, she asked, "You want to give it a try?"

"Now?"

"Yes, *now*. The contest, remember?"

Goodness. The last thing I needed was to get electrocuted or break my arm trying to catch an oven sliding out from the wall too fast. Not to mention the trauma that Elijah would experience when he came home and found me and Gabriella knocked out on the kitchen floor.

"Let's at least get help," I said. "Someone must live to tell the story."

"Fine." She tapped her phone. "I'll call my boyfriend. He's got tools and should be on break right now."

My anxiety shot to ten as we waited for him to come, watching even more videos to be sure we both understood what was waiting on the other side of that oven door. I owned a set of tools as well, thanks to my father, but I wouldn't pretend I knew how to operate them.

Gabriella's boyfriend was tall and thickly built, with a clean-shaven, handsome face and a quiet confidence that bordered on arrogance already. They made a cute couple, though I wouldn't have pegged them as "together" by the way he walked in without so much as a peck on her cheek. She didn't fawn over him or melt into smiles, either.

Gabriella introduced me to Lorenzo, and he got to work right away.

Reminded me of my last ten years with Eric. All business.

Gabriella stood beside him for a second, showing him one of the videos we'd watched. After less than a minute, he waved her off and barked, "I got it already."

My head snapped back fast because I just knew Gabriella was going to say something about his tone. But she didn't. She sighed, holding in the thoughts that were written on her face.

Lorenzo turned on the oven light and then opened the back door. "Tell me when the light goes off."

I felt embarrassed for her. Then angry. Then I decided it was best to mind my own business and be glad someone had come over to help us. Who was I to tell a young woman how to be with her boyfriend after it had taken me nearly thirty years to advocate for myself in my own marriage?

After Lorenzo had successfully killed the power to the oven, Gabriella and I served as assistants, handing him wrenches and screwdrivers.

Sweat began to form along his hairline before long.

"You need water?" Gabriella asked.

"No," he snapped. "Just… Quiet on the set, okay?"

The room was filled with the funk of his attitude and the sound of strained breathing and the occasional clink of metal on metal. When Lorenzo got to the point where he was ready to unhook the electrical wires, he started to unscrew the back panel first. Having watched several videos already, Gabriella and I both knew he didn't need to do that. We exchanged wary glances, but she stayed silent.

Seeing as we were all three huddled close, supporting that heavy oven, and Lorenzo was expending his energy and stretching his arms beyond their natural capacity, I spoke up. "You can disconnect the cords through the top panel."

He acted like he didn't hear me. Kept right on doing it the way he'd committed to.

"Yeah, that's what the videos showed for this model," Gabriella said a few wasted seconds later.

Lorenzo gave a heavy sigh and asked, "Do you want my help or not?" First, he laid his eyes on Gabriella. She didn't respond.

But when he poked those sassy brown eyes at me, I said, "No, I do not. We can finish on our own."

"Fine."

He let go of his corner, and all the weight landed on me and Gabriella. We struggled to push the oven back in place as he grabbed his little sorry tools and threw them in his piddly orange box.

I gave a count. "On three. One, two, three." Together, Gabriella and I restored the teetering appliance to a safe position.

"Really, Lorenzo?" Gabriella grunted at her boyfriend.

"Really. I'll see you at work tomorrow."

I gladly showed him out, wondering why I had the worst luck with handymen. *Note to self: Next time, find help online!* The internet could not do worse than Lorenzo and Wardell.

Left to our own devices, Gabriella and I exchanged a glance—hers full of youthful determination, mine tinged with a resignation that came from years of facing life's curveballs. We were two very different people in that moment, but we shared one common goal: fixing this blasted oven.

"I've got my father's tools," I offered, hoping the ghosts of past DIY attempts wouldn't come back to haunt us.

"The power's off, so we can't electrocute ourselves. We only need a screwdriver at this point," she reminded me, with that confident nod of hers that made me believe we could actually pull this off.

We fumbled through the final steps of the tutorial, the mechanics simple enough but somehow still daunting. The screwdriver slipped once, twice, but Gabriella caught it in midair, her reflexes quicker than mine. We kept pushing through, handing tools back and forth, our hands brushing occasionally as we tightened bolts and loosened screws. Each clink of metal felt like a tiny victory, and with every success, a little more of the tension between us eased.

But we did it. Together.

"On three. One, two, three." We freed the oven from its snug spot beside the cabinet and set it on the floor. It was a small one-hundred-dollar victory in the grand scheme of things, but monumental in that moment. In the aftermath, a spontaneous celebration erupted between us. A shared laugh broke the tension, and we found ourselves doing a little dance around the room, a salsa dance of sorts.

That's when I saw it. Tucked away in the dusty corner where the oven had stood, pressed against the cabinet wall, a slim, unassuming black box with rusted edges. "What's this?" I whispered to myself.

I felt Gabriella's warm presence behind my shoulder as I approached the box and gently slid it out from the cabinet, leaving a dusty outline.

"Dang, that's been sitting here forever," she remarked.

"You mean since, like, 1999?"

"Right! Ancient!"

"I was joking," I said.

"Oh. Sorry."

I turned the box over to find only more black tin. No writing, no engraving. It might have been a cashbox? A cigar box?

"Open it, Ms. Joyce," Gabriella urged.

I sat at the table, and she hovered so close that spirals of her hair brushed against my face.

I laughed. "Have a seat, girl."

She scooched one right next to me, holding her breath.

My heart raced, unsure of what we would find in Grandma Jewel's private business.

Had my father known about this box?

Slowly, I unlatched the mystery, careful not to damage the hinge. The first thing I saw was two folded stacks of money—wrinkled twenty-dollar bills on top—with dried-out rubber bands clinging to them.

Gabriella sang out, "Snap! Your grandma was ballin', baby!"

A musty smell arose as I laid the money in the top portion of the box. Then I gasped at the sight of the book that lay beneath. The green background had faded, but the cover text remained legible. "*The Negro Travelers' Green Book*."

"What the heck?" Gabriella asked.

"It's a Green Book. A list of places where it was safe for Black people to stop and get gas or stay while they traveled across the country," I explained. Honestly, I was afraid to touch it. The brittle, yellowed edges of the document seemed too sacred for human hands.

Gabriella obviously did not feel the same. She reached for the booklet.

"Careful, careful," I warned.

She complied, slowing her movements, opening the first page as though unfolding a fragile piece of history. "Wow."

I appreciated her reverence for this artifact, for my grandmother's property.

Suddenly, a packet of papers slipped out. We both scrambled to catch it before it hit the ground. And again, Gabriella did the honors of opening the papers.

"It's a list of foods for traveling." By the spark in her eyes, she had found the Holy Grail. "What? Wait...because they couldn't eat at most restaurants."

"Right," I confirmed.

She peeled off the top page from the papers and put a hand over her mouth. "It's a recipe for fried chicken." She looked at the second and third pages as well. "Pound cake. Spiced nut mix. Anything with potatoes or beans. All things that didn't take much space, either. This is amazing."

"It is," I agreed.

"This is why I love cooking. So much history."

When she got to the last page of my grandmother's insert, Gabriella let out a "Oooh! She's got names. And a ledger. See?"

Our heads bumped slightly as we surveyed my grandmother's meticulous accounting. There were names and dollar amounts and asterisks with the word *Owe* and cross-throughs with the word *Paid*.

And the money.

"Your grandma had a side gig selling traveling foods," Gabriella declared.

"I ain't mad at her," I said. "I could use a side gig right now."

"We could put her money toward the oven," Gabriella suggested.

"I don't know..." Was that the best use of these precious dollar bills?

"She obviously believed in financial independence," Gabriella lobbied.

"Yes, but... I just need a minute to process."

My housemate nodded. Impatiently. As though she wanted me to be past the moment already.

"So...tomorrow?"

"Gabriella. This"—I pointed at our new treasure—"changes things. This house...this money..."

"Right! What if she's hidden *more* money all over the place?"

Not exactly what I had mind, but it was a possibility.

"Let's just wait a minute."

Her shoulders slumped with resignation. "I think she would have wanted you to use it for whatever you need. And don't I get a vote? Am I not the person responsible for this problem anyway?"

We shared humorous sighs.

"We did a good thing today," I told her.

"We did, huh, Ms. Joyce?"

With that, Gabriella wrapped me up in a bear hug that was quickly interrupted by Elijah stomping into the house.

"I'm hungry!" he announced.

"What else is new?" Gabriella teased, and I joined in her laughter.

CHAPTER 10

Elijah, Gabriella's assistant for the morning, left the house with her to head to the breakfast contest. Gabriella had worked hard to perfect her dish with only a stove and a griddle, which was probably just as well, since they'd be cooking outside.

"What kind of breakfast cooking contest takes place on a lawn, anyway?" I'd drilled her the night before. We were packing her nonperishables in boxes—cinnamon, sugar, honey, pepper.

"The history of this contest goes back to the pioneer days. Open fire," Gabriella informed me.

"Hmph. I guess."

When I arrived about an hour later, the town square was alive with excitement as the breakfast cook-off commenced. Colorful streamers danced in the breeze while cheerful chatter filled the air. The mouthwatering aroma of sizzling bacon, sweet syrup, and warm spices enveloped me as I approached Gabriella's tent.

Gabriella greeted me from behind her table, her eyes shining with both joy and anxiety. "You made it!"

"Wouldn't miss it for the world." I tried to sound upbeat despite my own nerves.

"Grandma, we made three batches, and they're gone already!"

"I don't doubt it. You've got quite a chef here." I pointed at Gabriella.

"Thanks, Ms. Joyce. I'm so freakin' nervous." She wiped her hands on her apron.

"Let me have a taste," I offered.

"Behold, my honey-bacon breakfast nachos!" she exclaimed, gesturing proudly toward a platter piled high with buttered, crispy tortilla triangles, drizzled generously with honey, cinnamon, sugar, and crumbled bacon bits. Beside it lay a stack of informational flyers elaborating on the story behind her unique Blaxican cuisine.

I couldn't help but smile as I reached for a nacho. "Mmm, these are delicious!" I exclaimed, my taste buds delighting in the unique combination of flavors. "You've really outdone yourself, Gabriella."

"Thank you!" She beamed, her face flushed with pride. "I'm really hoping these will impress the judges."

As we chatted, townsfolk stopped by to admire Gabriella's dish and learn more about her culinary fusion. Joy filled my heart as I watched her animatedly share her passion for food, her eyes sparkling with enthusiasm. This young woman had such a bright future ahead of her. I just hoped the "Lorenzos" in her life wouldn't dim her shine.

Elijah's face lit up as he handed out samples of Gabriella's nachos to the eager tasters He clearly took pride in his role, beaming with each compliment about the dish.

"Gabriella, these are divine!" Eileen, who had rushed over as soon as she saw me, exclaimed after taking a bite. She read over the flyer as she chomped. "You have such a gift for combining flavors. We'd love to have you come to the library and share your story, your business information."

"Thank you so much," Gabriella replied, her cheeks flushed with happiness. "That would be great."

Of course, Miss Mary made her rounds. "Keep it up, young lady," she told Gabriella.

As the crowd around our tent grew, I noticed Gabriella's gaze shift toward another tent across the way. Her expression turned steely as she whispered to me, "See that woman over there? That's Mrs. Maine, my old home economics teacher."

I squinted to get a better look at Mrs. Maine. She looked like the sweetest woman on earth. "That woman? She could play Mrs. Claus in a movie."

"Don't let the white hair, bun, and glasses fool you," Gabriella warned. "That woman was evil."

"Looks can be deceiving." I raised an eyebrow. "Was she a good cook?"

"It's hard to say. She only made the basics in our class. She said we didn't deserve her best cuisine."

Mrs. Claus would never say a thing like that.

Gabriella grew a mischievous grin. "Go to her tent. Taste her food. Let me know what you think."

A snap and crackle preceded the announcer's voice. "Contestant numbers one through five, please prepare to bring your dishes to the judges in ten minutes."

"That's me!" Gabriella shrieked. "Ms. Joyce, you have to go scope her out. Did I tell you that this is my first contest?"

A bolt of electricity flew through me. "No. You. Did. Not."

"Please. I'm about to pass out. I have to know."

"Okay, okay. You and Elijah get busy making a fresh batch. I'll check out Mrs. Maine."

The way her face loosened up, you'd think I'd told her I was going to knock the woman's tent down. "Thank you."

Feeling like a secret agent, I strolled over to Mrs. Maine's booth, where she was serving up her own breakfast concoction: spicy chocolate and chili-pepper waffles. That didn't even sound right. *This is for you, Gabriella.*

"Hello, Mrs. Maine."

She paused, holding my sample midway between us. The chocolate-chunked waffle on the tiny plastic plate was a deep, rich brown, almost sinister in its appearance. I could see the flecks of spice in the syrup, promising a fiery kick with each bite. "Hello. Do we know each other?"

I gave my church-usher smile and took the plate from her. "No. My family has roots here, and I recently moved back. My housemate, Gabriella Santos, was a student of yours. She has so much to say about you."

"Does she, now?" she replied with a tight-lipped smile that didn't quite reach her eyes. "Well, I hope you enjoy my entry."

Taking a bite, I struggled to maintain my composure as the overdone spiciness hit my tongue. I coughed and sputtered, trying to catch my breath. I should have followed my first mind and passed on this one.

"Goodness," Mrs. Maine said, feigning concern. "It must have gone down the wrong pipe."

"Actually, it's...incredibly spicy," I managed to say between coughs before disposing of the rest of the dish. "Thank you."

I wiped my mouth with a napkin, trying to regain my composure as I walked back to Gabriella's tent. She was busy plating her honey-bacon nachos, each one arranged like a work of art. "Gabriella, believe me when I say you have nothing to worry about. Mrs. Maine's dish tastes like a sugary volcano erupted in my mouth."

"Really?" she asked, eyebrows raised.

"Trust me," I said. I took a moment to fan my tongue. "It's like a funnel cake and a firecracker had a baby."

Elijah erupted into laughter. But in his excitement, he stumbled and tipped over the platter of nachos. The carefully crafted bites tumbled to the ground, each second stretching into eternity. The nachos seemed to float before crashing down in a catastrophic sprawl. "Aaagh, no!" Gabriella cried out, hands flying to her cheeks. Elijah stared at the mess, eyes wide and filling with tears as he realized what he had done.

"I'm so sorry, Gabriella," he choked out. "I've ruined everything."

"Here, let me help," I offered, joining her on the ground. Together, we scrambled to rescue as many nachos as possible, the clock mercilessly ticking away above us.

"Time's almost up!" called the announcer, sending another wave of distress. "Five minutes."

Gabriella and I exchanged panicked glances, our hearts racing as we tried to make up for lost time.

"Okay, okay," Gabriella muttered under her breath, her hands moving quickly as she turned up the heat on the stove. "Remember the oven?" she asked me.

"Yeah."

Her confidence seemed to zip through me.

"We did it then. Let's get 'er done again."

Gabriella turned up the heat and slapped more bacon on the grill. The bacon sizzled furiously, spitting grease onto the stovetop. "Joyce, could you help me with the tortillas?"

"Of course," I replied, grabbing a pair of tongs and flipping the tortillas over in the cast-iron skillet. The scents of cinnamon and honey were now overshadowed by the unmistakable aroma of burning food.

Our outdoor kitchen was a whirlwind of activity as the three of us worked feverishly to salvage the dish. Elijah sprinkled cinnamon and sugar like nobody's business. But despite our best efforts, the bacon wasn't as crispy as it should've been, and the cinnamon and sugar hadn't had enough time to truly soak into the tortillas.

"Time's up!" the announcer called, signaling the end of the cook-off. Gabriella plated the nachos as best she could, her eyes filled with determination even as disappointment danced across her furrowed brow.

I squeezed her arm. "Gabriella, you did your best. It might not be perfect, but it's still delicious." It was also better than Mrs. Maine's, but I didn't want to try humor at the moment.

Tears welled up in Elijah's eyes as he watched Gabriella place the final garnishes on the plate. "I'm so sorry, Gabriella," he whispered, his voice cracking with emotion.

"Hey," Gabriella said gently, wiping away her own tears. "It's okay, Elijah. We all make mistakes. What's important is that we learn from them and move forward." She hugged him tightly with her free arm, offering forgiveness and understanding.

I took back all the bad things I'd thought about Gabriella. The tenderness she showed Elijah deserved some payback, and I made up in my mind that I'd do whatever it took to get her the kitchen she thought she'd signed up for when she moved into the duplex. The kitchen she deserved. Young folk need somebody in their corner, after all.

Elijah and I followed Gabriella to the judges' table. We stopped at the front row of onlookers, and she proceeded without us. I wondered if this was what a father felt like when he gave his daughter away at the altar. *Goodness gracious, this is nerve-racking.*

My grandson and I held hands when it was Gabriella's turn

to stand before the panel, the judges' eyes scrutinizing our hastily prepared dish. I could feel Gabriella's nerves radiating off her as she described the honey-bacon nachos with pride, not mentioning the mishap that had occurred just minutes before. The unique blend of flavors, inspired by her Blaxican heritage, shone through despite the imperfect presentation.

"Is the bacon fully cooked?" one judge asked, his eyes narrowing slightly in suspicion. The limp nacho chip in his hand had nearly lost its coating. It was clearly not Gabriella's best work.

Gabriella hesitated for a moment, then took a deep breath. Cleared her throat. "I did have to hurry with it because there was a mishap; my tray of food fell to the ground only five minutes ago." Her voice shook slightly but held firm, and I admired her courage. "We made another batch. Very quickly."

"Undercooked pork is dangerous!" Mrs. Maine called out from behind us, her voice dripping with condescension. Suddenly, all the judges spat out their mouthfuls, and one reprimanded Gabriella for giving them undercooked pork.

"Wait," Gabriella interjected, her voice wavering as she struggled to maintain her composure. "The bacon was thin-sliced, and the meat *is* done. It's just not as crispy as I wanted it to be, ideally, but the fat rendered."

"It sure was rendered; I saw it with my own eyes!" My words rang out just as loud and sure as Mrs. Maine's had. I didn't even know what "rendered fat" was, but I knew for a fact that Gabriella was honest and knew what she was talking about.

But despite my defense, the judges didn't take another bite. With a somber tone, the announcer said, "All right, folks, let's move on."

I watched as Gabriella managed to thank the judges even as

she gathered their barely touched plates. She tossed the uneaten food into the trash before leaving the stage.

As we walked back together, Elijah trailing close behind, townsfolk murmured encouraging words to Gabriella: "Better luck next time," and "I had some earlier and they were amazing."

But these small gestures didn't make it into her psyche. "Let's go home," she said, her voice soft yet resolute.

"Are you sure?" I asked, furrowing my brow in concern.

Gabriella simply nodded, her dark eyes glistening with the tears she'd bravely held back.

Together, the three of us began packing up the tent, working silently but efficiently. As I folded the colorful tablecloth, I made a vow to myself: Gabriella deserved another chance to win, and I intended to help her do so.

CHAPTER 11

I stared at my reflection in the full-length mirror, frowning at the floral sundress I had on. It was pretty enough, I supposed, with its bright pink and yellow flowers, but it wasn't really me. I'd spent a good forty-five minutes trying on and discarding outfit after outfit, each one feeling like a lie. Why should I dress up for Richard Tatum, of all people? We were just friends, catching up on old times. Besides, this was my new life, and I was done trying to impress anyone. Comfort and ease should have been my clothing priority, not whether Richard would be proud to have me on his arm.

"Who am I trying to please?" My choice made, I felt lighter, like I'd already shed a suffocating layer. A simple blouse, a pair of jeans, and canvas flats would suffice.

"Grandma, are you ready?" Elijah called from the living room. Poor child. I'd enlisted his help in choosing an outfit. He squeezed me in between zonking videogame monsters, but he wasn't happy about it.

"Coming," I replied, taking a deep breath before stepping out to face him.

Elijah looked me up and down, his eyebrows raised in surprise. "This? You don't look like you're going on a date. The dress was better."

"Good," I said firmly. "Because I'm not going on a date, I'm going as my normal, non-dating self. Richard is an old friend, and we're just going to support local artists tonight."

Elijah tilted his head thoughtfully before breaking into a smile. "Well, being yourself is always the best way to go, Grandma."

His words warmed my heart, and I smiled back. "You're absolutely right, Elijah. Thank you."

The evening air brushed against my skin as I walked up to the old Victorian just off the square. The once-private residence had belonged to the town's main doctor, I remembered. He and his wife were friends of Grandma Jewel, and I had been there once for a Christmas party.

Back then, I thought it was a slice out of an old movie. Now restored, it provided the perfect backdrop for art. Inside, the house-turned-gallery buzzed with conversations and the aroma of catered hors d'oeuvres. People milled around—artists discussing their work with grand gestures, patrons pondering designs with glasses of wine in hand.

My casual outfit felt stark in comparison to the room full of meticulously chosen ensembles. Yet here and there, I caught sight of others who had also opted for a more down-to-earth approach. I chuckled to myself, thinking back on all those events my ex-husband and I had attended, where my eyes might have critically lingered on someone who dared to break the mold. And now, here I was. Joyce Marrietta Hicks, mold-breaker.

I spotted Richard, dressed to impress in a charcoal suit. His face lit up as our gazes met, but I was determined not to let his charm faze me. *This is about friendship and art, nothing more.*

"Joyce!" Richard called from the entrance, smile bright.

"Hi, Richard," I replied, feeling excitement and apprehension.

"Wow, you look beautiful," he said, with that eagerness that reminded me of our high school days.

Beautiful felt over-the-top for my attire, my bare face, and my bushy hair behind a stretchy cloth headband. Especially from someone who was one step down from dressed for a symphony.

But I accepted his compliment, lest he deem me one of those women who didn't know how to do so. Eager men always home in on that kind of woman, one who hasn't already claimed her beauty.

No. I had to play like I didn't like him.

Which I didn't. *Do I? And why am I playing games, anyway?*

He gently guided me toward a lonely painting of a mockingbird, where he leaned in close to my ear. "I could sop you up with a biscuit."

The tickle of his breath caused me to jump. "Richard," I hissed, "you are crossing the line."

"Too strong? Too fast?" he guessed.

"Too *much*. I already told you that I am not trying to be in a romantic relationship. I need a friend right now. That's it. Are you capable of developing a friendship with me, without all this extra pressure?"

He paused for a moment, taking in my words. Then his head bobbed backward as though he'd been punched in the face with the truth. "I don't know."

"Try," I said. "Or else we can't see each other again."

He shrugged. "I'm just the guy trying to get the girl."

"Well, I'm not a girl, and I don't want to get *got*. So can we just enjoy the night as two people who are grateful to be alive, who've been through a lot of stuff, and who like art? No pressure?"

Richard took a drink of his wine. "You're switching up the rules. But I like it. Takes the pressure off me, too."

"Wonderful." I sighed. "I'm sorry I was so blunt."

I silently chastised myself for apologizing. Habits.

He laughed. "I don't think I would have truly heard you if you hadn't been blunt."

The spry crinkle in his eyes told me he *had* actually heard me. I mean, it was a shame I had to break it down for him like that, but it felt good to be clear about what I needed and what I didn't need. Him clawing on me and making passes all night would have only made a tough day worse.

"Thank you," I said, relieved by his response. We left the mockingbird alone and walked into a room just off the main corridor. The scents of old wood and fresh paint mingled in the air.

"This was the library," I remembered. "My grandmother brought me here once. Did you ever visit Dr. Maynard's house?"

"No. Two different sides of the tracks," he said.

"Guess you're right about that."

The next room we entered was slightly smaller than the others—intimate, almost. An overhead chandelier cast a gentle shadow across the floorboards. The walls were adorned with an array of paintings that felt deeply personal. This space retained the aura of quiet reflection, the books replaced by canvases of varying sizes. Some abstracts, others unbelievably realistic. Each telling its own story.

As we meandered through the room, our conversation flowed from one artwork to another. It was easy, like slipping into an old pair of shoes. The servers, moving gracefully through the space, offered trays of hors d'oeuvres and wine, which we took with gratitude. The wine, rich and smooth, seemed to ease the remnants of tension between us.

Somewhere between the abstract landscapes and the watercolor portraits, I found myself talking freely about my impressions of each piece.

Richard had a vast vocabulary when he wasn't busy impersonating Casanova.

It was amid this backdrop of eased defenses and shared appreciation for the art that we stopped in front of a small, somewhat melancholy work. The impressionistic oil painting depicted a single figure standing at the edge of a pier, looking out over a gray, tumultuous sea. The isolation and longing in the figure's posture resonated with me, mirroring the emotions swirling within.

Maybe it was the wine or the casualness that Richard and I both sank into during that hour, but I found myself opening up to him. "I've got so much to figure out, Richard. With my daughter. And my finances," I confessed, feeling vulnerable. "I really need to get the kitchen up to par and finish the construction at my duplex, but I'm going to need a job to pull it off. Can you believe it? Working again after retirement?"

"No offense, but I don't see the point in retiring, so long as you've got your mind and your health. That's why I never stopped working," he said. "Everybody I know either dies or finds a part-time gig after retirement."

I supposed he was trying to make me feel like less of failure for having to return to work, especially after all the hoopla people made over retirement. So I tried to force a smile, but it didn't work.

Richard's expression softened, and his voice was gentle as he spoke. "You said earlier that we've both been through a lot."

"We have."

He sipped from his glass. "All those trials and struggles made us stronger. Right?"

"Yeah. They did." I patted his arm.

"We come from a generation that knows how to make things work. How to dig in—work hard, keep trying, keep our faith. I feel sorry for kids these days. Everything's so convenient. They don't get to make as many mistakes as we did, you know? They ride the train to the top without trekking up the mountain. But they haven't developed the stamina, and their lungs haven't had the chance to gradually adjust along the way. So they can't enjoy the top because they took the convenient shortcut to get there."

"Hmmm..." I thought about Gabriella and how she had left the square when it was clear she wouldn't win. She was crushed by the judges' reaction to her last-minute platter. This experience was part of her mountain trek, I reckoned.

"Richard," I said, pausing in front of a vibrant painting of wildflowers, "thank you for being here tonight and for listening. As a *friend*. It means a lot."

"Of course, Joyce," he replied, his eyes sincere.

As Richard and I continued walking through the gallery, we approached a vendor selling various handcrafted items. He picked up a simple beaded bracelet and handed it to me. The white squares with black capital letters spelled out the word *strength*.

"Here, Joyce," he said gently. "I want you to have this."

"No strings attached?" I asked, arching an eyebrow.

"Absolutely not." Richard chuckled. "Just a reminder of all that's in you." We both laughed as I received it gratefully, touched by his gesture.

"Thank you, Richard," I said, sliding the bracelet up my wrist.

He paid the vendor and walked me back outside to my car, where we parted with a cordial hug. No pressure.

I returned home that evening feeling lighter and more contented than I had in a long while. As I entered the living room, I noticed that Elijah had made his way over to Gabriella's side of the house. They were watching the final scene of a movie together, their faces lit by the flickering screen. The scent of popcorn filled the air—but this wasn't just ordinary popcorn. This had a spicy, sugary smell. Gabriella, with her culinary genius, had somehow managed to elevate it into something extraordinary.

"Hey there, Elijah," I called softly, not wanting to interrupt their experience. He looked up and grinned at me.

"Hi, Grandma! Gabriella let me watch the movie with her. And this popcorn is amazing!"

"Of course it is." I smiled, walking over to them. "Gabriella's special touch, no doubt."

Gabriella beamed at the compliment. She swiped at her shoulder. "Well, you know how I do it. Gotta add a little zest and fire when I can." She glanced at the bracelet on my wrist. "Looks like you two had a nice time."

"I did. Richard proved himself a good friend tonight, and he gave me this as a reminder of my own strength."

"Beautiful," she murmured, admiring the simple piece of jewelry.

"Ugh, Grandma!" Elijah groaned, covering his face with his hands. "Did you kiss him?"

"Absolutely not." I chuckled, raising an eyebrow at Gabriella as she tried to suppress her laughter. "We're just friends, remember?"

"Aw, that's too bad," Gabriella teased, a playful frown crossing her face.

"Yay!" Elijah exclaimed, pumping his fist in the air. We all shared a laugh at his dramatic reaction.

"Thank you again for watching Elijah tonight."

"Of course, Ms. Joyce," she said warmly. "He's always welcome here on the..."

"East siiiiiide!" she and Elijah bellowed in unison. I guess those two had formed their own little popcorn gang.

"All right, kiddo," I said, running a hand affectionately through Elijah's hair. "Time to go back to the west side. Say good night to Gabriella."

"Good night, Miss Gabriella. Thanks for the popcorn and the movie."

"Night, Elijah. You're welcome anytime."

Elijah followed me back to our side, still chatting excitedly about the movie they had watched. As I tucked him into bed and listened to his sleepy chatter, I gave silent thanks for the few weeks I was spending with my grandson that summer.

"Grandma?" Elijah whispered, reaching for my hand as I stood up to leave his room.

"Yes, sweetheart?"

"Thanks for everything."

"Anytime, EJ," I whispered back, squeezing his hand gently before turning off the light and closing the door behind me.

Once Elijah was settled in his room, I decided it was time to call Terri and discuss my situation. The need for a job weighed heavily on my mind, and I hoped she would understand my predicament.

"Hey, Mom," Terri's voice echoed through the phone, her tone guarded.

"Hi, sweetheart," I said, trying to keep my own voice steady. "I wanted to talk to you about something important."

"Okay, what's up? Is everything okay with Elijah?"

"Yes, he's fine. It's just… I need to find a job," I confessed, bracing myself for her reaction.

"Mom, this is exactly why you shouldn't have divorced Dad," Terri snapped, her voice rising with frustration.

"I have money saved, and I have a retirement income. But remodeling a home takes money, and I might as well work since I'm still able."

"You wouldn't be in this mess if—"

"Terri, that's not fair," I replied, my heart sinking at her harsh response. "I'm doing my best to start over. I need a job, which means I'm going to need to send Elijah back as soon as possible. I need your support moving forward."

"Support?" she scoffed. "You're going to go back into the workforce, expose yourself to germs and bad attitudes and stress. You are retired. You're supposed to be volunteering, traveling, playing bingo. But you can't because you divorced Dad at the last minute. How is that a story anyone would want for their mother? I can't support it."

"Terri, there is no shame in working and providing for myself," I countered, glancing down at the *Strength* bracelet Richard had given me earlier in the night. I clung to that word as I faced my daughter's judgment. "I don't have a problem getting up and going to work every day, so long as it's for a good reason."

"Whatever, Mom," she muttered, clearly uninterested in seeing things from my perspective. "Do what you want. I'll ask Dad if Elijah can go there sooner."

"Good. Your father should be happy to spend a little more time with EJ. He is a delightful child. You and Chris are doing an excellent job."

She skipped over my compliment. "But this is not the example I want to set for Elijah. We're teaching him that if he works hard in school and gets a good job, one day he will retire and enjoy his senior years because of the education and the dues he paid. Seeing his grandma, who has a master's degree, get up every day to work for minimum wage does not support our theory."

"Terri. Dial it down a notch. Elijah is ten. He knows nothing about minimum wage or degrees or how the real world works. And you're not serving him well with this fairy tale you're painting, by the way. The economy can be rough. Plenty of people my age are still working. My friend Richard—"

"Richard? You have a *friend* named Richard?"

"Yes. And I have a new friend named Gabriella, and another one named Eileen, too, since you're askin'."

She made that tooth-sucking sound. "I gotta go, Mom. Bye."

"Terri, please—" I tried to appeal to her one last time, but she had already hung up, leaving our conversation unresolved.

My heart ached at the disconnect between us, but I couldn't let her negativity dictate my choices. I needed to forge my own path, even if it meant facing some disapproval along the way. Besides, I realized that Terri's problem wasn't with me, exactly. She was more upset that her ideas about how life should go were crumbling before her eyes.

Join the club, Terri. I'm the president.

"Grandma?" Elijah's voice wobbled as he stood in the doorway, clearly having overheard our tense exchange. "You're sending me away early?"

His wide, fearful eyes tugged at my heartstrings, and I immediately crossed the room to pull him into a tight embrace. "Oh, sweetheart," I murmured into his hair, stroking his back to soothe both his worries and mine. "I have to find a job. You need supervision throughout the day while I look and when I start working, so you'll have to go to your grandfather sooner than we planned."

"What if Grandpa won't let me come?" he whispered against my chest, his small frame trembling ever so slightly.

"I'm sure he will," I cooed.

"My mom sounds mad about it."

"Your mom is just...worried about me, and sometimes that comes out as anger," I explained gently, rubbing his back. "But I promise you, it has nothing to do with you. We both love you so much, and we want what's best for you. It has been great having you here for most of the month. And I'll be sure to get a schedule for you and Grandpa, just like I told you before."

"Really?" He pulled away, searching my face for reassurance. "No one's mad at me?"

"Really. No one has any reason to be upset with you," I confirmed, offering him a smile that I hoped conveyed certainty. That's the funny thing about children—they somehow feel responsible for what grown-ups do.

His expression lightened, and he wrapped his arms around my waist once more. "I love you, Grandma."

"I love you, too, EJ."

CHAPTER 12

The day before Elijah was scheduled to leave, Gabriella and I busied ourselves making a special meal for him. My chest ached at the thought, but I kept telling myself that I had to do what was best for myself this once. Tomorrow would be a difficult day for all of us, including Gabriella.

"What time are you meeting Elijah's mom?" Gabriella asked as she flattened the dough to make homemade tortillas. She'd gotten up before me to mix and let it rise.

"Late afternoon," I replied, taking a sip of hot green tea to get myself going for the day.

"You sure you don't want me to ride with you? It'll be dark on your way back. And everybody I know over the age of fifty is not down with driving at night."

I knew she was only trying to lighten the mood with one of her senior jokes, but it didn't work. "No. I don't want you to see me crying all the way there and back." My voice faltered at the thought of saying goodbye to Elijah, especially knowing he didn't want to leave.

Gabriella glanced over at me, her face full of empathy. "I'm really going to miss him, Joyce," she said quietly. "And I hate that it's all because of my culinary drama."

"Hey, now," I interjected, "don't you feel bad about that. This kitchen repair needed to happen no matter what. It's just life, and sometimes we have to adjust." But even as I attempted to reassure her, I couldn't shake my own sadness over Elijah's departure.

"Life be lifin'," Gabriella mused.

"So true."

Gabriella tested the grease with a drop of water. Satisfied with its sizzle, she said, "All right. Let's make these breakfast tortillas, Abuela's way."

"Sounds perfect," I agreed, pushing aside my worries and focusing on the task at hand.

Gabriella began by chopping up a medley of colorful veggies—red bell peppers, green onions, and tomatoes—while I whisked together eggs and a little milk in a bowl, as she instructed. The sizzle of butter melting in the skillet filled the kitchen with an inviting aroma that nipped at the gloominess we had been feeling. The knife chop-chop-chopping against the cutting board added a comforting cadence to the room, a soothing melody.

"Next, we'll add some spices," she said, handing me a small glass jar filled with a vibrant blend of cumin, chili powder, and smoked paprika. I sprinkled it over the vegetables as they cooked, watching as the spices released their rich, earthy scents into the air. They added depth to the complexity of the smells.

As the vegetables softened and became infused with the spices, Gabriella retrieved a package of smoked sausage from the refrigerator. We worked together to slice it into thin, even pieces. Each slice added to the skillet brought a new layer of savoriness, the smokiness of the sausage complementing the spices perfectly. The sound of the sausage sizzling and the sight of it browning amid the colorful vegetables was a sensory delight.

"Is this your family's special seasoning?" I asked, taking in the fragrant mixture.

"Yep, my abuela used a dash of it in almost every meal," Gabriella replied with a wistful smile. "It reminds me of home."

She suddenly grew quiet, her eyes distant as she stirred the contents of the skillet. "Joyce, can I tell you something? Promise not to judge?"

"Of course."

"My mom's side of the family came here from Mexico," she began hesitantly. "My grandfather crossed the border, looking for a better life. There was no work, no food to feed his family."

"Mmmm," I said softly.

She looked at me. "The other day, when we found the recipes for Black travelers, I thought about how amazing it is that both my Black ancestors traveling *across* this country and my Mexican ancestors escaping *to* this country had both packed specific foods for the journey."

Now it was my turn to be intrigued. "You don't say?"

"Yeah. I mean, I know it's, like, a hot political topic these days, but back when my grandfather came to America—across land and a river—he says they packed salty nuts and seeds. Canned foods. Water. And garlic and tobacco, to ward off snakes. He also wrote his name on his underwear, just in case he died of heatstroke or drowning."

"I can't imagine," I said.

"He got here and started working, took the classes, and became a citizen," she said. "He kept that underwear, though."

"You've got quite a few stories to share, Gabriella."

"This is why I love cooking. So much history."

"Your family's journey is a testament to the strength and resilience in your blood," I told her. "On both sides. You've got some kind of resilience in you. And that's why we gotta kick Mrs. Maine's behind next time!"

Gabriella's full mane trembled with her laughter.

"Yes! Crush Mrs. Maine!"

And in that small kitchen, with the smell of warm spices and freshly cooked tortillas wafting around us, we found solace in each other's company—a bond that I hoped would endure long after the last bite of breakfast had been savored.

Together, we filled the tortillas with our mixture of veggies and meat, and topped them with a creamy cheese sauce that she whipped up in the same skillet we'd used earlier. Every single bite of these burritos would be full of flavor.

How Elijah slept through our conversation and laughter, let alone the irresistible aromas, was beyond me.

"Gabriella, I'm going to check on Elijah. He's usually up by now," I said as I wiped my hands on a dish towel and left the kitchen.

I made my way down the hall, my footsteps echoing softly on the laminate floors. The door to Elijah's room was slightly ajar, and I could see his outline in the dim morning light. He was sitting in the rocking chair, knees drawn up to his chest, wearing different pajamas from the ones he had gone to sleep in. His bedding was in a heap on the floor, and a towel covered part of his mattress.

"Baby, are you okay?" I asked, taking a cautious step into the room.

Elijah buried his face in his knees, his voice muffled as he spoke. "I peed in the bed, Grandma. I'm sorry."

My heart ached for him; I could feel his embarrassment radiating off him in waves. I crossed the room and rested a hand on his shoulders. “No worries, EJ. Everyone has accidents sometimes.”

He looked up at me, tears welling in his eyes. “I still don’t like it when it happens.”

“I’m sure you don’t.”

“Please don’t tell Gabriella. I don’t want her to know.”

“Of course I won’t,” I assured him, giving his arm a gentle squeeze. “Why don’t you go ahead and take a shower? I’ll take care of the laundry.”

“Okay,” he whispered, sliding off the rocking chair and heading toward the bathroom.

As he closed the door behind him, I gathered up the soiled bedding and carried it to the laundry room, making sure not to catch Gabriella’s eye. My mind raced with worry for my grandson.

Both of my kids had been completely potty-trained by age three, and we never had a slip-up, except for the time Eric Jr. refused to step away from a video game because he didn’t want to lose. He won the game against Terri, but he lost control of his bladder in the celebration, and she never let her brother forget it.

Elijah, at ten years old, should be long past his bed-wetting days, in my estimation.

I stood in the hallway, listening to the sound of the shower running behind the closed bathroom door. I slipped back into my bedroom and called my daughter.

“Hey, Momma,” she answered, her voice hurried. “What’s up?”

“Terri, I need to talk to you about something that happened with Elijah this morning.” I launched into an explanation of the situation. “Is this normal for him?”

"Ah." Terri sighed. "He only gets that way when he's feeling anxious. It's not unusual, but it hasn't happened in a while."

"Could it be because he's going to his grandpa's house soon?" I wondered aloud, my mind racing through possible reasons for his distress.

"Maybe," Terri replied, sounding distracted. "Look, I have to get to my next seminar session. We can talk about it later."

"Wait," I pressed, unwilling to let the conversation end just yet. "Is there any way Elijah could just go home and stay with his father instead? Maybe that would help with his anxiety."

"Mom, I said I can't talk right now. I'll call you back when I have more time."

"All right," I relented, the weight of worry settling heavily on my shoulders as we hung up.

As I stood in the dimly lit hallway, the scent of breakfast tortillas wafting from the kitchen, I couldn't shake the nagging feeling that I needed to find a solution for Elijah. My grandson deserved the best summer possible, and I was determined to do whatever it took to make that happen. But first, I needed to learn more about what was causing his anxiety and how I could help him through it.

I stood there, lost in thought, my fingers absently tracing the delicate wallpaper lining the hallway. The sound of running water ceased, and I knew Elijah would soon be stepping out of the shower, freshly washed and hopefully feeling a bit better about his morning ordeal.

"Focus, Joyce," I whispered to myself, straightening my shoulders. "You'll figure this out. You always do."

I took a deep breath and returned to my room, steeling myself for the next conversation I needed to have. Calling my ex-husband, Eric, was never an easy task, but discussing Elijah's well-being was more important than any lingering discomfort between us. I dialed Eric's number and waited as the line rang.

"Hello?" Eric answered, cautiously curious.

"Hi, it's Joyce," I said, trying to sound as casual as possible. "I wanted to talk to you about Elijah."

"Is everything okay?" he asked, his voice portraying a hint of concern, which brought a small relief.

"Things are fine. I—I just thought we should discuss his upcoming visit with you. He might be anxious."

"Anxious? Why?"

"I'm not sure..." I hadn't given much thought to how I might explain that our grandson didn't want to be with my husband for the same reasons I didn't want to be with him. "I've already researched some activities for you two to do together, so maybe that will help him feel more...excited," I sidestepped awkwardly.

"All right," Eric conceded. "But what does this have to do with anxiety?"

Honestly, I hadn't expected him to pay enough attention to catch on to my diversion.

"Well, since he's been here with me, he's expressed that he's feeling like maybe you don't want him around, and I'm asking you to be sensitive to his feelings."

"Fine," he replied, a touch of annoyance creeping into his tone. "But I still don't understand why he's so worried."

"Look, I don't know all the details myself," I admitted. "But I do know that he's been so worried, he had an accident last night."

"An accident?" Eric asked, incredulous.

"Yes," I said softly. "He wet the bed."

"Joyce, he's ten years old! When I was his age, I had a part-time job already. He needs to grow up."

"Eric, he's still a child," I snapped back, my patience wearing thin.

"He's a young Black man, and I wish you'd stop filling his head with all these ideas about feelings and emotions. That's *your* thing, not his."

See, now, why'd he have to go and say that? "Eric, we all have feelings, no matter how old or how young we are," I said, trying to keep my voice steady. "Unless you're constantly shutting them down."

I counted to ten, for my grandson's sake. "This isn't about me or you."

"I know how to babysit my own grandchild. I'm not gonna coddle him. He's got his games. TV. He'll be fine."

This was a no-win conversation. "All right, then," I said. "I'll send you the information about fun *activities* in email."

"Go right ahead," he replied, and we ended the call.

As I hung up the phone, I couldn't help but worry that I had made things worse by telling Eric about Elijah's accident. My intentions were good, but I knew all too well that even the best-laid plans could go awry.

This business of putting my own needs first... Maybe it wasn't for the old Gen Xer in me. We sacrificed *everything* for our kids. I felt like I was sending Elijah to boot camp.

I paced back and forth, my mind racing with thoughts of what-ifs and worst-case scenarios. What if Eric made a snide comment? What if he compared Elijah to himself at that age, implying he was weak or a disappointment?

I sighed heavily, my shoulders tightening as I walked back into the kitchen. "Elijah should be out in a minute."

Gabriella looked up from the glass she'd filled with juice,

her dark eyes filled with concern. "Everything okay?" she asked gently.

"Just talked to my ex-husband, Eric," I began, my voice shaking slightly. "He doesn't seem excited about Elijah's visit."

Gabriella frowned, setting down her knife. "Elijah is amazing. What's your ex's problem?"

I nodded in agreement, feeling oddly relieved to have someone else affirm me without question. It felt good to have someone on my side.

"Miss," Gabriella said earnestly, "you and I need to figure out a way for Elijah to stay here in Robin Creek for the summer. We can't let him go from all this"—she gestured at the beautiful spread we'd created in Elijah's honor—"to a grumpy old man with Pop-Tarts."

"I appreciate that, Gabriella," I replied, touched by her kindness. "But I haven't found a job yet, and I won't have anyone to watch him while I job hunt."

"I could switch shifts with somebody at work if we need to. Once you know your schedule," she tried again.

"I can't ask you to do that."

"Hold on..." she mused, tapping her chin thoughtfully. After a moment, her face brightened. "I have an idea! Let me call my cousin." She pulled out her phone. "Hey, Lisa!" Gabriella greeted cheerfully. "Quick question: Do you know of any full-day summer programs for ten-year-old kids around here?"

I held up a finger to stop her because I'd already been down that road.

"Actually, yeah," Ana replied loud enough for me to hear the full conversation. "There's a recreation center on the rich side of town that has a great program. It's expensive, though."

"Really? That's fantastic! Thanks, Ana!" Gabriella beamed before ending the call.

"What do you think?"

"I'd already looked around—how did I miss that one?"

"I'm guessing you only looked for activities, not all-day stuff."

She had a point.

"But do you want him with the rich kids? Probably Mrs. Maine's grandkids. Ulk!"

"You have taken Mrs. Maine too far. Anyway, Elijah's parents are from the suburbs," I mused. "He'll be fine there. We just need to figure out the logistics."

"Let's do it," Gabriella said firmly, her eyes shining with determination. "For Elijah."

After getting details about the program via the internet, I texted Terri. Would you be able to cover the cost of a summer program for Elijah's summer day camp here? I sent a link to the program that showed the weekly cost and enrollment fee.

I hit send and waited for her response, my stomach twisting with its own brand of anxiety.

A few minutes later, my phone buzzed with a reply from Terri. I can cover it, but I am sure he will want to stay longer if he makes friends.

That's fine. Thanks. Let your dad know. I sighed in relief. I was sure this was what my daughter wanted all along. For EJ's sake, I was on her side.

As we sat down to breakfast, I decided to broach the topic with Elijah. "Hey, buddy," I began, trying to sound casual, "how would you feel about staying here in Robin Creek and going to a summer program?"

His eyes lit up like fireworks. “Really, Grandma? I can stay with you all summer?” He beamed, his excitement contagious.

“Absolutely,” I said, grinning at him. “Your mom agreed to pay for the day-camp program as long as you stay the whole summer. Are you up for it?”

“Thank you, Grandma! Thank you!” He hugged me tightly, his happiness pulsing through the embrace.

“Looks like we make a pretty good team, huh?” Gabriella chimed in, her smile matching Elijah’s enthusiasm.

“Definitely,” I agreed, tousling Elijah’s hair affectionately. “Now, young man, it’s your turn to do the dishes after we eat.”

Elijah groaned for good measure, but the smile on his face said he’d wash dishes every day if it meant he could stay with us.

So much for putting myself first. And I was glad about it.

CHAPTER 13

I led an excited Elijah into the recreation center, his feet skipping with glee from the car to the front door. The children's reception area was a hub of activity, with vibrant murals of sports icons. Colorful chairs and a fish tank completed the ambience, promising all who entered that this place would be fun.

Really, the whole scene stoked nostalgia for my teaching days and how the first day of school had brought a renewed sense of hope to children, parents, and teachers.

The staff greeted us with warm smiles and friendly hellos, immediately putting me at ease about my decision to enroll him in their youth day camp.

"Okay, Elijah, you go have breakfast with your new friends." I gave him a gentle nudge toward the bustling cafeteria. "I'll take care of all the paperwork and catch up with you later."

"Thanks, Grandma!" he called over his shoulder before disappearing into a crowd of children.

I made my way to the office of Mr. Drew, the camp administrator, to fill out the necessary forms. He'd filled his space with hand-drawn artwork from campers and a collection of educational awards and certificates he'd amassed over his career. Mr. Drew himself looked to be in his early fifties, but it was hard to tell. People who work around kids have a certain youth about them. He had a kind face and a smile that sparkled with passion for his work.

Listing Terri and Gabriella as alternate emergency contacts, I found myself touched by how important Gabriella was becoming in my life. She wasn't just my housemate anymore; she was a friend and someone I could rely on.

"How did you hear about our summer camp?" Mr. Drew asked casually as he looked over my completed forms.

"A friend," I replied. "I'm new to the city. Retired from teaching and moved back here to my grandmother's home." *Goodness gracious, I'm turning into Miss Mary. TMI.*

"Oh!" He gave me that if-you-know-you-know look that everyone who spends their days with kids knows. It's a thankless job that most wouldn't trade for anything. "You've worked with kids, too?"

"Taught several elementary grades, team leader," I said proudly. "Lots of experience signing kids up and making sure everyone's happy and accounted for."

"We're glad to have Elijah here."

"Well, I hadn't planned on enrolling my grandson in day care, but I'm job hunting now and needed a place for him to go."

"Ah, I see." Mr. Drew leaned back in his chair, thoughtful. "Well, if you're interested, we're actually looking for someone to manage and coordinate adult educational and recreational programs part-time. Our last person found a remote position, and we can't really compete with that. But, uh... Would you like to apply?"

"Really?" I busted out a bright smile at the unexpected opportunity. "I'd love to!"

"Great! When you leave, go past the weight room and you'll see the main offices. You can fill out an application there."

A few weeks later, after a strong reference from Eileen, I found myself sitting in the recreation center's conference room on my first day as a program coordinator. I was only guaranteed twenty hours a week, but it paid better than a minimum-wage job would have offered, so I think I came out pretty good, given the math.

Yessss!!!

The mandatory training video about blood-borne pathogens droned on in front of me, but despite the boredom, I felt a sense of accomplishment. I had landed this job right when I needed it.

As I tried to focus on the video, my phone buzzed with a text message. Glancing down, I saw it was from Eric. My stomach tightened as I read his words: Will I get any time with Elijah this summer?

He was trying to play the victim, but I decided to take the high road. I'd be more than happy to trade off Friday and pick him up again Sunday night, I replied. Would you meet me halfway?

No. You're the one who inconvenienced me, came his predictable response. I could practically hear the smugness in his voice as he typed his next message. It's really sad that you're so lonely you had to kidnap our grandson for company. Richard must not be very amusing.

My hands trembled with anger as I stared at the screen. How dare he? Was it Terri who had told him? Or had Elijah said something to his mother? Perhaps word had gotten around town and back to Eric. But in that moment, I realized it didn't matter how he found out. What my ex-husband thought of me was irrelevant.

Have to go was all I replied before putting my phone away. I wouldn't give him the satisfaction of engaging in his petty attempts to undermine me. Instead, I focused on the training video and the promising future that lay ahead of me.

The door to the training room swung open, and Gabriella appeared with a bright smile on her face. "Hey! They said you'd be in here. How's it going?"

I paused the video and turned to face her, grateful for the distraction. "It's going fine. Thanks for using your lunch hour to get Elijah so he can go to the library for the LEGO club meeting."

"Ah, no problem," she replied, waving off my gratitude. She glanced at the computer screen and made a face at the fake blood oozing from a fake cut on a young actor's leg. "Ugh. Blood?"

I laughed. "Tell me about it. But I suppose it's necessary for this job. People get hurt from time to time."

"I guess," she agreed, nodding. "Last week, the new dishwashing guy slammed his hand in the door."

"How?" I tried to imagine.

"We have no idea." She laughed. "Maybe he should have watched some safety videos, too. Gotta go pick up Elijah. See you at home tonight."

A few hours later, I finally clocked out, relieved to put the mandatory training behind me. Eager to see Elijah, I headed to the library. I arrived halfway through his LEGO club meeting, so I decided to join the Chapter Chatters group that was already in session.

"Joyce, how nice to see you!" Christine exclaimed as I took a seat among them. The others nodded and echoed greetings as well.

After our welcome session, the group continued discussing

a book about a woman who discovered her son was involved in a scandal at school—a prank gone wrong. Although I hadn't read the book, I found myself enjoying their easy banter and thoughtful insights.

"Have you read any good books lately?" Lupita asked, bringing me back to the present discussion.

I said, "Haven't had much time to read lately. But I did discover an old copy of a Green Book underneath my grandmother's stove."

The ensuing *ooohs* and *aaahs* led to me sharing how Gabriella and I had talked about the foods people carry from one life to the next, then a spontaneous sharing of favorite recipes. Shrimp étouffée, triple-chocolate torte, and Texas-style brisket.

"We should have a potluck," Sonia suggested.

"Oh no. I don't do potlucks," Althea said with a shake of her head.

"No?" Eileen pressed.

"Me, either," I seconded.

With a perplexed look, she asked me, "Why not?"

"Working at a school, there was always somebody bringing food into the teachers' lounge. And people would come right in after touching their students' heads and tying their shoes, and put their hands right in a bag of chips. So unless I get first dibs, I don't eat food that other people have picked over."

Eileen waved away my concerns. "That's an easy fix; we'll all be sure to wash our hands."

Althea contested, "No, ma'am. I love y'all, but with cats and dogs and hoarding and different levels of cleanliness standards in different people's homes...I don't. I can't."

Valeria added, "I ended up in the hospital one evening after a spread at work."

Eileen scoffed. "Are y'all serious? What kind of Southern ladies are we if we can't have a potluck now and then?"

"What if we make a meal together?" Lupita suggested. "At somebody's house. Everyone can participate, and we'll all know that we all washed our pots, pans, and hands—"

"And nobody's cat licked the bowl," Althea said.

"Sounds good to me," I said.

"Fine. A do-it-together potluck," Eileen agreed. "When?"

"Some time before we all get busy preparing for the Fourth, or Labor Day," Christine warned.

Heads nodded.

"I know just the person to guide us through our meal prep," I said. "My housemate, Gabriella."

Eileen exclaimed, "Oh! She made the breakfast bacon nachos at the county cook-off?"

"Sure did." I beamed with pride. "She's an excellent teacher. If we bring her a few recipes, she'll add her magic to them and we'll have ourselves the best one-cook potluck in the county."

"Sounds good to me," Sonia agreed.

"No animals at your place?" Althea confirmed.

"No. But there is a ten-year-old boy there." I laughed.

They all laughed, knowing that kids can be the germiest, which led to another round of sharing stories about the extravagant messes our children made while growing up. Feeling right at home with these seasoned women, I threw in my story about the time Eric Jr. and Terri emptied an entire bag of sugar all over my kitchen.

Before long, the closing time for both the LEGO club and Chapter Chatters came upon us. We tabled the date and time for the cook-and-share night until I could talk to Gabriella, but everyone was still excited.

I gathered Elijah and decided I'd better start pricing ovens, given that I'd all but volunteered my home for a cooking escapade. Well, if I didn't have enough money to buy a stove by the end of the summer, we could still cook at someone else's house, I reasoned. I'd still bring Gabriella, assuming she'd agree to teach. *What was I thinking?*

I guess I'd been thinking of how things used to be. I'd get a bright idea and then just do it. Never thought twice about how much money it cost when I was married. But I had to slow down now. Count my pennies.

This is my new life.

But I wasn't upset. In fact, I was happy to have a life where I had honest people around me. True friends are priceless.

As Elijah and I stood in the oven section of McCloud's, the only Robin Creek home-appliance store, my mind wandered to the ongoing remodel of my grandmother's house. I knew that buying a new oven was an essential part of completing the project, but as I surveyed the various models on display, I realized there was more to it than I had thought. There were ovens with Wi-Fi connectivity, offering remote control via smartphone apps. Some boasted advanced convection technology for more even cooking, and others had preset cooking modes for everything from roasting a turkey to baking artisan bread. There were models with integrated temperature probes for precise cooking, self-cleaning features, and even steam-cooking options for healthier meals.

What in the world?

"Grandma, this one has voice command," Elijah noted.

Are we cooking with robots now?

Feeling slightly overwhelmed by the array of high-tech

features, most of which seemed more suited for a professional chef than for my own needs, I decided to call Gabriella for help.

"Hey, Gabriella, you off work?"

"Clocking out now."

"Would you mind joining Elijah and me at McCloud's? I could use your advice on picking out a new oven."

She responded with a chirp in her tone. "I'll meet you there."

When Gabriella arrived at the store, a wave of relief washed over me. Her cheerful presence was a welcome contrast to the sterile, fluorescent-lit showroom filled with stainless steel appliances. Together, we began to explore the various ovens on display, each one boasting more features than the last.

"Look at this one, Joyce," Gabriella said excitedly, pointing to an oven with a built-in air fryer and a touchscreen display. "Can you imagine all the meals we could whip up in this beauty?"

The salesperson, Leonna, who wore a few service pins noting her accomplishments with the store, complimented Gabriella on her knowledge of cooking. "I don't think you need me here at all!"

Finally, the last oven on the aisle left me, Gabriella, and Elijah in complete awe. The Celestia Gourmet Precision Elite was a marvel of modern kitchen technology. Its sleek stainless steel exterior gleamed under the store's lights, and its large glass door promised a clear view of whatever culinary creations it would hold inside.

Leonna described its features to us. "This model boasts an intuitive touchscreen control panel..." I swear, the theme song from *Rocky* started playing as she spoke. Celestia seemed to offer an endless array of cooking options, from a precision baking mode to a specialized roast function. It even had a unique feature that allowed for sous-vide cooking, a method usually reserved for kitchens in high-end restaurants. The oven boasted smart technology, capable of being controlled remotely through a smartphone app, and the app could suggest recipes based on ingredients you had on hand. Finally, the surface had been treated with a substance to resist fingerprints, scratches, and smudges.

"Grandma, that oven is a boss," Elijah remarked, his eyes wide with admiration at the sight of this cutting-edge appliance. You know a stove is a bad mutha-shut-your-mouth when a ten-year-old looks like he's about to cry just looking at it.

Gabriella was practically salivating, and my mind reeled at the list of features. I think the only thing it *didn't* do was plate your food.

But when Leonna turned over that price tag, I thought somebody had written their phone number on it, there were so many digits.

Elijah gulped. "Whoa. I think you could buy a car for that much money."

"Maybe," I agreed.

"But look at it!" Gabriella straightened an arm and outlined the perimeter. "And listen!" She knocked on the stainless steel. "It's solid. It will last for decades."

"Lifetime warranty," Leonna declared. "This brand is family owned. They stand by what they sell."

"They have to, as much as they charge," I said.

As the three of us stood there with mouths agape, Leonna offered, "And we match competitors' prices, so you won't find a better deal within fifty miles."

"By the way," Gabriella mentioned casually, "the next cooking competition is in August. I'd love to have a new oven before then to practice with."

I gawked. "No pressure."

"No pressure. I'm just sayin'," Gabriella said.

I glanced at the price tag and winced. "Yeah, I'm not sure if that's going to work, especially with the future plans to separate the house further."

Elijah, who had been quietly observing our conversation, piped up with a question. "Why do you need to separate the house more, Grandma?"

Gabriella smiled at him and ruffled his hair. "Right. I don't plan on moving anywhere anytime soon. Unless someone sweeps me off my feet, which isn't going to happen in a year's time."

"Neither am I," I added, realizing that there really was no rush to finish dividing the house. The only urgency came from wanting to share a great oven with Gabriella, to encourage her culinary dreams and create delicious memories together.

"Then we can just wait on the duplex separation," Gabriella declared, determination sparkling in her eyes. And in that moment, the future felt a little less uncertain, with the knowledge that we were both committed to making the best of our shared lives and our shared kitchen, one meal at a time.

Just as I was settling in to the idea of owning the Celestia, Lorenzo appeared out of nowhere, like a gust of wind that suddenly changed the temperature. They must have been sharing locations or something because he knew exactly where to find Gabriella.

He said something to her in Spanish, and she nodded, a hint of concern flickering across her face.

"Excuse us for a second," she said. They stepped away to the next aisle over.

I, for one, was grateful. I needed a moment to contemplate my first big purchase alone. Yes, I'd orchestrated the house remodel alone, but it was necessary. A huge, fancy stove, though? Right now?

I caught Elijah craning his neck to watch Gabriella and Lorenzo through the dishwashing machines.

"Let's not be nosy, Elijah," I whispered, gently nudging him back to the task at hand.

He sighed, relenting. "All right, Grandma."

I returned my attention to Leonna, who was obviously hoping for a sale. "Could you tell me more about the financing and payment options for these ovens?"

"Of course!" She smiled, launching into an explanation of various plans and discounts available.

As I listened, my mind kept wandering to Gabriella and Lorenzo, wondering what was going on between them. But I reminded myself that it wasn't my place to pry. I needed to focus on finding the right oven for our kitchen. So Gabriella could beat Mrs. Maine and, maybe, I could host the no-germ potluck.

When Gabriella returned, her eyes were slightly red, and her cheerful oven-happy demeanor had vanished. "I have to head back to work," she said quietly. "Someone called in sick last minute, and they need me to cover the shift tonight."

"Are you sure you're okay?" I asked, concerned.

"Yeah, I'll be fine." She forced a weak smile. "You two finish up here, okay? You know my vote. But I understand the situation. Just let me know."

"Will do," I replied, giving her a reassuring pat on the arm before she left the store.

Elijah looked at me with furrowed brows. "Grandma, it looks like Gabriella was crying."

I said gently, "Don't worry. She'll be okay."

Inside, I felt a knot forming in the pit of my stomach. Gabriella was usually so transparent, her emotions like an open book. To see her mask her feelings so quickly—it wasn't like her.

"Okay," he agreed hesitantly, though the concern lingered in his eyes. "But didn't she just get *off* work?"

He looked up at me with those big brown eyes, searching for reassurance. "People have to work double shifts sometimes," I told Elijah, trying to calm him. "Haven't your mom and dad ever had to stay late at the office?"

"I guess. It seemed like Gabriella and that guy were arguing."

"Stay out of grown folks' business, EJ," I admonished him. "Now, tell me how things are going at day camp. Have you made any new friends?"

He paused for a moment before launching into a tale of his latest adventures at the youth center. It was clear that he was having a great time, even if he couldn't shake his concerns about Gabriella.

He wasn't alone. I was worried about her, too. Fancy new oven or not, I hoped she wouldn't have to spend all her life working double shifts at someone else's restaurant. Or crying after a distressing conversation with her partner. For all she had done to help me and Elijah, she deserved so much more.

CHAPTER 14

I awoke the next morning with a sense of unease. My first thoughts were on the fact that I woke due to sunlight instead of sounds in the dark signaling Gabriella's return. She hadn't come home last night after leaving the appliance store with Lorenzo, and it worried me. Every scary movie I'd ever seen, every true crime show I'd ever watched, haunted my imagination.

I tried to brush off my feelings as I prepared breakfast for Elijah and myself. As we ate, I glanced at my phone every few minutes, checking for any messages from her.

Nothing.

I sighed and decided not to overthink it. One thing I'd learned from my own children was that my need for communication could be overwhelming to people who were accustomed to asynchronous conversations.

"All right, Elijah," I said, trying to keep my concerns from seeping into my voice. "Time to pack your lunch so we can leave."

"Okay, Grandma," he replied. Thanks to his time with Gabriella in the kitchen, Elijah was eager and able to make his own lunch. He made a simple turkey sandwich, threw some chips in a plastic bag, grabbed a banana, and asked me for cash to purchase a cold drink from the machine.

"You got it," I replied, with what I realized was a little too much cheer. It was weird being in the kitchen without Gabriella or the mention of her. It alarmed me how quickly Elijah caught on to this grown-up game of Don't Mention the Obvious when it came to fearful news. He was wise beyond his ten years. I know people mean that as a compliment, but it's not, because that often means the kid didn't get to have a childhood.

So I decided to let him engage with his feelings on our way to the day camp. "You got anything on your mind?"

"Miss Gabriella," he whispered.

"Me, too. But you know what? She's a grown-up. She doesn't have to tell us where she is all the time, you know?"

"I know."

Really, I was two inches away from calling 9-1-1.

Once I had dropped Elijah off, I headed to work, where I forced myself to focus on the task ahead. Today, I would learn the new software for scheduling and uploading workshop descriptions, taking payments, checking registration, and compensating the facilitators. It was a big day, and I couldn't afford to let my concerns about Gabriella interfere.

As I settled into my desk, I reminded myself how grateful I was for this job. It was giving me the confidence I needed to prove that I could still function well and lead an independent life. In fact, I realized just how much I needed work—more than I had initially thought.

"All right, Joyce," my coworker Susan called out cheerfully. "Are you ready to dive into this software?"

"Ready as I'll ever be," I replied, forcing a smile.

"Great! Let's get started, then," she said, pulling up a chair beside me. She smelled of patchouli and lavender, the kind of fragrance that made me think she'd once been a free-spirited hippie with dreams of changing the world. The faded, intricate tattoos on her forearms only added to that impression. Susan split her time between the recreation center and the city manager's office. I needed to learn this system so she wouldn't have to run back and forth, and that required my undivided attention.

As we worked through the program, I felt a sense of accomplishment and pride. My brain felt like it had done somersaults, but it was still sharp, and I could adapt to new situations.

When our first break came, two hours and two notebook pages full of handwritten notes later, my concerns about Gabriella resurfaced. So I called over to her workplace.

I was happy when a female voice answered the phone. "Hello, this is Joyce. I'm with the city of Robin Creek, and I'm trying to reach Gabriella Santos. Is she there?" So far, so good. No lies. I *did* work for the city's Parks and Recreation Department.

"I'm sorry, but she's busy prepping for the day. May I take a message and have her call you when she gets a free moment?"

This was some old-school phone micromanaging. No wonder folks kept their devices on them at all times! My true crime mind conjured up this idea that the woman on the phone was Lorenzo's other girlfriend. She and Lorenzo had kidnapped Gabriella. They were holding her hostage in a back alley. And it was a good thing I hadn't given her my last name so they couldn't come looking for me.

"You said she is present at work, though, right?" I double-checked.

"Yes. Are you, like, her mom?" The voice attempted a laugh

that came out more like a snort. Somehow, that snide question erased my thoughts about the kidnapping. The woman on the phone was too goofy to kidnap Gabriella.

"No. I'm with the city. I'll call her later." My trembling hands ended the call. I ate a few graham crackers, went to the ladies' room, and then returned to my desk a few minutes early to continue working.

"Hey, are you okay?" Susan asked, probably noticing my furrowed brow.

"Yeah, I'm fine," I lied, shaking my head to clear away the concern. "Just trying to absorb all this information."

"You're doing great," she reassured me. "Take your time."

"Thanks," I said, smiling genuinely at her encouragement. Time to get back to work.

Before lunch, I had a decent grasp on the software, and I felt more confident in my ability to handle it. I wished Terri could have been there to see me glide through the workflow.

Somebody called for Susan to come to the front desk, so we decided to break for lunch. But before I could log out of the computer and get my purse, Susan reentered my office carrying a small bouquet of flowers. There were daisies, sunflowers, and soft pink carnations, with tiny sprigs of baby's breath delicately woven between them. "These just arrived for you."

"Really?" I said, my curiosity piqued.

As Susan placed the bouquet on my desk, a smile crept across my face. The vibrant colors and delicate petals seemed to brighten up the room instantly. I opened the card attached to the bouquet and read it aloud.

"'Happy new job, friend. From Richard.'"

Aw, that's sweet of him, I thought, feeling a warmth spread through me. I reached for my phone and dialed his number, eager to thank him for his thoughtful gesture.

That was when I saw I'd received a text from Gabriella, finally. Sorry I missed calls. Phone died. Might stay with Lorenzo again tonight. Talk to you later.

She missed calls, messages, *and* texts! And did she really think that a dead phone was a decent excuse? That's right up there with saying *My alarm clock didn't go off.* Whose fault is that? Furthermore, this wasn't her second time using that one. *She needs another phone.* The only thing that staved off the anger was a sense of relief. This message had come from the real Gabriella; a kidnapper would have created a better story.

"Hey, Richard. Thank you for the flowers. They're lovely," I said as soon as he answered.

"Of course, Joyce," he replied. "I wanted to congratulate you on your new job. Have you gone to lunch yet?"

"No, not yet," I admitted.

"Would you like to join me at that small café near your workplace?" he suggested.

"Sure, I'd like that," I agreed, grateful for the chance to spend some time away from the worries about Gabriella circling overhead.

When lunchtime arrived, Richard pulled up in front of the recreation center, and we drove to the nearby café, a charming little spot with checkered tablecloths and mason jar glasses. It was the kind of small-town café where the waitstaff knew everyone's name and asked about their kids, and the menu hadn't changed since 1985—good, simple comfort food.

As we sat down at a quiet table, I thanked Richard again for the flowers. He flashed me a charming smile. I noticed the flirty glint in his eyes.

What was I thinking? This man had sent me flowers and taken me to lunch. This must look like a date to him. "Richard, I appreciate the gesture, but are you sure you can handle being just friends with me?" I asked, raising an eyebrow.

He sighed and leaned back in his chair. "Joyce, I'll be honest. I've always known how to pursue a woman, but being friends with one is uncharted territory for me. I just want to know if there's any chance at all for something more. In the future, I mean. After the friendship is firmly established."

I studied his face, noting the sincerity in his expression. A part of me recognized his desperation. We were both in a predicament neither of us could have imagined when we were younger. No one says *I can't wait to be by myself again in my golden years!* If we had known, we might have made different choices. You just never know sometimes.

But while I thoroughly understood these things, Richard had to know this wasn't a good look. Seemed like he was asking me to commit to the possibility of a romantic relationship, which felt as equally smothering as if he'd asked me to be his girlfriend.

Is that what I'd be at my age, anyway? A girl*friend?*

"Richard, I enjoy your company, and I'm grateful for your friendship. But right now, that's all I can offer you. I can't commit to anything more."

"Well, at least you didn't say flat 'no.' There's hope."

I blinked slowly. "Hope."

"Yeah. I just need a little hope that anything could happen, you know?"

The waitress arrived with our ice water and took our food order as well as my request for coffee. I glanced at the menu but couldn't fully focus, my mind still on Richard's words. *Hope? Hope for what?*

"Richard, do you have any female friends?" I asked before sipping my water.

He looked thoughtful for a moment before answering. "Well, yes, but they're all women I'm not attracted to. Not my type."

"And what, exactly, is your type?"

His lips curved upward, like he'd been waiting for this question.

I rolled my eyes to let him know this was not the time to give me a corny line. Anything even close to one of those bad pickup lines would make me walk back to the recreation center if need be.

He laughed at my expression and shook his head, presumably hard enough to dislodge the foolishness he'd considered saying. "Okay, okay. No romantic overtures."

"Thank you in advance," I said.

"Okay, hmmm..." His gaze drifted up and to the left. He was actually thinking of a non-frisky answer to my question, apparently. "Since you are my *friend*, and nothing more, I'm going to tell you the truth."

I slow-blinked. "That is ideal."

"Right. Here's the thing. What I really want is an old-fashioned woman. She cooks, laughs at my jokes, goes to church, is obsessed with keeping the house clean. She fusses about everything, keeps me in line. She makes sure I don't miss my doctors' appointments, she buys all the kids and grandkids Christmas gifts and puts both our names on them. You feel me?"

Friends don't judge. Though his list of desires in a relationship was self-focused, I simply nodded and said, "Uh-huh. I see."

"Is that wrong?"

"It's not for me to determine if what you truly want is right or wrong. It is what it is."

He rubbed his chin slowly. "Would you want to be this woman? Not to me, but to *anybody*?"

"Yes. If we were both getting what we needed from the relationship, I would gladly fulfill that list."

He quickly turned the spotlight on me. "Okay, and what do *you* want to receive in a relationship?"

"I'm not on the market."

"Hypothetically. Speculatively."

I was always a sucker for big words. "I have yet to *crystallize* my wish list."

"Oooh, you pullin' the teacher on me today?" he chided.

I laughed. "You started it."

"You play Scrabble?"

"No, sir. I don't *play* when it comes to Scrabble. I *obliterate* in Scrabble."

He laughed. "I've got to see that for myself."

The waitress arrived with our food and my coffee, placing the respective orders in front of us. Richard said grace over our meal before we took our first bites. The food was decent, but it didn't have Gabriella's flair. I found myself missing her creative touch, the way she'd elevate even simple ingredients into something fantastic. In the culinary sense, I was getting spoiled.

As we ate lunch, my thoughts drifted back to my first date with Eric. We had both played the roles that society had prescribed for us: He tried to see how far I would let him go, while I spent the evening showing interest without seeming too available. Good girls didn't make it easy, after all. What a confusing dance it was, where boys tried to gain a reputation while girls tried not to lose one. It was all too much then, and it still felt like too much now.

"Richard, I appreciate your feelings, but I don't want to lead you on," I said, returning to the present. "Let's just focus on building a friendship."

He nodded slowly. No googly eyes. "You're right, Joyce. I value what we have now, and I'm willing to be a friend if that's what you need, because the truth is, I need one, too. In fact, I kind of like this no-pressure thing."

"Good," I replied, feeling relieved. "Now, may I ask you a question?"

"Go."

"Tell me about your wife," I asked, curious about his past relationships and how they might have shaped him. To keep from qualifying my question, I stuffed my mouth and chewed.

He hesitated for a moment, then began. "I assume we were like most couples back then. I was the protective and providing husband; she was the nurturing and God-fearing wife and housekeeper." He paused, his voice growing somber. "Up until she cheated on me."

I considered his words, feeling a pang of empathy for his hurt. "Did you like being the provider and protector?"

"Mostly, yes," he replied with a shrug. "It was easy, in a way. I didn't have to think too much about it. I enjoyed my work, loved my kids and my wife... It all seemed good, as far as I could tell."

"I don't know your ex-wife, but I know how our generation was raised. I don't believe that a woman of our time would cheat just for the sake of cheating," I mused, remembering how constrained we had felt by societal expectations. "Perhaps there were deeper issues at play."

Richard looked thoughtful, his eyes meeting mine with a vulnerability that touched me. We sat there, two people with histories and fears, trying to navigate this new chapter of our lives together.

"Joyce," Richard began, his voice hesitant, "what happened between you and Eric?"

I sighed, stirring my coffee as I considered how to answer. "If I'd stayed in my marriage much longer, I might have ended up cheating, too," I admitted, a weight lifting from my chest as I spoke the truth. "I gave Eric clear warning. But he chose not to grow. I wasn't willing to wait another fifteen or thirty years. That's what happened to us." I looked up at Richard, gauging his reaction.

Richard scratched his head and shrugged. "That ain't what we were raised to do."

"Maybe that's why you and I both are single right now," I said.

"Touché."

I suggested gently, "I'm guessing you being with me as a friend will teach you what you need to know for the woman who comes next."

Richard seemed to take my words to heart, mulling them over. "So you're my *practice* friend."

"Yes."

He smirked. "I think you've got a lesson to learn, too."

"What would that be?"

"To have hope. Faith. Believe again."

"What, exactly, am I believing and hoping for?"

"Good days ahead," he said.

A bell of truth rang within me, stopping me mid-chew. *Good days ahead*. "Hmph."

He winked at me and his face broke into a grin. "It'll come to you later."

In that moment, I felt something shift between us. We had a new understanding, a deeper connection. We were two souls navigating the uncertainties of life, learning to be friends with each other in ways we never imagined before. Felt real good.

CHAPTER 15

"Grandma, what's for dinner?" Elijah asked, tugging on my sleeve, his eyes wide with curiosity. You'd think they didn't feed them two snacks and lunch at the day camp, the way he claimed starvation when I picked him up.

"Let's go out tonight," I suggested, forcing a smile. "Let's go to the Mexican restaurant in town where Gabriella works. Maybe we can surprise her."

"Yay!" Elijah clapped his hands.

At the restaurant, we were shown to a small table near the window. I scanned the room, searching for Gabriella among the bustling waitstaff, but she was nowhere to be seen. Instead, my eyes locked with Lorenzo's as he cashed out a customer. His gaze bored into me with unspoken hostility, making my blood run cold. I glared right back at him, determined not to let him intimidate me. Meanwhile, Elijah was engrossed in the word-find puzzle the waiter had given him, oblivious to the tension in the air.

"Can I get extra guacamole, Grandma?" Elijah asked without looking up, his pencil scratching against the paper.

"Of course, sweetheart," I replied, patting his hand gently.

My mind, however, was racing with questions and concerns about Gabriella. What was going on? Why hadn't she come home or responded to my messages? And why did Lorenzo look at me like that?

Let's just focus on having a good time, I told myself, trying to shake off the unease. As I glanced around the restaurant once more, I silently prayed that Gabriella was safe and sound, and that she and I would have a long conversation about it tonight.

"Here are your drinks," Chandra, our young waitress, said with a forced smile as she placed the glasses of water on the table. Her gaze darted away nervously, and I noticed her squirrelly twitch.

"Thank you," I replied, taking a sip to moisten my parched throat. "I was going to ask about the chicken burrito..."

Chandra hesitated for a moment, then shook her head. "I'm sorry, ma'am, but I can't serve you."

I blinked in confusion, feeling a surge of indignation rise within me. "Excuse me? What do you mean you can't serve us?"

"Please," Chandra whispered, glancing around anxiously. "Gabriella says you should leave."

"Leave?" I repeated, incredulous.

Elijah looked up from his kids' menu. "But we just got here. Is Gabriella okay?"

"Gabriella's fine," Chandra assured us, her voice barely audible. "She just doesn't want any more trouble. She'll explain everything later. At home."

As much as I wanted to protest, to demand answers right then and there, I knew that causing a scene wouldn't be in anyone's best interest—especially not with Elijah present. So, swallowing my frustration, I nodded reluctantly.

"All right." I sighed, reaching for Elijah's hand. "Let's go, sweetheart. We'll get dinner somewhere else."

"Okay, Grandma," he replied, his brow furrowed in confusion as he slid off his chair.

"Promise me Gabriella is okay," I whispered to Chandra one last time before leaving.

"I promise," she whispered back, her eyes filled with sincerity.

As we exited the restaurant, Elijah's small hand clutched mine tightly, a mask of confusion stuck to his face. I tried to steady my breathing, wrestling with the wild emotions thundering through me. It was obvious that something was going on—something I couldn't quite put my finger on. What could it be? If he hit her, I was gonna let him have it!

"Grandma, what happened?" Elijah asked, his voice quivering slightly.

"Nothing you need to worry about, baby," I reassured him, giving his hand a gentle squeeze. "We'll just find another place to eat tonight, okay?"

"Okaaaaay," he stretched out his respectful curiosity.

I stomped back to my car with Elijah in tow and backed out of my spot, wondering if I should leave or call the police. I circled the small lot and spotted Gabriella's car, which made me feel a little better. Just as I was about to exit the property, I saw Gabriella's mass of hair bouncing down the back stairs. She waved me down, and I took a breath of fresh air as I scanned her face. No bruises or marks, thank God.

I lowered my window as Elijah nearly hopped over into the driver's seat on top of me to see Gabriella for himself as well.

"I'm sorry I haven't called you back."

"Hi, Miss Gabriella!"

"Hey, Elijah. It's good to see you." Her eyes filled with tears that she blinked away. "I'll be back home soon."

"Great!" He settled back on his side of the car.

I whispered, "Are you okay, Gabriella?"

"Yes, Ms. Joyce. I appreciate your concern. I'm not in danger. Lorenzo and I are…trying to work things out. Without interference."

"Interference? As in, nosy people?"

"No. I mean…well… He thinks I've been acting different since I moved out and… We want to see if we can work it out. Just the two of us. No interference. You know he has in-law trauma from his ex's family."

Is that a thing?

As far as I could see, the only two people Gabriella had been around were me and Elijah. Didn't take a genius to figure out his insinuation. I didn't know whether to be relieved or insulted. Gabriella's calm demeanor soothed my fears, but her words made me wonder what was really going on.

"Plus, he's letting me use the stove and oven after hours, to practice my recipes." The fake grin on her face told another story.

"Gabriella, we can get the stove. You don't have to—"

She caught a tear before it fell. The phone in her apron pocket lit up as it vibrated. "I have to get back to work. I'll be home. Soon."

Whatever was happening, I knew one thing for certain: I wouldn't rest until I found answers.

CHAPTER 16

Every small Texas town has at least two restaurants: Sonic and Dairy Queen. Elijah was a fan of both and readily agreed that we should stop at Sonic. He considered it a special treat to park outside, roll down the windows, and wait for food between colorful menus dividing parking spots instead of idling through the drive-through.

To pass the time as we waited for our food, I asked Elijah about how things were going at the day camp. This led to a ten-minute speech about his new friends. One of them, Jamieson, was enamored by Greek mythology and had brought books to excite Elijah as well.

Try as I might, I could not give my grandson my undivided attention. *Without interference*. What exactly did that mean? And which one of them had come up with that phrase?

"Grandma, do you know how many kids Zeus had?"

I managed to catch the question. "Oh, I don't know. Ten?"

"No. A hundred!" Elijah's eyes shone with wonder. "And his wife was not happy about it."

"I wouldn't be happy, either," I replied, glad for the distraction.

"That's a lot of cooking and laundry. Who did he expect to watch all of them while he was out traveling across the world?"

His eyes furrowed. "Zeus didn't travel."

"No?"

"No. He's, like, the *big* god in Greek mythology. He didn't have to travel anywhere because he's everywhere. Maybe you're thinking about Odysseus. That guy traveled all over the Mediterranean Sea trying to get back home to his wife."

"I stand corrected."

"Grandma, do you believe in God?"

"Yes, I do."

"Then why don't you go to church anymore?" he asked with genuine curiosity.

Back when I was a child, we didn't ask grown-ups questions. They told you what to do, you did it, and there was little conversation outside of those directives. My father would sometimes entertain my inquisitions, much to my mother's chagrin. She wasn't raising a daughter who didn't know her place, which is to say she wasn't raising a sassy, contrary little girl who made people feel uncomfortable. "No man wants a disrespectful wife," she'd say.

Elijah wasn't being socialized as a girl, but he was still a child, and my mother would have cringed at him questioning me as well as the question itself. Not because it was about God, but the fact that he'd wondered if I believed in God because I hadn't taken the boy or myself to church. I didn't grow up in one of those families that practically lived in the sanctuary, but we were regular members with a decent attendance record and a huge white Bible with gold trim perched on the living room coffee table.

"I don't know, Elijah. I guess I haven't really thought about church much lately. Not since I moved."

"Oh. Okay."

"But I do believe in God," I clarified for the record.

"Cool. Me, too. Not Zeus god. *Real* God."

"Cool," I echoed his calm and collected nature.

I prayed he wouldn't ask me to take him to church while in Robin Creek. Me and God had…let's call it a "falling-out" recently. I still talked to Him in a thankful, reverent way. I just didn't like how He'd set up the whole entire world with women on the bottom, and it seemed everyone—Him included—was perfectly fine with us carrying the world on our shoulders. From birthing babies to carrying water pails to being stuck in loveless marriages because most of the female-dominated careers are front line and low paying…yeah. I had a chip on my shoulder. And going through the divorce wringer squeezed a lot out of me, including my faith in people, in the general goodness of humanity. Faith in myself.

Thankfully, Elijah didn't say anything more about church or God or anything in that neighborhood.

When our food arrived, we decided the temperature outside was so pleasant, we might as well eat in the car. This was yet another childhood rule broken.

"Grandma, this food is not like Gabriella's."

I gasped. "I know, right? Yesterday, I ate lunch with a friend at a nice little café. Those people have nothing on Gabriella."

"Man, I really need her to come home."

"Me, too, EJ."

"When are we gonna get the stove? She said she's gonna show me how to make old-fashioned cinnamon toast."

My mouth watered already. I could live on oven-made cinnamon toast, and I was certain Gabriella had a Blaxican twist that would take it to another level. No matter what she and Lorenzo were up to in their no-outsider zone, I was certain of one thing: She was still cooking up masterpieces, which meant he was the beneficiary of all her good cooking while Elijah and I were reduced to fast food.

But I couldn't "interfere." I reminded myself that Gabriella was twenty-six. Not a baby. Grown enough to have lived with her boyfriend before she met me, and grown enough to move out on her own and pay my rent. Eating amazing food had been a bonus. So had her sweet laugh and her silly jokes, and the way she'd embraced Elijah like he was her little brother.

"We've gotta get that oven" slid out of my mouth.

"Let's get it," he said while chomping on his last french fries.

"Get what?"

"The oven. Let's go buy it, and maybe Gabriella will come home," he said.

"I don't think—"

"You need an oven anyway, don't you?"

I pulled the corners of my lips downward, pondering his words. "This is true."

"So why not get the best one? Gabriella will be extra happy to come back, and you will have your oven." Then he flashed me a ridiculously charming, full-mouthed smile with those oversize two front teeth typical of ten-year-olds, and bits of french fries clinging to his gums.

Made me laugh so hard I nearly choked on my onion rings. "Boy, you are something else."

Next stop: McCloud's. All the way there, I second-guessed myself as I worked the math in my head: my paycheck, the cost of the oven, the tax, delivery and installation. I could put it on my emergency credit card.

Is this an emergency? Not exactly. But I did need an oven, regardless. At least, that's what Elijah said.

At McCloud's, Celestia awaited us in all her stainless steel glory. Elijah and I stood in front of her again, taking in her beauty. She was even more attractive the second time around, with the bit of sunlight left in the sky streaming through the windows.

Joyce. It's an oven. A box that heats up food, I told myself. But it was a lie, because Celestia was more than an oven. She was a shiny friend.

"Back already?" Leonna approached wearing a sneaky smile. She had us and she knew it.

"Yes. We're going with the Celestia."

"An excellent choice. Follow me."

Elijah beamed like he'd just won the lottery, while my chest tightened with anxiety. Who in their right mind would pay so much for an oven? I wrestled with myself all the way to the check-out counter. In my training at the recreation center, Susan told me about how they decided which classes to offer every year. "We do market research to see what people sign up for so we don't waste resources. We have to skim at least a little profit to pay the bills around here," she'd told me.

So if Celestia's manufacturer went through all the trouble of making the machine, I couldn't have been the only person in the world purchasing it. People like me, people like Gabriella, people all over the world were buying Celestias, right?

Leonna smiled nervously as she walked me through the buying process, reassuring me that I was making a smart, elevated purchase. "I have *never* seen one of these returned to the store."

What's her commission, anyway?

Since the oven came with a solid warranty, I passed on the

store's offer. We talked through delivery options next. Given my work schedule, I opted for a Friday-afternoon delivery. All this conversation led to the final numbers and me whipping out the credit card and inserting the chipped side into the reader.

I had a flashback of the first time Eric and I purchased a luxury vehicle. A BMW. I could hardly believe we were signing our names to the papers, about to spend the next four years of our lives paying a car note that was half the cost of our monthly mortgage. But Eric had insisted that with his new promotion came new lunch meetings and golf appointments, and he needed to look the part of a middle manager. "Live a little, Joyce."

Signing the receipt for Celestia didn't feel like living. It felt like smothering. I took deep breaths as wrote my name with the stylus on the tiny screen and clicked "OK."

"We're all settled, Miss Hicks," Leonna chirped.

Hicks? Oh, yes. I am Hicks again. I'd gotten the new credit card using my maiden name. Which meant I was the only one responsible for this bill. Not Gabriella, not Elijah. *What have I done?*

"Thank you," I squeaked as I took the foot-long receipt from her and rolled it into my wallet. Suddenly, the food from Sonic wasn't setting so well in my stomach.

"The delivery team will give you a call Thursday to confirm the time. If you need anything between now and then, please don't hesitate to give me a call. I work most weekdays from twelve to close."

"Okay. Thank you."

"Grandma, we did it!" Elijah squealed.

"Yes. We sure did."

The first thing I did when we got home was take two pink

antacid pills. Calmed my stomach. I had written a large check to the contractor when they worked on this house, but that was all in the name of profit. It made sense to turn Grandma Jewel's house into a duplex, especially given the housing market. Folks were scrambling for affordable housing all over the country. I could make money and help somebody else at the same time if I invested in a remodel.

But an overpriced oven? In my circumstances?

My stomach rumbled again. I needed to stop worrying about Celestia before I made myself sick.

I gave Elijah permission to run out to play with his neighborhood friends before it got too dark, then I lay on the couch to practice more deep breathing and regulate my nervous system. *Goodness gracious*. To date, I had not experienced a panic attack, and I had no desire to.

I pulled myself off the couch and gave my body a big head-to-toe stretch. This oven, this house, my divorced status all fell under the "everything" umbrella. I needed to keep moving forward.

So I took the next step that made sense. I called my previous contractor—no more local referrals, thank you—to ask about resuming the work, starting with the oven. I got his voicemail and left a message.

Then I washed my face in the bathroom, a final step in reclaiming my sanity for the day. I returned to the kitchen and saw that I'd missed his call, presumably due to the sound of me running water in the sink.

"Miss Hicks, this is Jerry with Southern Sons Remodeling. I got your message about the oven installation Friday. I'm afraid that won't be possible to resume unless you've had someone else take care of the numerous items I shared in my last report. I'm headed out to an event with my family tonight. You can reach me in the morning. Take care, now."

So much for today's sanity.

CHAPTER 17

When I'd first gotten notice from Southern Sons via email that they couldn't complete the full reconstruction in time, sure, I opened the attachment. I'd scrolled to the last page and saw the amount needed to continue the work, which might as well have been the same as the national debt because, either way, I didn't have the money to proceed.

With that, I had closed the document and finished packing the last of my bags at my home in Austin while Eric seethed in his man cave. His man cave had its own bar, along with a theater. It was the perfect hideaway for someone who loved to be alone as much as he did.

But that day, as I rolled and stuffed several pairs of black slacks into a lightweight suitcase, he left the cave door open, filling the bottom floor with sounds of gunfire, cussing, and the sharp sound effects of a violent action movie. Though Eric had never hit me, he had a way of agitating me all his own. He'd play music so loud that I couldn't think straight, or burn several sticks of incense, knowing I couldn't stand the smell or the feel of thick, smoky air.

For the record, I could be petty as well. I've been known to make up one side of the bed for weeks at a time. There's an art to it.

Anyway, when I got the email about the newly discovered problems and the estimate for what it would cost to fix them, I put the matter out of my mind, choosing to worry about one thing at a time. Packing and getting to Robin Creek took priority. And when I'd arrived at Grandma Jewel's place and looked around, I liked what I saw. Beautiful exterior and interior paint. White, shiny baseboards. Working lights. Whatever the Southern Sons still needed to do didn't seem dire.

When your car still gets you from point A to point B with no problems, it's easy to ignore a check-engine light. Especially when you don't have extra money.

Now that I had reopened the email and paid attention to the problems, it all made sense. Gabriella wasn't to blame for the oven disaster because that side of the house with the kitchen and laundry room needed rewiring. The plumbing system needed significant upgrades to support increased demand once an additional laundry room was added.

My heart sank at these first two revelations. It was only a matter of time before things fell apart if I installed Celestia, let alone finished the duplex separation.

Additionally, the heating system needed an upgrade with new insulation; otherwise, the upcoming winter months might make the house unlivable, depending on how Mother Nature rolled in. No matter what, I had to make changes. Time mattered now.

Gabriella had come in late the night before, so we didn't get to talk about whatever had happened with her and Lorenzo. Their issue was no longer a priority for me, given the message from Jerry and my scan of the documents he gave me months ago. In a way, I was glad I hadn't scoured the estimate. I might not have left Austin when I did.

Elijah and I were up and out before Gabriella woke up. He and I parted ways at the recreation center, him heading to the camp and me to the offices. The flowers from Richard were holding up nicely, and my framed picture of Elijah scuba diving—a gift from Terri—made me smile despite everything.

No sooner had I logged into our system than Jerry followed up with me again.

"Ms. Hicks, hello again. How are you?"

"Hello, Jerry. I'm fine. Thanks so much for your message. How are you?"

"Oh, I can't complain. Just wanted to follow up with you about the duplex. Did you get the other work done by someone else?"

I managed a laugh. "No. I haven't done anything except mess up my oven."

"Yikes! Sorry to hear that," he said in a wincing voice. "Yeah, that wiring can't be overloaded. According to my records, that oven was the oldest appliance in the kitchen. The new stuff will turn off before it overheats like that, so I wouldn't say you're in danger at this point. You just need to make the changes before you can move ahead, and definitely before winter with the heating situation."

"I gathered that," I told him. "The problem is, I don't have the money to do all those things. Not until I've been on my job a while longer. I'm wondering if we can prioritize, maybe. Do things in stages."

"Certainly, I'm willing to do that," he agreed. "Um...I don't want to insult you, but have you by chance checked in with SLAP?"

"No. I don't know who Slap is, and I'm not interested in another off-the-record contractor," I said frankly.

Jerry laughed. "No. I'm talking about the Senior Living Advocacy Program. S-L-A-P. In Lubbock. They can sometimes help with upgrades, installing ramps and rails, things to help people stay at home as they age. They might be able to help you, though your circumstance is different."

"No, I haven't called SLAP." I laughed at myself. "But I can. I'll let you know what happens. Thank you."

I got a number and made an appointment to visit SLAP that afternoon. I got hold of Gabriella by text, and she said she'd pick up Elijah if I was running late.

An hour after I got off work, I found myself signing in for my appointment at SLAP's West Texas regional office. The office was a bustling hub of information and assistance, its walls papered with an array of large-print notices and flyers, all aimed at supporting the senior community. There were comprehensive guides on healthcare rights, notices about upcoming workshops on financial planning for retirement, tips for navigating Social Security benefits, and QR codes to scan for more information.

Aside from joining the AARP and getting a few Tuesday discounts, I really hadn't considered myself an outright senior citizen. Yet there I was, with silver hairs streaking through my pulled-back, puffy ponytail. All I needed now was long compression socks and nursing shoes, which, coincidentally, sounded like heaven. Every time I hauled myself up from the chair at work, I felt a pulsing in my legs. It wouldn't be long before I joined the long-socks club.

"Ms. Hicks?" An unnaturally blond girl, with a clump of hair humped on top of her head held in place by a gold clasp, called my name. Her bright smile and piercing grayish-blue eyes—reminded me of a Siberian husky—caught my attention right away. I liked her modest denim skirt with a flared red blouse. She looked like a first-year teacher, all cheerful and untarnished by reality.

"Right here." I pushed off my chair's arm to stand. *Gracious, I am old* for real *for real.*

"Hi, I'm Jennifer. I'll be your liaison. Come this way."

"Thank you."

I followed her and the floral scent of her body spray down a narrow hallway, past two more liaisons with name tags outside their offices who were busy talking on their phones. Once inside Jennifer's office, I realized how bare the other two offices seemed in comparison. Jennifer, again in true new-teacher style, had decorated hers with an array of brightly colored posters, each bearing sports-inspired motivational quotes. A small, lush plant sat happily in a sunlit corner of the desk, its green leaves adding a touch of life to the room. On her desk, a collection of quirky, fun-shaped paperweights held down a neat stack of papers, and a ceramic mug painted with cheerful sunflowers served as a pen holder. She also had several pictures of what I assumed were family members. Her parents, one brother, and grandparents.

Jennifer had made this 10x10 office her own. It made me feel right at home.

She got straight into the work. "I read through the information you supplied online, and I'm hoping we can help."

"Me, too, because I have a lot that needs to be done."

"Let's get started."

I showed her the email from Southern Sons, my receipt for Celestia, my banking information, my first few paycheck stubs, my rental contract with Gabriella—everything she asked for to document my case, income, and expenses. I gave her information about my bank accounts, my next of kin. Everything except my shoe size. She worked with clinical precision. Her fingers typed rapidly on the keyboard while her other hand flipped through the pages I'd presented like she was sorting laundry.

Jennifer entered the information and figures into the computer. She had two screens open: one for typing, and one for reference. Turns out, that new-teacher feel meant new SLAP liaison. The book was open, and she intended to follow those guidelines with integrity.

"Hmm." She paused and bit her thumb. Her brow furrowed as her eyes scanned the figures, and a flicker of something unreadable passing across her face. "It looks like you don't have enough money."

I nodded. "Yes. That's why I'm here, for help with the remodeling."

"No." She shook her head. "I mean, you don't have enough money for your daily living expenses. *Before* the remodel."

"My bills are paid on time."

"What about food? Electricity? Emergency funds?" Her perfume seemed to thicken the air.

"This *is* my emergency, and I've come here for funding," I said.

Jennifer's eyes scanned the screens again. Then she faced me, her eyes drooping with sympathy. "Ms. Hicks, according to our calculations, you are living below the poverty level."

"Wouldn't be the first time an old, single woman found herself in this predicament." I laughed, hoping she'd join me. But she didn't.

I swiped the smile off my face. "I'm a bit short for now," I said. "But when I turn sixty-two, I'll start drawing my full teacher pension. I just have to make it until then. I'm trying not to touch my savings any more if I don't have to. If I keep my job at the recreation center, I'll be fine, don't you think?"

She pursed her lips. Sighed. "What about the fire with the original oven?"

"There was no *fire*," I corrected her. "It was an overheated burner. My tenant took care of everything."

I could tell by the way her eyes stayed steady on me that she didn't believe me. "Speaking of your tenant. She's paying way less than market value for her side of the duplex."

"I know. That's because when I originally advertised it, I thought there'd be two separate units. I lowered the amount significantly when I realized I'd made a mistake in the advertisement," I admitted. "Anyway, Robin Creek is a small town. People help each other out. I was just glad to get someone willing to stay, since I didn't complete the duplex."

Jennifer shook her head slightly. "I hate to say this, but your tenant may be taking advantage of you, Ms. Hicks. It's quite common for people to underpay senior citizens."

A wave of irritation washed over me, my jaw tightened, and my hands clenched into fists in my lap. The only person starting fires was Jennifer, with her suggestion that I was being exploited, coupled with the underlying insinuation that my age made me inherently vulnerable. *What kind of training did she get for this job?* "I assure you that Gabriella is not taking advantage of me. And I may not have much disposable income, but there are plenty of people making it on much less. Is it a crime to be poor these days?"

She gave me a patronizing smile. And then she asked, in that slow, kindergartner-speak tone, "Have you suffered any falls? Or memory loss?"

My eyes narrowed as I fought to maintain my composure. "Jennifer, I don't know exactly what you're huntin' for, but I assure you I can take care of myself. The time may come when I need someone else, but it ain't today." I reached across her paperweights and snatched back all my papers.

She jumped back, pressing against her seat cushion. "Ms. Hicks, it's okay. I can get you help."

"I don't need help. I withdraw my request."

"I'm afraid it's not that simple," she said.

I froze.

"Since you're over sixty, and I do believe you're in danger, I have to report this to Adult Protective Services. I—I hope you understand."

My lips trembled as I attempted to formulate a word, a phrase, a sentence in response.

Jennifer pointed to her on-screen manual. "It says that if a client shows signs of financial distress, isolation, or any signs of neglect, I am required to report the situation to the proper authorities for further assessment." She looked up at me. "I'm sorry, Ms. Hicks, but these are the guidelines I must follow."

"I don't care what your screen says. Common sense ought to tell you that I only need help with these one-time repairs," I managed to say. My shaky voice betrayed me, and I took a big gulp of air to steady my brain.

Jennifer's face flushed. She bit her bottom lip for a second. "There's no need to be alarmed."

"You *have* alarmed me, Jennifer. Sincerely."

"I understand. Someone will be in touch again soon. Just as a follow-up."

"Don't you send nobody to my house," I all but threatened her in my native Southern drawl. After all these years, I still managed to sound just like Grandma Jewel when she got riled up and lost her religion.

Jennifer must've seen something in my eyes, because she recoiled slightly, probably thinking I was hiding the depths of my despair. She softly stated, "Ms. Hicks, if your home is unlivable, we can help you find another place to stay. From what you've shared, it sounds like things might be...spiraling."

"I am not spiraling," I said slowly, trying to keep my voice steady. "I am managing just fine."

Jennifer's expression didn't shift. She was in full-on official mode now. "It's important to take these things seriously. If you've felt overwhelmed or neglected basic needs—"

I threw up my hands, exasperated. "Neglected? Look, I'm not some charity case. You've got this all wrong."

Jennifer typed something quickly, clearly making note of my reaction. "I just want to make sure you're safe."

The finality in her tone hit me like a boulder. It's amazing how one person can decide something about you—a judge, a teacher, a social worker—and everything changes.

I stood and pivoted to leave her office, not waiting for her to walk me back to the reception area. The room seemed to spin for a moment, my legs unsteady as I forced myself to walk away from the desk. What a waste of time, effort, and gas money. Worse, now I was on the state's radar as an old woman in distress. Broke, possibly duped, and noted as irrational. Just like my daughter and my ex-husband had said. Just as I had feared.

I'd gone there for help from SLAP. But SLAP slapped *me* instead.

CHAPTER 18

Thanks to my abbreviated visit to SLAP, I made it back in plenty of time to pick up Elijah from day camp. The light makeup I'd put on that morning had been all but swept away by my river of tears.

"Grandma, what's wrong?" he asked as soon as we got in my car.

"I don't want to talk about it right now."

The air between us swelled with anxiety, however, and I decided I'd better say something, because one thing I know about children: They often internalize things and wonder if they're to blame whenever adults have problems.

A few blocks from the house, I concocted a suitable explanation for my reddened eyes and sniffles. "EJ, I'm dealing with some sadness, but it has nothing to do with you."

"Wh-what are you sad about?"

"Grown-up stuff. *Old* grown-up stuff." I snickered.

"Are you gonna be sad all day?" he pried.

"That's a good question. I don't know," I answered.

"Okay. 'Cause I was just thinking, if you're still sad after dinner, we should go get a huge snow cone."

A laugh barreled up from my belly, full and light, taking a bit of my cares with it. "You make me happy, EJ. I'm so glad you're here." I reached over and tried to tickle his neck, but he clamped his chin down in defense.

I'd barely parked the car in my driveway when he jumped out and ran toward Gabriella, who was sitting on the porch, drinking wine at 6:15 p.m. My mother would have had a hissy fit over the sight of a woman drinking alone outside in daylight for all the neighborhood to see. Being my mother's child, it gave me pause, too. And yet, if her day had been anything like mine, getting drunk on the porch seemed like a proper finale for the evening. My feelings of frustration and humiliation from the SLAP meeting wore on me like a heavy coat.

"Hey, Elijah! I missed you!" Gabriella hugged him with one hand and held on to her glass with the other.

"I missed you, too! And guess what?"

"What?"

"We got the amazing oven for you!"

Leave it to EJ.

Gabriella's eyebrows shot up and her mouth dropped open. "What?" She shifted her eyes from Elijah's to mine, searching for confirmation as I walked from the car and up the steps to join them. "Where is it?"

"It's scheduled for delivery tomorrow. But we need to talk about that."

Elijah unfurled himself from their lingering hug and threw me a questioning glance.

"Let's get you a snack," I said to distract him for the moment, and gave Gabriella a nod to signal we'd discuss the situation later.

"I made mozzarella cheese sticks," she offered, which sent Elijah racing through the door and straight to the kitchen.

I joined him at the table, savoring Gabriella's immaculate creation. The aroma of fried bread bits filled the air. True to her craft, she had seasoned the breading, stuffed bits of jalapeño into the cheese, and created a creamy dip on the side. The first bite shifted my attitude. The world was not a total loss, because these homemade cheese sticks had survived.

"Grandma, can you make cheese sticks like this?"

"No, siree, I cannot."

He giggled. "How did she get so good at cooking?"

"Practice on top of a gift from God."

"I want to cook like her when I grow up," he declared with a mouth full of gooey cheese. "'Cause you were sad before you ate these cheese sticks. And now you're happy. I want to make people happy with my food. That's what I'm gonna call it: Happy Foods."

Again, his words filled me with laughter. "Sounds like a good plan, EJ."

He took off with his neighborhood friends on that extra bike, and I joined Gabriella on the porch again with a glass of my own. What good were all my manners today?

"Mind if I join you?"

"Please do."

She scooted over on the wooden bench to give me ample room. I tilted my glass toward her and she poured. The ruby red liquid splashed into place quickly. "Whoa! That's enough. You trying to drown *all* my sorrows away?"

Gabriella laughed. "Isn't that the purpose?"

I took a sip, sweet and robust. The evening air was warm but carried a soft, cooling breeze that made sitting outside on the porch incredibly pleasant. The sun had just begun to dip below the horizon, and the crickets and cicadas were tuning up for their nightly songs. It was moments like these that made the slower pace of small-town life so appealing. And yet, our problems knew no zip codes.

"You want to walk to the park and swing?" she suggested.

"Swing?"

"Yeah. That's what I do when I need to clear my mind. Swing and remember what it's like to be carefree."

Sounded like a good plan to me. I changed into a pair of sneakers and jeans. We left a note for Elijah in case he came looking for us and walked a few blocks to the park. Gabriella carried the wine and our cups in a backpack. There was one family—two parents and two kids—playing in the newer part of the park, with colorful slides and climbing frames, which left Gabriella and me to ourselves on the old, abandoned swings fifty yards away.

The sun had begun its descent, which gave us a bit of privacy. We had about a minute of unfiltered joy, swinging so high our bottoms lifted at the crest. The rush of air past my ears, the fleeting moment of weightlessness at the swing's peak, brought an exhilarating freedom that I hadn't felt in years. For those brief moments, the complications of life seemed to melt away, replaced by the simple, pure joy of flight.

But my stomach wasn't feeling it, as my roller coaster days were far behind me. "Gabriella, we're gonna be sick!"

"I know, right?"

We both came back down to earth—reality—and slowed to rocking back and forth. Gabriella abandoned her swing long enough to open her backpack and pour more wine for us. Somehow, we managed to swing and keep our wine cups from tilting.

"So what happened with Lorenzo?"

She countered, "What happened with Celestia?"

"I asked first."

She threw her head back. "Ugh! Ratchet. He is ratchet."

"'Ratchet'? Is that the same as trifling?"

"Close." She pulled her head straight again. "I never thought he was the one. Never thought we'd get married or anything. But I didn't know he could be such a… Ooh! I don't want to cuss around you, Ms. Joyce." She took another sip.

"Say what you gotta say."

She stacked up pretty much every cussing word and phrase in the book, one on top of the other, to describe this man, some combinations I didn't even realized matched. Then she took a deep breath. "That felt good."

"Glad to be here for you. You still haven't told me what happened."

Two blocks over, Elijah and his friend zipped by on their bicycles. He threw us a wave, which Gabriella and I returned.

"God, I hope Elijah won't turn out like Lorenzo."

"He won't," I assured her. "He wants to be like you. A chef whose food makes people happy."

She smiled. "Awww. He's so sweet. And kind. Most kids are. What happens to boys between ten and thirty?"

"According to the wisdom of Earth, Wind & Fire, the world makes a heart cold over time."

"Earth, wind, and who?"

I'd forgotten who I was talking to for a second. "They were an R and B band. In the seventies."

She sipped again. "*Cold heart* is the right phrase. Frozen. Solid. Lorenzo wants me to move back in with him, get married, start a family, and become a partner in the restaurant. Like, yesterday."

"He proposed?"

"No. He didn't. He just named off all these things he wants us to do, like it was a checklist."

"Wow."

"Yeah," she huffed. "It's like he's never seen a final episode of *The Bachelor*."

I could only follow with "Oh."

Gabriella twirled her head and faced me. "You've never seen a final episode, either?"

"I haven't seen *any* episodes."

She smacked her forehead. "Ay yi yi. What am I going to do with you?"

"Just like you've never heard of Earth, Wind & Fire," I reminded her.

A smile snuck across her face, and we both laughed at ourselves, sipping wine across these swings and across this generational gap.

"The thing is," she continued, "I want those things, too. A husband, a family, a place to cook and bring people happiness, like Elijah said. But his presentation was all wrong because his heart is so freakin' cold. He wants me to join *his* life, not make *our* life together. You don't like him, do you?"

She'd blindsided me with that one, but I recovered with, "It doesn't matter what I think of him. Do *you* like him?"

"I used to," she whispered. "Is that how all relationships go? You start off great, getting to know each other. Hanging out, eating. Great sex. Move in together. Then—Bam!—the world and everyday life snatches all the magic away?"

She got me again with the "great sex" part. When I was her age, my friends and I didn't talk about sex. I never talked about sex with other women. With anybody. I just wove it into my marriage, right along with the extra laundry.

"Since I just left a thirty-year marriage and the ladies in my library group said I'm still in my anti-man phase, I decline to comment."

"Joyce. You were married thirty years. You're an expert, in my opinion."

"But I'm divorced. We failed."

"Oh my gosh, seriously? I'd put a three-year relationship in my Win column. Even schools aren't that cruel; they give you an average for the grade. I'd give your marriage no lower than a C for thirty years, on effort and extra credit alone."

I stared at an oncoming car, considering her words. My words. *We failed* because our marriage ended. I did feel like had a scarlet "D" embroidered onto my blouses since the divorce.

"No one in your family stayed married for more than thirty years?" I double-checked.

"They stayed married as long as they could or until somebody died. My parents were already split up when my dad died. My grandfather died young, too. My half brother and his wife have been married almost ten years, but she's the meanest person alive. I don't see it lasting."

"Hmph."

"Me and Lorenzo... We were good the first year. And then this other side of him brought out this other side of me, and now I can't do it." Her face crumpled and tears leaked from her big brown eyes. Poor Gabriella. She was so smart, beautiful, and kind. She had no business crying over somebody who didn't or couldn't appreciate her.

"If you can't, then don't. Stay here, get yourself together, and wait until you meet someone who wants to add to your life as much as you're willing to add to his."

She cried, "But what if he never comes along?"

"So be it."

"I want kids!"

"You also want those kids to have a father who teaches them how to love, who won't let this world make their hearts grow cold," I told her, thinking of my own daughter. "I endured my husband's coldness for the sake of my children's financial well-being without understanding that I was setting a model in place, setting up the next generation to repeat the pattern. I thought my love and self-sacrifice could make up for my husband's shortcomings, but it didn't. It couldn't."

Gabriella hiccuped. "Dang, Ms. Joyce. You went in on a sistah."

A drop of wine escaped my lips as I chuckled. "Sorry, sweetheart."

"No, I needed to hear it. Lorenzo is great at running a business, and he can be sweet when he wants to, but overall, he's got an attitude problem and I don't want to pass that on to my imaginary future children. I said it first right here with you." She raised her glass. "To kind men?"

"To kind men."

As we toasted, Richard came to mind. He was kind, as a friend. Annoying as a suitor.

"What's up with Celestia?" Gabriella wasted no time "going in" on me, too.

I took a big gulp.

"That bad?"

"Worse."

"Get a refund. We can buy a cheaper oven. We could even scrape by with a toaster oven for now," she said.

I smacked my lips. "A toaster oven, Gabriella?"

"I'm just sayin'. I've made it this far without Celestia." She rolled her neck as she hissed the name. "I can make it to my own business without her."

"I wish it was that simple. When I called the old contractor to install Celestia, he promptly said he couldn't do it unless I'd had that whole side of the house rewired. He referred me to the Senior Living Advocacy Program, SLAP."

Gabriella swatted at the air clumsily. "Slap, baby, slap!"

"Slow down on the wine."

She grabbed her swing's chain links again. "But SLAP is good, right?"

"Wrong. I went there and told the lady I needed help, showed her my bills. Next thing I know, she's talking to me like I needed every syllable spelled out. She basically said I don't have enough money, my house is unsafe, and she's going to send someone from Adult Protective Services to check things out."

Gabriella's eyes widened. "What. The. Total. Heck?"

"Yep."

"Why?"

"Because that's what her computer told her to do." I mimicked the way Jennifer touched her monitor, as though it were an almighty wise adviser.

Gabriella's head lolled to the side. "I...I totally know how you feel. When I was seven, I was taken into CPS custody for a little while."

My mouth dropped open, and my heart fell, too. "Gabriella, I'm so sorry."

"It was...temporary. Only a few days, while they confirmed my mother's story about how I broke my arm when I fell off my bike. I had other bruises on my body. Did I tell you I was a beast when I was little?"

I could certainly imagine her as an athletic, curious child with a penchant for adventure. "Sounds about right."

"Well, me and some other kids in the neighborhood were always playing rough. Riding, like, four people on a bicycle. Rolling in tires. Daring each other to see who could hold their breath the longest or stand the most pain before crying uncle. And I was always up for a dare."

I nodded.

"So I was pretty rough. And the day I was trying to ride on the back tire of my bike, I fell and broke my arm. The nurses had me take off my shirt. When they finished with the cast, a social worker took me away."

I gasped at this, but quickly realized I wasn't helping the situation. Her eyes were rimmed with tears. "It was the scariest thing. I felt like I was being kidnapped."

"I'm so sorry."

"But the people who took me in were actually super nice. No horror story there."

"I'm glad to hear that."

"I'm just saying," Gabriella noted, "I know how it feels when 'the man' gets involved in your life. For better or for worse. But the truth comes out in the end, you know?"

"Let's hope so," I said.

She asked, "So what are they saying will happen next?"

"Someone from APS will call or come by, I imagine."

"Wow. Just wow."

A sad silence spread over us, soft but all-encompassing. Then Gabriella said, "We'll fight 'em, Ms. Joyce."

"Thank you, Gabriella," I said. My tears came again a few seconds later, so quickly it surprised me. I had cried in the car.

Alone. But I hadn't cried in front of anyone for years; not even at my father's funeral when the soloist sang "Precious Lord." That day, I had numbed myself, stepped outside of myself, and thought about practical things—*Do we have enough food for the repast? Will my heels sink into the damp earth at the gravesite? Who sent those beautiful purple flowers?*

Expecting a visit from APS should have been easy compared to seeing my father lying in a casket. Yet there I sat, fully in my emotions as tears trailed down my face again, feeling the sadness in a way that I didn't allow myself to feel before—especially not around another person.

But swinging outside with Gabriella and sharing our lives, watching her sadness come, have its moment, and leave—crying in her company felt normal.

I poured more of the humanizing wine into my half-filled glass. The evening breeze picked up, weaving through us, lending a sense of calm to our shared moment of vulnerability. The squeak of our swings' chains a sweet soundtrack of its own.

"We'll formulate a plan. When we're completely sober," she qualified.

"Yeah. Sober will be best."

And we both cracked up like we were watching old reruns of *Good Times*.

CHAPTER 19

As the morning light brightened my bedroom, I lay there, cocooned in the soft sheets, pondering the direction my life had taken. It's funny how life can change in a second. An accident, a well-meaning word spoken, an overheated oven, a computer's calculation, a social media algorithm—all these can impact the trajectory of someone's life, without any one person to blame.

The word *blame* rang in my brain. Did I blame myself? Why did I feel the need to blame anyone at all? What if this was all a part of God's big plans? Part of how life panned out? In my sixty years of living, I'd seen enough good people suffer to understand that you don't have to do anything wrong to find yourself struggling. In school, we taught students that if they worked hard enough, long enough, they would eventually become successful.

The longer I lived, the more I realized this was a lie. Nothing is promised. Eat, drink, and be merry, like the birds chirping outside do. Their tweeting alone brightened a melancholy morning.

My thoughts wandered to Richard's words about faith as well. *Good days ahead.* I decided that, with all the uncertainty, the best I could hope for was a good day right now. Today. I imagined myself smiling throughout this Saturday, hugging EJ, laughing with Gabriella. She had the day off, which meant she'd surely be cooking up a storm.

The sound of laughter drifted through the house, pulling me from my introspection. I could hear Elijah and Gabriella chatting in the kitchen, their voices a comforting melody. They were my "eat, drink, and be merry" crew, and I was thankful for them.

The smell of breakfast hadn't reached me yet. Maybe I could get in there and help with whatever they were cooking. I tossed off my covers, stretched through my normal morning aches and pains, took care of my hygiene, and padded down the hallway to investigate.

"Good morning!" I greeted, surprised to find them both eating cereal—a far cry from Gabriella's usual culinary magic. "What's all this?"

"Grandma Joyce, we have an adventure planned for today!" Elijah beamed, his eyes sparkling with excitement. "It's called the Kitchen Chef Showdown."

"Yep," Gabriella chimed in, her grin wide. "I'm entering another cooking contest soon, and—"

"Gabriella, that's wonderful!" I interrupted with joy. "You need to get back out there, keep trying. And beat Mrs. Maine. She's your Bobby Flay."

"Okay, okay, Ms. Joyce. I see you tryna stay current with your analogies," she sang. "Brownie points for you!"

"We're making brownies?" Elijah asked eagerly.

"No. It's an expression. She gets points for knowing about Bobby Flay." Gabriella returned her attention to me. "This contest is one where you have to make an impromptu meal. We're heading to the farmers market to pick out some random ingredients, and then we'll have our own little cooking challenge, right here. Like the *Chopped* cooking show. We have to make a meal out of the ingredients, no matter what."

"Oh, wow." I played along, clinging desperately to my earned brownie points. Unlike *Beat Bobby Flay*, I'd never seen *Chopped*, but I got the gist. "Mind if I join you?"

"Yes!" Elijah said, pumping his fist into the air. "Our challenge is going to be amazing."

I made myself a quick bite—toast and eggs—and we were off to the farmers market just outside of town. Leave it to Gabriella to have us hunting for the oddest ingredients in a place that felt like a global marketplace. The clashing smells, the vendors bellowing for us to taste-test their foods, and somebody's goat running around with a broken leash. This was quite the experience already.

Once there, I first partnered with Elijah to gather his secret ingredients. I took in the fragrant aroma of ripe peaches as Elijah, eager to get started, grabbed my hand and led me through the stalls.

"Grandma, look at these huge watermelons!" he exclaimed, pointing at a pyramid of massive green-striped fruits. "They're bigger than my head!"

"That's pretty big," I teased, rubbing the crown of his head with my knuckles.

He jerked away. "Anyway!"

We joked and pointed at various spices and foods. Elijah was torn between jackfruit and fennel. "They both look so weird. Jackfruit is like a green porcupine, and fennel is like a deformed onion."

"Have you tasted them?" I asked.

"No. You?"

"Nope. But I'm sure Gabriella can make something delicious out of one or the other."

He settled on the fennel, which I hid in my basket underneath a sales flyer. Then it was his turn to shop with Gabriella.

"All right, buddy, time to switch partners," Gabriella announced, tapping him on the shoulder. "You help me find something now."

"Okay, Grandma, you're on your own!" Elijah called over his shoulder as he scampered off with Gabriella, leaving me to navigate the remaining stalls solo.

I already knew Elijah was going to divulge the fennel before we even left the market, so my ingredient had to be off-the-charts challenging if I wanted to adequately prepare Gabriella for the contest.

Just as I was pondering my options at an herb stand, I felt a tap on my shoulder. Turning around, I found myself face-to-face with Richard.

"Joyce! Fancy seeing you here," he greeted me warmly. "What brings you to the farmers market?"

"Actually, we're doing this cooking challenge to help Gabriella prepare for her next contest," I explained, my excitement shining through. "Elijah, Gabriella, and I are picking out secret ingredients for each other; with Gabriella's guidance, we're gonna make a meal out of them. It's like that cooking show, *Chopped*. You ever seen it?" I asked like I'd seen many an episode.

"Can't say that I have," Richard said.

I laughed and admitted, "Neither have I."

Richard joined in my chortling. "Sounds like fun, though. Mind if I help you pick out something?"

"Sure, I'd appreciate the input," I replied, grateful for

the company. Optimism chased away a fleeting shadow of apprehension.

We wandered the market together, discussing various possibilities. At one point, Richard picked up a bag of dried chilies, a wicked grin spreading across his face.

"How about these?" he suggested. "They'll definitely add some heat to the challenge."

"Those look perfect," I agreed, but then hesitated. "Although we're working with a limited kitchen setup right now. We don't have an oven."

"No? Is there something wrong with your oven?"

Suddenly, I felt my shoulders tense with his words. He had that move-aside-and-let-me-fix-it tone, one that I recognized well from my ex-husband. Though Richard's question didn't come with the condescending glare that usually accompanied Eric's solutions, it triggered me nonetheless. "Oh, we'll be fine."

"Joyce, are you okay?" Richard said, his brow creasing with concern.

"Really, it's fine," I replied quickly, not wanting to delve into my current living situation. "We make do with what we have."

"All right, if you say so," Richard relented, still looking worried.

I took the chilies from him and dropped them into my basket.

"I can't wait to hear how this meal turns out," he said.

"Thanks, Richard," I responded, feeling grateful for his support. All the while, I scolded myself for how quickly I'd shoved my new friend's concern aside. What if he knew a master oven-installer? A reputable electrician who wasn't flirty or mean? How long would we stay friends if I kept shoving him away?

"Richard," I said, struck by a sudden impulse, "why don't you come over for dinner tonight and taste the results of our challenge?"

He hesitated, looking thoughtful. "I might be able to make it, but I'm not sure. Depends on how the rest of my afternoon goes with my errands."

"All right, no pressure," I replied, trying to sound casual despite the fear rising in my throat. *Have I hurt his feelings?*

We continued walking together toward the checkout line, discussing our respective days. When it was my turn to pay, I made sure to have my mystery item bagged separately in a brown sack to keep it hidden from Gabriella and Elijah until the big reveal later.

"Thanks, Richard," I said. "I hope we can make something interesting with these ingredients."

"You've got quite the challenge. I'll let you know if I'm free."

"Like I said, no pressure either way. Have a good one."

"You, too, Joyce."

That evening, Gabriella, Elijah, and I gathered in the kitchen, revealing our chosen ingredients. The countertop was littered with a seemingly mismatched assortment of items: fennel, dried chilies, peaches, and lamb.

"Wow. This is so all so odd," Elijah declared. "Dried chilies, Grandma? Really?"

"Okay, team," Gabriella announced, rolling up her sleeves. "Let's put our heads together and figure out how we can turn this into a meal. Ideas?"

Elijah and I both shook our heads.

He bowed out. "You're the chef. I'm just the assistant."

"Ms. Joyce?"

"I'm with Elijah."

Gabriella nodded. "Okay, I see how it is. But that's all right. It's giving me good practice for the competition."

She held my chilies to her nose. Her chest expanded as she

smelled my contribution. "These are amazing." She inhaled the peaches next. "Yes, yes, and more yes."

Elijah and I stood still, watching her handle each ingredient, smell it, take it into her whole being. It was magic, really.

"This is gonna be good," she said. If I didn't know any better, I'd think the girl was intoxicated from the smells and textures alone.

"Our appetizer will be fennel salad. Main course, peach honey-grilled lamb chops. I'll throw in some potatoes for good measure."

My mouth was watering already.

"What about the dried chilies?" Elijah asked.

"I'm going to grind them and add them to my own spices for the pork chop...or maybe see if it goes with the fennel. We'll figure it out as we go. You two ready?"

Elijah nodded, I shrugged—what did we have to lose in this experiment?

Gabriella put me to work removing the seeds from the dried chilies first. She took her time showing Elijah how to cut the fennel bulbs, then carefully supervised him with the mandoline and a special glove to protect his hands.

As we cooked, we each offered suggestions. Salt and pepper for the salad, chives and bacon for the potatoes. Gabriella took charge of the main course; she expertly seasoned the lamb chops with the freshly ground chilies, her hands moving with the confidence of a master chef.

The kitchen buzzed with activity, the air filled with the fragrant blend of sweet and spicy. Elijah accidentally dropped a peach slice, and his face fell in disappointment. "Oops! Sorry, I messed up," he mumbled, looking up at Gabriella and me.

Gabriella laughed it off amid the sizzle of the lamb chops.

"Elijah, in cooking, there's always room for a little mistake. It's all about how we recover and keep going," she reassured him, her voice warm and encouraging.

Bolstered by our support, Elijah dove back into his task with renewed vigor, his small hands skillfully maneuvering around the cutting board. As the lamb chops were seared to perfection under Gabriella's watchful eye, I coated the salad, drizzling the lemon-and-olive-oil dressing over the fennel with a flourish.

"Here. Taste." Gabriella offered Elijah and me a spoonful of the braise, and we gave it a total of four thumbs-up.

"This meal deserves my good china," I declared, making a beeline to my closet and fetching a box I hadn't planned to open any time soon. My mother had given us the set when we married, and I used it only twice a year: Thanksgiving and Easter. But in the spirit of seizing the day, and in light of this five-star dish, I figured why not?

I unboxed the dishes to their *ooohs* and *aaahs*.

"It's like we're kings and queens," Elijah marveled.

"We are," Gabriella said. "Kings and queens of this house. And we should enjoy it."

Just as we'd finished preparing the table, the doorbell rang.

"Who could that be?" Gabriella asked, glancing over at me.

"My word. Must be Richard," I muttered, retrieving my phone from my apron pocket. Sure enough, I'd missed a call and two texts from him confirming he was coming. "I invited him over earlier when we ran into each other at the farmers market."

"Richard, huh?" Elijah inquired, his eyes narrowed with suspicion.

"An old friend of mine," I reminded him, trying to keep my tone nonchalant. "He's here to try our Kitchen Chef Showdown masterpiece."

"Really?" Gabriella chimed in, throwing me a mischievous grin over Elijah's head.

"Friend," I repeated as I removed my apron.

I walked over to the door, where Richard stood with a bottle of wine in hand. "I hope it's okay that I came over without a final confirmation," he said hesitantly.

"I'm sorry. Elijah, Gabriella, and I got so busy cooking, I didn't realize my ringer was off. Sure, come on in."

"Whatever you're cooking smells incredible," Richard remarked, handing me the wine. "You three must be quite the team."

"Indeed, we are," I replied. He followed me to the kitchen, where he exchanged pleasantries with Elijah and Gabriella.

I added an extra place setting at the table, anticipation building as we awaited the judgment from our guest. And though I was nervous about sharing our culinary experiment with someone else, I also felt a sense of pride in what we'd accomplished. We had taken a hodgepodge of ingredients and turned them into something wonderful—just like the unlikely friendship that had blossomed between us all.

"This looks amazing. I almost don't want to eat it," Richard said. "But I will."

We all laughed at his joke and absorbed his compliment.

"Wait," Elijah said, holding up a hand. "I want to say grace first." We all bowed our heads as Elijah began. "Dear God, thank you for this food and for bringing us together today. We're grateful that we know how to make something great with whatever we have. Amen."

Hope sang in my heart with Elijah's simple yet profound words. He was right. Life had thrown its share of curveballs my way, but Elijah's simple prayer reminded me that there was still beauty in the mess.

As I took my first bite of the salad we had all created, I let out a sigh of satisfaction. The flavors melded together in a way that surprised and delighted me. I glanced around the table, noting the smiles on everyone's faces as they dug into their plates.

"Joyce," Richard said between bites, "this is incredible. I can't believe you all came up with this using all ingredients from the farmers market."

"Me neither." Gabriella chuckled. "But it was a group effort." She high-fived Elijah.

Elijah nodded enthusiastically, his mouth full of food. "Yeah, Grandma Joyce picked out the chilies."

Richard gave a friendly nod in my direction.

As we sat there, chatting and laughing while the sun dipped below the horizon, I knew that this was a moment I would treasure for years to come. In the company of my new makeshift family. In that moment, it felt like everything would fall into place. Eventually. In the good days ahead. I just wanted them to get here already.

CHAPTER 20

I stood in the Dollar General store, clutching a few home decor items and air fresheners. The place was nothing fancy, but it had a charm that suited my new life on a budget. I picked up a simple picture frame and a pretty tablecloth with a floral design. Maybe it wasn't much, but I hoped these little touches would make the duplex feel like a welcoming, stable home.

Gabriella would like this, I thought as I snapped a photo of the tablecloth with my phone and sent it to her. Her reply pinged with a thumbs-up emoji and a Looks great, Ms. Joyce! message. Our text conversation continued back and forth until she finally wrote, You've got this! Don't be nervous. APS will see u r doing your best.

Her words were a comfort, but my hands still shook like a chihuahua as I approached the cash register. The cashier, a young woman with a friendly smile, noted, "I haven't seen you here before. You new to the area?"

"Sort of," I replied, trying to force a smile, but my nerves were so rattled, it came out more like a grimace. "I spent summers here when I was younger."

"Welcome back, then," she said cheerily. We exchanged a bit

more small talk, but I could hardly focus on her words. This afternoon's visit from Adult Protective Services weighed heavily on my mind.

"Have a nice day," the cashier said as she handed me my receipt. I mumbled a thank-you and hurried out of the store, my heart pounding.

I was hoping for a chance to explain that this was all a huge misunderstanding from the very beginning of the visit. Then, hopefully, I would exchange another pleasant goodbye as the caseworker left with a smile.

Back at home, I plugged in the air fresheners and felt a renewed surge of determination. I went through each room, covering each surface and checking every nook and cranny with disinfectant wipes. The faint scent of lavender filled the air as I moved from room to room, thanks to my new diffusers. I made sure all the light switches worked and that the water ran clear from every faucet.

"Everything is going to be perfect," I murmured to myself, trying to calm my nerves.

In the laundry room, I checked on Celestia again. She was covered with blankets, so as not the raise suspicions about my spending. I was certain splurges weren't allowed, if the APS folks went by the same book as the SLAP group.

The doorbell rang.

I froze, my heart clawing its way out of my chest. Taking a deep breath, I wiped my hands on my apron and answered it.

"Hello, Ms. Hicks," said the woman standing on my porch. She was dressed in a crisp navy suit, white blouse, and black kitten heels. Her stern expression reminded me of a tax auditor—someone who wouldn't hesitate to point out any flaws. "I'm Anya Bryson from Adult Protective Services. You were referred to us by the Senior Living Advocacy Program, and I'm here to ensure your living situation is safe and meets your needs. May I come in?"

My knees went weak with nerves. Anya wasn't the same person I'd talked to a few days earlier when I'd reluctantly agreed to the appointment.

"Of course," I managed to reply, stepping aside to let her in. Her smile walked a fine line between tight-lipped professionalism and warmth, which only served to intimidate me further.

"Would you like some tea, coffee, or water?" I offered, desperate to utter words so I could breathe.

"No, thank you," she declined politely, glancing around the room with an observant eye.

I wished Gabriella had stayed home from work or that I had invited Richard over to charm our visitor. But it was too late for that now.

Everything will be fine, I thought, even though my insides felt as jiggly as Jell-O. I just need to get through this visit.

Anya scribbled notes onto her electronic clipboard. I wondered what she could possibly be writing down so soon. "You've barely been in the house," I joked nervously. "What's there to write?"

Anya looked up at me, her expression unreadable. "I can smell the air fresheners you've used," she said, her voice neutral. "While it's a nice gesture, a strong scent can sometimes cover up potential concerns that may need addressing."

My stomach dropped. I'd only wanted to make my home inviting and pleasant for her visit, and now it seemed like I'd made a mistake. Again. I bit my lip, trying to suppress my regret.

"Let's begin with the interview portion of the visit, Ms. Hicks," Anya continued, shifting her attention to me. "I'll be asking you a series of questions to ensure your well-being. Do you understand?"

Her tone made me bristle, but I swallowed my pride and nodded. "Yes, I do."

"Great."

I gestured for her to sit on my couch and wondered if my cushions were soft enough, firm enough, upholstered well enough. Would they say it presented a knee hazard for being too low, a hip hazard for being too high? My worst-case imagination was in overdrive.

Anya swiped to a new page on her clipboard and readied her stylus.

In this monetary pause, I took the opportunity to interject the speech I'd been practicing nearly all morning while at work. "Miss Bryson—"

"Please, call me Anya."

I swallowed a little relief. "Anya. I'm afraid there's been a misunderstanding. When I went to SLAP, I asked for help with my electrical wiring so I can get an oven installed. I'm perfectly stable, mentally and financially—I only had a hiccup in my plans. Somehow, Jennifer—that was her name—fell under the false impression that I'm struggling, being scammed, and incapable of caring for myself. None of that is true."

Anya nodded and said, "That's good to hear. I understand that there might have been a miscommunication at some level, but, like me, those of us who serve our senior population would rather err on the side of caution than underserve."

My translation, despite her politeness: *Lady, I'm doing my job.*

"I can respect that. I'm just sayin', I hate to see you wasting your time with me."

Anya scrunched up her lips, apparently thinking. Then she said, "Ms. Hicks, I understand that you're single and living alone, correct?"

"I have a tenant," I said. "And I'm making friends at the library."

"Yes. But you don't have family or anyone with a close, non-transactional relationship?"

I didn't answer the question. "I'm not the only one in the world in my predicament. This whole visit is ridiculous. You should be retraining Jennifer, not investigating me."

"I understand how this might feel invasive and unnecessary. Or even humiliating," she stated.

"To say the least," I agreed. It was a small relief to know she wasn't reading a script off a screen.

"Sometimes, when people live alone, they don't recognize the changes that are occurring in them and around them. And loved ones don't pick up on the signs of, say, early dementia. And how would they know if you were having blackouts or placing yourself in harm's way if they're not around? How would anyone know if you're struggling?"

I gave her a perfectly reasonable answer. "You'd know because I am cogent."

Anya smirked. "Your vocabulary certainly suggests that you are not experiencing cognitive decline." She jotted something on her forms.

Yes!

With that, I resolved to let this woman do what my taxes were paying her to do, then let her get along her way, to someone who might actually need her services.

"Let's start with your routine," Anya launched. "Can you describe your daily routine, including how you manage personal care?"

"I get up most mornings around seven. Get myself and my grandson, Elijah, ready to go to the recreation center. He goes to the day camp and I go to my job—"

"Oh, you have a job?" she interrupted me.

"Yes."

"Hmm." She flicked a finger across her screen. "Didn't know that. Are you volunteering, or is it a paid position?"

"Paid. I'm an administrative assistant." I gave her the details of my job description so she'd lose any remaining doubt about my mental faculties.

"Thanks. And what about after work?"

"Let's see… I run errands, watch a little television, maybe take a catnap. Then I pick up my grandson no later than six, and we get ready for dinner. Sometimes I cook, sometimes Gabriella cooks. Well, mostly it's Gabriella. She's an amazing cook."

Anya smiled.

I continued, "We might watch a movie or sit out on the porch while Elijah plays with his friends. And then we settle in for the night. Do it all again the next day."

Anya tilted her head. "When do you take care of your hygiene? Baths and such?"

I didn't realize she'd want to know *all* my personal business. "Oh, at night. I like to take plenty of showers and baths."

"Perfect."

The first question seemed simple enough, but with each one that followed, my anxiety grew. How do you manage your medications? How do you manage your finances? Who would you call if you needed help? Have you experienced any falls or injuries in the home recently?

Every question felt like an accusation, and I fought to keep my composure as she probed into areas of my life I'd rather keep private. I answered, though, and tried to keep that "hostile witness" spirit at bay.

"Tell me about your relationship with Gabriella," she asked, her eyes still on the screen. "She's your tenant, correct?"

"Y-yes," I stammered. "We share the kitchen, but we have separate living quarters. We get along well."

Anya pressed, "Does she contribute positively to your overall well-being?"

"Of course," I answered more firmly this time. "Gabriella is kind and supportive. We're friends, and she's always there for me when I need someone to talk to."

"All right." Anya made a note and glanced up from her notes. "Looks like we're done with the interview portion of this visit. Let's move on to the inspection, shall we?"

"Of course."

We started in Gabriella's side of the house. The living room was immaculate, with her colorful throw pillows neatly arranged on the couch and not a speck of dust in sight. Anya nodded appreciatively as she walked through the space, her digital pen hovering above her tablet but not making a mark.

"Looks like your tenant takes good care of her space," Anya commented.

"Gabriella is very responsible," I agreed, hoping my living quarters would fare just as well.

We moved on to my side. The bedrooms were tidy, with Elijah's things put away and the bed made. But when we got to the bathrooms, Anya's forehead wrinkled as she opened the lower cabinet and noticed some water droplets on the pipes under the sink. "This could lead to mold, which is very dangerous for the respiratory system, especially for seniors," she warned me, jotting down a note.

She checked the windows, toilet, and tub. "It's not major, but you might want to reseal the caulking around the bathtub and sink in the bathroom that wasn't remodeled. That helps prevent mold, too."

My heart sank at the thought of hidden dangers lurking in my home, but I tried to focus on the fact that it was something fixable. I could handle this.

In the laundry room, Anya turned her attention to the hot-water heater. It was rusty and, I noticed for the first time, seemed to lean ever so slightly to one side. "This is a crucial fix, for the sake of your hygiene," she said, adding another note to her growing list. She was using that tablet to take pictures.

"Of course," I murmured, feeling the cumulative drag of all the repairs pulling me down. "I'll make sure to get that taken care of."

"Good," Anya replied, her tone steady as a metronome. Back in the day, Anya could have been a telephone operator with that even tone of hers. Or a poker player, the way she played it calm.

As we wrapped up the inspection, I couldn't shake the feeling that my fresh start in life was turning out to be more complicated than I'd imagined. Yet with each discovered issue, I also felt a growing determination to prove that I could handle it all and live life on my own terms.

"Let's take a look at the kitchen, since this is the area you've expressed concern about."

We moved to the kitchen, where Anya inspected the electrical outlets and appliances. "Ms. Hicks, the wiring in this kitchen is quite outdated," she said, her fake pen poised above her notebook. "If the electricity isn't repaired soon, it's definitely a dangerous situation. Let's make this the priority."

My heart raced as I tried to keep my composure. I wanted to say, "Duh! This is why I reached out in the first place." Frustration bubbled within me, and I found myself desperate for a moment alone. "Excuse me for just a moment," I said, trying to sound casual. "I need to use the bathroom."

"Of course, take your time," Anya replied, continuing her inspection of the kitchen.

As soon as I closed the bathroom door behind me, I leaned against the sink and took a few deep breaths. Gabriella's words echoed in my mind: *We're in this together.* I turned on the faucet, splashed cold water on my face, and faced myself in the mirror. I looked tired, but determined. For the first time, I noticed the faint gurgling noise the water made as it flowed from the tap. It struck me that this sound might hint at a more serious plumbing issue.

Wait—has it always sounded like that? I'm paranoid.

All I wanted was to get Anya out of my house so I could regroup and think straight again. I wiped my face with a towel, took one last deep breath, and returned to the kitchen.

Anya stood at the sink, her eyes fixated on the wine bottle Gabriella and I had opened the other night. "Do you or your tenant frequently drink alcohol?" she asked.

"No," I replied, trying to sound as casual as possible. "Gabriella and I only had a drink the other night at the park. Just a little celebration of our own. That's not illegal, is it?" So much for a neutral consternation.

Anya's eyebrows rose in surprise and concern. "Well, I should let you know that drinking in public parks is, actually, illegal in this county," she said.

My heart dropped as another wave of fear washed over me. Is she also some kind of lawyer? I didn't know that—it was an honest mistake. And today, every little detail was being scrutinized by this woman from Adult Protective Services.

"Thank you for telling me," I managed to say. "It won't happen again."

Anya nodded and closed her notebook. "Ms. Hicks, I'm really just wondering if Gabriella, who is paying so little rent, might be taking advantage of you. And if she's a good influence. Is there anyone else in your family who can help care for you? Your children? A close niece or a nephew?"

Tears threatened to spill over as I shook my head, answering no to all her questions. It felt like salt in the wound, knowing that my family wasn't around to help me through this time.

"All right, Ms. Hicks," Anya said softly, clearly noticing my distress. "I'm going to give you fifteen business days to address the issues we've discussed today."

"Thank you," I whispered, wiping away a tear that had escaped. "I appreciate your understanding."

"Take care, Ms. Hicks," Anya said as she walked toward the door. "And remember that there are resources available to support you in this process."

Resources, my foot. I didn't want anything from the state or any of its nonprofit friends if it would only add to my stress.

"I'll contact you to set up a time for a second inspection and to follow up on any concerns related to emotional and social support," Anya informed me.

"Thank you, Anya. I'll do my best," I replied, trying to sound confident despite the fear gnawing at my insides. I walked her to the front door, feeling incredibly vulnerable as I watched her walk away.

"Lord, help me," I whispered as I closed the door behind her. It was then that I noticed Miss Mary approaching with mail in hand, her eyes following Anya's retreating figure.

"Joyce, honey, I know that woman and that car," Miss Mary said, shaking her head as she handed me the mail. "What did she say to you?"

I couldn't hold back any longer. My tears flowed freely as I told Miss Mary about Anya's visit, the problems with the house, and the fifteen-day deadline. As I spoke, it felt like I was releasing a pressure valve inside me, allowing all the pent-up emotions to escape.

"I'm sorry for blubbering all over you like that," I said, wiping my eyes again. "I just feel so overwhelmed trying to get this house fixed up while still getting my feet under me in this town."

"Oh, hush, you just let it all out," Miss Mary tutted, patting my shoulder. "A good cry cleanses the soul. And Lord knows you've had a time of it."

Miss Mary looked thoughtful for a moment, her gaze drifting off into the distance. "You know, I've known that child's people for a long time," she began, her voice gentle and reassuring. "Her grandparents died when a rotting tree fell on their house, and ever since then, she's been a stickler for dotting all the i's and crossing all the t's in the name of protecting people."

I blinked, surprised by this revelation. It suddenly made sense why Anya was so thorough, her demeanor bordering on severity.

"Anya means well, Joyce," Miss Mary continued, meeting my eyes. "And she won't budge on her convictions. So you'd best follow her rules. And get you some more players in the game."

"Players?" I asked, my brow furrowing in confusion. "What do you mean?"

"More people to help you, honey," she clarified, her eyes twinkling with determination. "You can't do the stuff you just told me about all on your own. You need support from friends, neighbors, in addition to professionals to fix every problem in this here house."

I sighed, feeling both grateful for Miss Mary's advice and overwhelmed by the thought of finding help. "I don't even know where to start," I admitted, my hands wringing together anxiously.

"Start by asking around," Miss Mary suggested, her voice warm and encouraging. "Talk to people at church, at the grocery store, or even down at the community center. There are plenty of folks in this town who would be willing to lend a hand if they knew you needed it."

"But would they really?" I asked, doubt creeping into my voice. "I'm not exactly...well known around here."

"Joyce, that doesn't matter," Miss Mary insisted, placing a comforting hand on my arm. "What matters is that you're in need, and people will step up when it counts if you ask."

Her words resonated deep within me. I knew she was right. I had to put aside my pride and ask for help if I wanted to keep my home and prove myself as an independent woman.

"All right," I agreed, nodding determinedly. "I'll start asking the few people I do know. And thank you, Miss Mary, for the advice."

"Child, independence is overrated. We all need each other sometimes," she replied with a knowing smile. "Now, you'd best get moving. Three weeks will be here before you know it, and you've got plenty of work to do."

CHAPTER 21

It was past time for me do the math and make some hard decisions. My prized nest egg was getting all scrambled up, and I only had thirteen more business days to get myself together before Anya Day. Thirteen days to prove myself safe and sane, to get the stamp that would allow me to stay in my home, without state supervision.

I'd wasted time moping and feeling sorry for myself. I justified that "waste" with the fact that Anya couldn't count July 4 as a business day.

Take that, APS.

Somewhere in there, Eric Jr. called to ask how things were going for me in Robin Creek. I told him everything, which felt surprisingly good. But he's no Dr. Phil. "Don't worry, Momma. If you have to move in with me, I gotcha."

No big speech, just a simple last-resort solution. "Thanks, son."

I had no intention of moving overseas, however. I needed to exhaust all domestic options first.

My first move, which broke my heart, was to exchange Celestia for a much less expensive model. About half the cost of Celestia, to be exact. Gabriella and Elijah understood that sacrifices had to be made because the cost of having a certified electrician with experience in older homes to travel from Lubbock to Robin Creek and rewire the north side of the house was gonna be twice the cost of Celestia. I knew this already from my conversation with the remodeling company. If I hadn't been a little miffed at them for turning me on to SLAP, I might have asked them for a referral.

Nonetheless, during my Monday-morning work break, I made the call, pushed the numbers to get past the automatic answering system, and talked to a representative at the investment company so I could withdraw funds. I had to audibly reply "Yes" to the notification that this would lower my payments when time came for me to get monthly disbursements. *Didn't need that reminder.*

They asked if I was withdrawing funds to pay medical debts or taxes. "No."

Why all these questions to withdraw my own money?

The transaction was finalized at the end of day, East Coast time, with the close of the stock market. They cut a check the next day and overnighted it to me. I had the money for the repairs in hand by the time I got off work Wednesday.

Standing in my bedroom and holding that five-figure check, I had to be grateful. I whispered my thanks to God because, despite all the hassle and the fact that this withdrawal would probably haunt me until the day I died, I didn't know what I would have done without the money I'd saved outside of my state pension.

I thought about my coworkers MaryAlice and Faye, who were single mothers barely making it on their teachers' salary. At one point, MaryAlice qualified for food stamps, and Faye had moved back home with her mother at the ripe age of forty-five to make sure her son could finish college. They had nothing else except their state pension, which was why they hadn't retired yet even though they were both older than I was. Almost all our friends who'd retired before me complained about how the state teacher-pension plan only increased once every twenty years or so, unlike Social Security, which had a cost-of-living increase. At 3 percent inflation annually, all it takes is about three years until you're making 10 percent less than your original retirement check—which is only about 70 percent of your last employment check.

"Retirement is a blessing for sure," MaryAlice had said as they helped me box dry erase boards and markers. "I'm going to try for a promotion to instructional coach soon, get my salary average up higher."

"Sometimes we have to play the game," Faye added.

I'd never struggled to make ends meet or pay unexpected bills when I was with Eric. The last time I'd suffered through money problems was in college, when I lived off excess student loan disbursements. I made great friends with the girl who landed the mailroom work-study job. She'd call my dorm hall when she saw a check come for me, and I'd throw on a jogging suit and race to the administration offices, waiting outside the window until she opened that wooden door for me and all the other desperate souls awaiting money from loans, friends, and family.

Of course, I had to pay all that loan money back later, plus interest. But it had been worth it, allowing me to eat a steady diet of ramen noodles in college, and later giving me a career I enjoyed. I tried to frame this significant withdrawal from my retirement fund in the same light: I'd keep my grandmother's house, eat Gabriella's good cooking—hot oven broiler and all—and enjoy the rest of my years in peace, knowing my home was safe and sturdy.

The Chapter Chatters met that evening, a fact that made my heart feel nice and toasty. Miss Mary's words still resonated through me as I found a parking spot in the library's lot. This town, the people of Robin Creek, had been nothing but good to me. Except Wardell and Lorenzo, but there were always a few bad actors. Gabriella, Richard, and the women in this group had welcomed me sweetly. Hadn't required anything of me except to show up and be myself, and for that, I appreciated them.

Elijah happily skipped off to his LEGO group, and I entered the main portion of the library looking for Eileen. We usually got a chance to speak before she started the group, but she was nowhere in sight. I entered our usual meeting spot ready to share the proposed dates for our cooking party that I'd told Gabriella about. But immediately, I sensed tension in the room. Partying was the last thing on their minds. The chairs were arranged in their usual circle, but the empty one in the center seemed to loom larger than the rest.

"Eileen's in the hospital," Sonia informed me.

The words landed with a force I wasn't prepared for, like a punch in the gut.

"She had a ministroke," Valeria added, shaking her head. "They say she'll recover, but she needs to take it easy."

"Then why are we here instead of the hospital?" I asked.

"I'm thinking the same thing," Christine said. "But her family's asked for privacy."

"And by 'family,' we mean the son who's never around," Althea added. "The irony."

I stared at Eileen's empty seat, processing the news.

"We've all been praying for her since it happened," Sonia said.

"And I lit a candle for her when I got the news," Lupita added.

That was my first inclination that there was some sort of back-channel communication between them. "When did it happen?"

"Yesterday morning," from Christine. "My sister works at the hospital. She let me know, and I shared it with the group."

Trying to hide my offense, I said flatly, "Well, I didn't get a message."

"I'm sorry," Christine apologized. "When we first met, you said you were only coming because you took your grandson to the LEGO club."

"And Eileen said you were just getting situated in town. We didn't want to bother you," Althea concluded.

My mouth dropped as I eyed each one of their faces. They stared back at me as though their collective excuse was valid. Wait… Was this the impression I had given them? That I didn't want to be bothered? That I wouldn't want to know if our leader had had a stroke?

"I don't know what kind of monster you all think I am, but I do want to when know somebody in this group goes down," I managed to say with a chuckle.

"Girl, stop being so dramatic," Althea said. "You're new. We don't know you like that yet."

I took my stance. "Well, I'm here to stay. You all and my housemate are the closest people I have to family living in this town. I'm all in."

"Great." Christine smiled at me. She lifted a card from her purse. "Sign it."

Writing my name on that card next to well wishes from the others felt like signing my name to the sisterhood roll. *You are sorely missed, Eileen. Praying for your swift healing and return! With Love, Joyce.*

"I propose we do something different tonight," Lupita said. "Journaling."

Half the room snarled, the other half cooed. I was a snarler. Writing just wasn't my thing. Ever since my first-grade teacher, Mrs. Batton, had rapped a ruler on my knuckles for incorrect pencil grip, I've had a thing about printing words on paper. Word processors and, later, computers saved me from reliving that traumatic memory.

Lupita ripped lined paper from a spiral notebook she had waiting in the wings. "Everybody take a few sheets. Get one of these books off the shelf so you'll have something to write on. I have a few prompts we could use. Does anyone need a pen?"

"This ain't school," Valerie fussed.

Thank God I'm not the only one.

"It's free therapy," Christine countered. "We're all feeling down because of Eileen. If we write a little bit, then share either what we wrote or how it felt to write, we'll leave a little lighter."

Sonia shrugged. "It's worth a try." With that, she tilted the scale in favor of journaling.

"Okay, ummm… Let me open my app." Lupita hummed out loud.

All of a sudden, I felt Mrs. Batton looking over my shoulder, warning me that I'd better not "scribble scrabble" all over this beautiful white paper.

I'm sixty, not six years old. I'm not Li'l Joy. I'm Big Joy. Biiiiiig Joy. Joyce. Hicks.

Lupita directed, "First, let's take a minute to close our eyes and breathe slowly, in and out. Get the oxygen flowing through the system, get centered. A minute starts now."

Those sixty seconds felt as good as a steaming-hot bubble bath. My joints tingled with a warmth I couldn't put words to.

"Now, for the next ten minutes, let's either freewrite or write about what it means to enjoy life in this season."

Lupita freed me from Mrs. Batton with the word *freewrite*. Even scribble scrabble must be acceptable with a freewrite. So that's exactly what I did first. I drew a gaggle of eights for the heck of it. Smiled at them and myself.

You see those, Mrs. Batton?

Then I remembered that Mrs. Batton had gray hairs on her head over fifty years ago; she was probably long gone.

Rest her soul.

And then I wrote.

> *Sorry for thinking ill of the dead.*
>
> *I don't like writing because of her. This isn't going well.*
>
> *A lot of people have ruined things for me. Not Eileen, though. She's nice and I hope she gets well because she deserves it. She deserves life. Is that a thing? Does anyone deserve life? Probably not. It's a gift. Something that lands in your lap and you either open it and use it—whatever it looks like, whatever size, however many days you get—or you let it sit in that box.*
>
> *Who is you? You is me. This is my life. My gift. I want to use it. Put it on and wear it, smell it, flaunt it, bling it out!!!*
>
> *Other times I just want to sit with it. Cherish it. Adore it, all by myself. And be thankful for it.*
>
> *I hope Eileen gets better.*
>
> *I hope this business with the house repairs doesn't take away my joy.*
>
> *Too passive.*

I won't let it take my joy. This is pipes and wires and man-made materials and money that was never intended to last forever. If I let this stuff steal my joy, everything else is up for grabs.

No. I'm gonna be glad to have my home, my new friends, my family. My grandson. They are all a gift, too. Even if I have to move to Dubai with Eric Jr. It's not the worst thing that could happen.

Beep-beep-beep. Lupita's alarm signaled the end of ten minutes.

Valerie whined, "Awwww."

"Really?" Althea quipped, and we all laughed.

"That was definitely free therapy." Valerie sighed. She stretched her neck on both sides and let out a belch. "Sorry. It's cleansing."

"All righty, then," Sonia exclaimed. "You got pretty comfortable there."

"That was nice, Lupita. Thanks for the suggestion," I had to agree.

We took turns talking about our experience. Everyone said we needed to do more journaling, more deep thinking, more relaxing.

"I can't wait for Eileen to get back. She's gonna love it," Christine said with a hopeful grin.

Instead of rushing out to get Elijah, I kept one eye on the library lobby as I hung around with the ladies a few minutes after our official dismissal time. The air felt lighter now, as if the weight we'd all carried in earlier had somehow been lifted.

This is what friends do, I told myself. *They hang out.* "Fellowship" is what my mother would have called it.

And it felt good.

My celebrations continued the next day. "This a win-win," I kept telling myself as I traveled on to the bank to make the deposit. There was no early-withdrawal penalty, since I was over fifty-nine. For once, my age worked *for* me instead of against me. "Besides, it's just money. And if the problem can be solved with money, then it's not a real problem."

Eric used to say that all the time. I used to believe him, because that was the two-income lifestyle we lived when we were together. But things were different now. I had always imagined myself retiring someday, with all my income sourced from something I'd done when I was younger. Be it Social Security, investments, pension, selling a house, my husband's retirement, or even kids taking care of me.

What I hadn't imagined was the idea of legal intervention, of someone declaring me incapable of caring for myself, making decisions for me based on rigid government guidelines, forcing me to withdraw large lump sums of money, telling me who could stay with me and how many days I had to prove myself competent or find myself without a home.

"Depositing only?" the teller asked. Due to the check amount and possibly the fact that my account was newer, I had to deposit in person.

"Yes, thank you."

"Great." She did her business and handed me the receipt for our transaction, which I examined and then tucked safely into my wallet. My nest egg was smaller, but my immediate problems were solved.

Or so I thought, until I returned home from the bank to find my ex-husband's Audi parked in my driveway.

CHAPTER 22

Elijah scooted forward in his seat, straining against his seat belt, and clutched the dashboard. "Is that Grandpa's car?"

Eric's ebony-brown arm was draped along the driver's-side doorframe. You live with a man for thirty years, you know the curve of his arm, the way it rests like it owns the space around it. A part of me wanted to think it wasn't him, that I was imagining things. I checked the license plate to confirm what my own eyes had seen. "Sure is him."

My stomach clenched as my mind spiraled, conjuring possibilities faster than I could shut them down. My first thought was that my ex-husband must be dying. Or at least sick. And he had come to either make peace with me or beg me to take care of him. The next thing I considered was whether or not we should be buried together. *Why didn't I think of this before?* And my children—bless their hearts—losing their father at such an early age. Eric Jr. would surely fly home soon.

My throat felt lumpy, full of rocks. *Calm down. Talk to him first.*

"Why is he here?" Elijah had his own worries, his voice tinged with an unmistakable nervousness. It wasn't just curiosity; there was a quiver beneath his words.

"Let's find out."

Eric watched Elijah and me through his side-view mirrors as we exited my car. Is he in pain? All the instincts I'd mastered throughout our marriage reignited. Instinctively, I wanted to take care of him. I guess that's what happens when you're programmed to take care of others.

The sweat on Eric's forehead said he'd been waiting outside for a while, though being hot never bothered him. We argued constantly over thermostat settings.

I stopped at his open window. "Hello."

"Hello." He barely looked at me. His jaw was tight. Angry.

My sickness theory dissipated. "What are you—"

"Hey, Grandpa!"

"Hey, EJ! Good to see you. Missed ya, buddy."

Elijah smiled sheepishly. "I've just been...you know...taking care of Grandma. You came to visit us?"

"Need to talk to your grandmother for a minute." He moved to unfurl himself from his vehicle, so I took a step back and gave him space. I had not seen my ex-husband since the previous Thanksgiving holiday, when we briefly crossed paths at Terri's house. I ate with her, my son-in-law's family, and Elijah first, at 12:00 p.m., mainly because she needed help with the final touches.

Eric Sr. came over at 3:30. He wasn't due to arrive until 4:30, but he'd said he'd wanted to be situated for the NFL pregame show.

Terri was both embarrassed and infuriated that her father and I were taking different "shifts," as she called them. I was staying in my coworker's guesthouse at the time. "Can't you both act civilized so I don't have to stagger serving people on Thanksgiving Day?"

"He's the one who didn't want to eat with the rest of us," I reminded her.

Seeing Eric at my grandmother's home felt like an invasion. How dare he show up in my Robin Creek world without a life-threatening disease? "Is everything okay?"

Eric stood erect now and shoved his hands into his jeans pockets. "You tell me, Joyce. How are you?" I detected a hint of sincerity in his voice, like he thought maybe I was the one sick.

"I'm fine."

"Can we go inside?"

"What's this about, Eric?"

"Inside. Please. I've been baking in this sun."

It wasn't like him to use the word *please*, at least not with me. Despite my apprehension, I let him inside the house and escorted him to the kitchen, where he accepted my offer for a glass of sweet tea.

Eric moved slowly, deliberately, as if every step was calculated to maintain control. He settled into one of the kitchen chairs with an air of practiced ease, but there was something about the way he did it—how he pulled the chair out with a grating scrape against the floor, the way he sat down heavily, leaning back and rolling his shoulders—that set my nerves on edge. He drummed his fingers on the table. His eyes didn't quite meet mine, instead roving around the room with a barely concealed criticism, as if he were inspecting the life I'd built without him.

"Looks nice," he finally complimented. "But where's the oven?"

"It broke. I'm gonna replace it. Next week," I quickly declared, not wanting to give him an inkling of wonder about how I was doing without him. His opinion of me shouldn't have mattered. I knew this. Yet somehow it did.

"Oh. Good," he said.

I leaned my bottom against the main counter and planted my

hands beside me, making my elbows look like cricket legs. Eric made me uneasy, to say the least. I wasn't afraid of him, not in the same way you'd want to keep your distance from a venomous snake. More like not wanting to get near a cat you don't know. It won't kill you, but it sure can scratch.

Elijah entered the kitchen, cautiously. "Can I…get a snack?"

"Yes," I answered at the same time Eric said, "No."

"Okaaay," Elijah slurred, wondering which one of us to obey.

Eric, who had no idea of Elijah's daily schedule, answered, "We'll let you know when it's time for a snack."

Elijah turned and walked back down my hallway.

I crossed my arms. "I know you didn't drive all this way for tea."

"No. I didn't. Can we talk?" My ex gestured toward a seat at the table.

There, in the slight downturn of his eyes, sat an ounce of regret that calmed me enough to join him.

He took another sip of tea, then started. "I'm here because Terri asked me to come."

"Terri called you?"

"Apparently, someone called her. Some kind of senior citizens' care organization called her, asking questions."

"What?" A bolt of indignation shot through me. "What questions?"

"Questions about your welfare. They wanted to make sure you were…well."

"And they sent you, my ex-husband, to check on my welfare?"

"*Terri* sent me."

Weren't there laws against this? Yes, I had listed my daughter as my next of kin—but this? Didn't I have rights when it came to unproven allegations regarding my health? Who would I sue first for this humiliation?

"I'm perfectly fine," I told him. "Sorry you wasted a trip."

He raised an eyebrow. There was more he needed to say.

I waited, clenching my teeth.

"Terri asked me to bring Elijah home with me."

I felt a sharp, nauseating twist deep in my gut, as if someone had just punched me there. I swallowed. "Eric, there is no reason for Elijah to leave. He's just fine here."

He glanced at the empty space where my oven used to be. "He might be too much for you to handle. And is he safe here?"

"Of course he's safe," I spat back. "The person who called Terri was overreacting to my request for help with replacing the oven."

"I thought you were getting it fixed next week?"

"I am."

"Then why did the repairman call the authorities on you?"

I cringed. "No one has called the authorities on me. I went voluntarily, upon the repairman's recommendation, asking for help. It's a long story, and I don't have to answer your questions. Elijah is not in danger. I am fine. You can go home now."

"Terri's wishes. Not mine," he repeated as he pressed buttons on his screen, then held his phone to his ear. "I'm calling her now."

My skin prickled with irritation. I wanted him to leave. Get off my property.

He managed to keep the smirk off his face, but his body language said, *Maybe you really are cracking up, woman.*

This was how he operated. Passive-aggressive. Makes you doubt yourself enough to give him the benefit of the doubt. How did he manage to bundle all those moves at once? I felt myself slipping back into his spell while we waited for our daughter to answer the phone.

She didn't, which kind of surprised me because I thought for sure she'd answer her daddy quicker than me. Either she was extremely caught up in work, or she had grown tired of her father's endless demands without any effort to return the favor.

"I'll have her send you a text," Eric said. He took the final gulp of his tea and stood. "I need to get back on the road. Can you help Elijah pack his bags?"

"You help him," I said. "I'm not your personal servant."

That was when the smirk he'd been trying to hide peeked out. "How long you been waitin' to say that, Joyce?"

Well, I had a smirk of my own to share. "Since our wedding day," I stated coolly.

The corners of his lips dropped, and his silly grin fell with it. "You're acting like we had a terrible marriage. A terrible family. You know I love you. You never wanted for anything, Joyce. And I was faithful to you. That alone is better than 90 percent of what you would have got from anybody else."

I opened my lips to continue, but then I shut them. First, because we had different definitions of love. Second, because this was all déjà vu. *He still doesn't get it. He may not ever get it.*

Back to the real subject. "You don't have to take Elijah, Eric. I will get in touch with Terri later today and let her know that I made an executive decision to keep him."

"There you go again, unilaterally making decisions that impact everybody else. I'm not driving back out here again to get him. He's coming with me. Now. Per his mother's orders."

Eric was one volume notch away from yelling. I grew up with my father yelling a lot. He wasn't angry; he was just loud. Loudness always made me shrink, and Eric knew exactly how to approach close enough to the line that it was debatable as to whether or not he'd raised his voice.

"Paw-Paw, stop." Elijah had entered the kitchen again. "Fine. I'll go with you. Just don't yell at Grandma."

While it was nice to know I wasn't the only one who'd classify Eric's tone as "yelling," my chest caved at the sight of Elijah's tear-filled eyes. His attempt to protect me nearly crushed me. Children shouldn't be caught up in the middle of grown-up issues.

"Pack your bags. Let's go," Eric ordered our grandson.

"Yes, sir." Elijah obeyed.

I wanted to shout, to grab my grandson and tell him he didn't have to go, he didn't have to bow to Eric's commanding voice. But my words got stuck somewhere between my mind and my throat, tangled up with old fears and fresh anger. Every part of my body crossed. My ankles, my arms, my stomach, inside. This was one of the main reasons we'd divorced; it was Eric's way or no way at all. Well, it was kind of Terri's way, too, according to Eric. Facts aside, it was the way my ex-husband showed up in times like these that reinforced my determination to stay single and solvent. I would never again second-guess myself for leaving him.

I excused myself to the hallway bathroom and tried calling my daughter again. Voicemail. I texted her a piece of my mind: Why did you send your father here for Elijah? You don't think I can watch my own grandson? Why didn't you call me first?

No answer.

A flash of my reflection in the mirror caught me. This woman staring back at me was frazzled. Annoyed. The extra creases on my forehead and the way my ample lips managed to press into a tight line—all of it pointed to a lack of peace. What was the point of moving to Robin Creek if all this stress followed me?

Thoughts of the ladies in the journaling group came to me suddenly. The last time I'd felt truly peaceful was when we were together. Writing. Talking. They'd welcomed me into their sisterhood. I sure could use a sister right now.

If Gabriella had been in the kitchen, she would have said something to Eric, no doubt. Then again, Eric reserved his snarkiest self for me and me alone. He would have presented his charming nature for a stranger.

I jumped at the knock on the door. "Grandma, I need to get my toothbrush."

I took a few deep breaths to calm myself. Closed my eyes. I had to be strong for Elijah. With a tiny smile on my face, I opened the door and let him inside. "Don't forget your deodorant, too. Can't have you smelling like onions when you go back to Austin."

He pushed past me. No laughter. Not even the slightest grin. He was angry, by the tightness around his lips. God knows his expression looked exactly like the one his mother wore throughout most of her teenage years, pulsing temple and all.

"Summer will be over before you know it," I whispered to him.

A tear rolled down his cheek as he slammed the drawer door shut and threw his toothpaste into his backpack. "It's not fair."

"What's not fair?"

"That nobody else—not you or my dad or my mom—wants to spend time with Paw-Paw, but I'm the one who has to go stay with him."

His tone and his words were borderline disrespectful, something I don't allow from children to grown-ups. My momma would have popped me in my mouth for saying something like that about an elder. Even if it was 100 percent true, as I suspected in this case. It sounded like Elijah was speaking words he'd overheard from his parents. I'd always suspected my son-in-law wasn't too keen on Eric. And now that Terri had all but admitted her father was getting on her nerves, I could see Elijah's point. Why should he have to put up with a cantankerous old man who had so little patience for children?

"Let's go, EJ!" Eric called.

A whimper escaped from my grandson's throat. I hugged him tight. If Eric could have seen us, he would have said I was "babying" the boy. Making him too touchy-feely. Often, Eric had said he was hard on the kids because I was too soft on them. "Gotta balance it out," he'd said. Like it was some kind of mathematical equation.

All I knew was that Elijah's face wasn't so stressed after we finished hugging. "EJ, you're a wonderful young man. You are kind, you are helpful—Gabriella can tell you that! And you know how to get along with people. I saw that with the way you made friends with the LEGO group. Your grandfather is a person, too. And he does care about you…in his own way. I need you to remember that. Okay?"

He nodded dutifully.

"And as soon as you get another break in school, I'm gonna see about coming to get you," I promised him.

He brightened a bit. "When's the first holiday?"

"Labor Day? Columbus Day?" I guessed. "Definitely the week of Thanksgiving."

He sniffed and dried his face. "Okay. I love you, Grandma."

"Love you, too, EJ."

The walk down our short hallway to the kitchen felt like that movie *The Green Mile*. Okay, I'm being dramatic. But anybody who's ever dropped their child off with a reluctant babysitter knows, it feels kinda wrong the whole way there. I know from my years as a public-school teacher that kids sense when a person doesn't want to be bothered with them, no matter if they're being paid to do it or not. Sad when it's someone in the family bringing all that sadness to a child.

Eric wasted no time with goodbyes. He put a firm hand on Elijah's shoulder and guided him out of the house and to the car.

"Thanks for the tea," Eric said.

Should have poisoned it. "Mm-hmm."

I wondered, in that split second, if Eric had removed me as the beneficiary on his life insurance policies. All of them, which I'd managed while we were married. Funny what you think about after the man you once loved turns into a crotchety old grouch.

Just as we were walking down the steps of the front porch, Gabriella pulled up next to my car. Elijah tore away from Eric and ran to hug her as she got out of the driver's side.

"What's going on?" she asked him, returning the hug.

"I'm leaving," he muttered into her hair.

"Wait—what?" she asked.

It was then that I saw the red around her eyes, the slight swell of her nose and cheeks. She'd been crying even before Elijah clobbered her.

"I'm going with my Paw-Paw."

Gabriella protested, looking at me first, Eric second. "Why?"

Eric didn't bother to answer her. "Come on, Elijah. We've got a long trip ahead."

Elijah peeled away from Gabriella and trudged to the passenger's side of Eric's car.

The question marks crossing Gabriella's face landed squarely on my shoulders. She approached me, shaking her head.

"We can talk about it later," I whispered. My composure was just a millimeter from slipping completely, so I didn't even look at Elijah when I said goodbye. I trained my eyes on Eric because the anger was easier to manage than the pain from how he'd so callously ripped Elijah from my home.

Gabriella stood next to me, draping one arm across my shoulder for support. Together, we stood as a united front, waving at the car while Elijah's little hand slowly waved back.

As soon as the car was out of sight, tears sprang from Gabriella's eyes as she squealed, "Just when I thought this day couldn't get any worse."

CHAPTER 23

Gabriella and I got real tipsy together that night. Slurred speech and all. Empty wineglasses and an open bottle sat between us, the cork rolled somewhere out of reach. Between sobs for Elijah, I told Gabriella all about what happened with Eric. "He's got some nerve, driving all the way here without so much as calling me first. Who does that?"

"Someone who thinks you're just going to open the door and let him in," Gabriella said.

"Hmmm," I thought out loud. "Well. I did let him in."

She nodded and swallowed hard. "Of course you did. You're not rude like him. He knows you're always going to show up in kindness and love. That's who you are, Joyce. Don't let him make you something else."

"Rrrrright," I agreed.

"But me? I wouldn't have let him in," she said. "He's lucky I wasn't here. We could have had one of those—what do you call them?—standoffs. We could have held Elijah hostage!"

"Sounds violent."

She shrugged. "Don't start none, won't be none."

We both decided Eric was quite a piece of work, to put it mildly. Then Gabriella told me what was on her mind. Turns out, she and Lorenzo broke up. To which I replied, "Good riddance!" because my filter was off.

My ex-husband had basically kidnapped my grandson at my daughter's command, I was dipping into my nest egg early, and Celestia was gone. What did I have to lose by holding my tongue?

"I know, I know," Gabriella agreed. "I just don't want to be lonely. You know?"

I did know. When I was a young woman, being lonely—read, not tied to a man—was almost a sin. Some women enrolled in college just to find an upwardly bound man, not to actually get a degree. A woman unbound to a man was problematic. Even though laws had changed, depending on where you lived you could still run into trouble renting an apartment on your own, financing a car, or getting certain jobs. Employers couldn't discriminate blatantly anymore, but they still worried that a single woman would mean scandal in the office. And it went without saying that a woman would be paid less than a man to perform the exact same job.

That's how the system worked. A woman without a man faced an uphill battle. Being lonely was only one of her worries.

Gabriella was too young to remember days like that. I didn't want to invalidate her thoughts by reminiscing on the days before she was born, so I said, "You learn a lot about yourself and about life when you're lonely."

"I know mysssselffff," Gabriella insisted. "Gabriella Santos! And I'm a boss in the kitchen!"

"That, you are!"

The chirping insects agreed loudly as she poured us both another glass of wine. She'd added a small table and two lawn chairs on her side of the back porch, giving us our own private outdoor living space. We'd doused ourselves heavily with anti-mosquito spray, so we could stay out all night if we'd wanted to.

"And I'm Joyce Hicks. Retired teacher. I taught hundreds—thousands—of kids to read! And I left my non-loving husband, and now I just love on myself. And I'm gonna fix up this house before that APS woman comes back, if it's the last thing I do!"

"I wish I could help," Gabriella said. Then, without warning, she burst into tears, the kind of deep, guttural sobbing that shakes the whole body. Her shoulders heaved violently, as though the weight of the world had just been dropped on her.

My heart clenched in empathy. "Oh no. No, no, no, no. You're going to be all right, Gabriella," I comforted her, though my own voice was shaking at that point. It hit me then that this child had carved a deep place in my heart already. She loved hard. Cared for people with a fierce loyalty that was rare and beautiful. This was one of the reasons Elijah was so drawn to her.

The last time I'd been this close to a slobbering young lady was when Mrs. Rivers, one of the kindergarten teachers, had found out she was pregnant with her third child while her second child was only four months old and her first one was barely potty-trained. Now, why she decided to take a pregnancy test during her teacher-conference period, I'll never understand. But there she was, coming out of the restroom in the teachers' lounge looking like God had just texted her and told her she wasn't gonna make it in.

"I can't do this!" she wailed and fell onto me, much the same as Gabriella now. By the time we'd finished our talk, I'd convinced Mrs. Rivers that her children would be close—best friends. And they'd have one another for all their lives, practically. I figured this because families used to have stair-step kids all the time back in the day; it was expected. Encouraged. What started off as hectic could later yield a beautiful harvest.

So I amplified my empathetic skills. "Gabriella, sweetheart, I know it might not seem like it now, but you've got your whole life ahead of you. There will be lot more opportunities to fall in love."

"No, it's not just that. When we broke up today, Lorenzo fired me. That's why I'm home so early."

"He fired you?" I screeched.

"Mm-hmm. And now Lisa, who's, like, the last family member I really talk to, is mad at me, since she's married to Lorenzo's cousin. It's wild. Mmm, mmm, mmm."

Her mumble traveled through me. Made me want to fight somebody, like a mother would for her child. "We're gonna make it through this, Gabriella. Together."

"Yes, ma'am," she cried. "Can we get Elijah back?"

I sighed. Now it was my turn to cry. "I've been thinking about it. We probably could, if Terri ever calls me back. But maybe that wouldn't be the best move." I blinked the tears away. "We've got lots to do around here in very little time. Having him underfoot could slow us down," I admitted to myself as much as her. "I'm gonna...start asking around for help. With friends—no more eager senior-support organizations. They all need numbers, you know?"

Gabriella sat up again. "Maybe they really do think you're in danger. You can't get mad at an underpaid government worker for actually doing their job, you know. We should be grateful, probably."

I squinted at her. "Whose side are you on?"

"Yours! I'm just saying. Let's get this house together, get those people out of your hair, get me a job, get Elijah back at least for a little while, and move on." She'd solved all our problems with one run-on sentence.

"Sounds like a plan."

She added, "We're gonna need help. You got friends?"

I fired back, "You got friends?"

"All my friends are Lorenzo's friends. They're not gonna betray him by helping me. What about your new friends? The library ladies?"

"We need people with strong backs and knees," I told her. "All the money's going into the stove. Professionals will handle that. But the other stuff will take some good old elbow grease. Young folk would be best."

She knocked her elbow against mine. "If they're like you, they got this! And what about Richard? He likes you. He'll help."

I rolled my eyes. "I'm not trying to use the man."

"Just tell him what's up. Be like, 'Bro, I'm in a bind with the gub'ment. I need your help. You in?'"

The way she imitated my voice sent me into a fit of giggles. She followed with laughter of her own.

"So just ask him?"

"Yes," she repeated. "And the ladies at the library, too. I will cook a big meal for everyone when we finish, whatever you all want."

She should have known by now that I can't turn down her cooking. I needed the promise of it, actually, to move past my heartbreak over Elijah's untimely removal.

Somebody added me to the group text—probably Christine, since her husband had my number—to let me know that that we were all meeting up at Eileen's tomorrow instead of the library. She was at home recovering now, and her sister had given us permission to drop by to bring and share dinner with her for only an hour or so; she didn't want to wear Eileen out with too much company.

It was the perfect opportunity to ask for the group's help over one of Gabriella's delicious side dishes. Good food never hurts.

Between morning and evening job interviews, Gabriella prepared something I had never even thought to put together: sweet potato and black bean taquitos. "I've heard of it, but never tried it or put my own flavors to it."

She let me taste one as soon as they cooled off. "Oh my word!" I said with a mouth full of her delicious creation.

She giggled and said, "I put a hint of cinnamon in them for sweetness."

Whether she'd put cinnamon, nutmeg, lemon pepper, I neither knew nor cared. I finished chewing. "I don't know how on earth you come up with these recipes, but they are everything."

"Actually, I got the idea from the Green Book. It said potatoes or beans. I figured, why not use them both? With my Blaxican twist, of course." She snapped the lid onto my glass container full of taquitos. "Keep them covered until you get there."

"Can't guarantee I won't eat a few on the way."

"Patience, patience, Ms. Joyce."

"It's not only because these taquitos are irresistible. I'm really not a 'potluck' person," I admitted. "Too much going on in people's houses. No regulation."

Gabriella put a hand on her hip. "Seriously? I've been working in kitchens for almost ten years. You have no idea what people do to your food behind the veil."

"True," I had to agree. "Somebody might be mishandling meat

at a fast-food place, but the food's so full of chemicals, the germs don't stand a chance." I'd meant it as a joke, but Gabriella's face said it was not funny to her.

"Joyce, listen to me." She put her hands on my shoulders and faced off like she was my boxing coach and I was losing the fight. "Preparing food, giving food, is a way that people show love. You reject their food, you reject them."

I nodded slightly. "I can see how you'd say that, being a chef and all."

She leaned in closer. "Focus. These people—the ones with too much going on in their homes—are the same ones you're about to ask for help in your home. Do you want friends or not?"

The question pushed against my face with such force, I was glad Gabriella held me still. *Do I want friends or not?* I stumbled through my response. "I mean… I like people—and I do want friends."

She asked, "You have social anxiety?"

"No. I'm fine being around people. I just don't want to be around them a lot."

"Cool. Nobody's trying to be with you twenty-four seven, either. They have lives, too. I'm just saying, if you want to make friends in a small town, you need to be friend-ly. Not in a performative way. Authentically."

I nodded. Genuine and authentic, I could do. It was all the pretense for Eric's job and Terri's dance team and Eric Jr.'s leagues and even the Parent-Teacher Association that had worn me down. Made me leery of people. And, according to Gabriella, maybe it wasn't their fault. It was me who had put these expectations on myself to show up a certain way. Proper. Polished. Put-together.

"Another thing," she continued. "You can't be judgmental and beg for help at the same time. I need you to change your energy around this potluck, okay?"

"Not sure how to change my energy, but I'll try."

"I mean change your attitude. People can feel what you're thinking because it comes out in your body language, the things you say, the things you don't say. It's your vibe. Got it?"

"Got it. Thank you."

"You got this."

I left with Gabriella's words swimming around my head. *You can't be judgmental and beg for help at the same time.*

I parked at the address shared in the group text. The house was modest but inviting, with white siding that had seen better days but still held on to its charm. A wide front porch stretched across the front, its floorboards worn and weathered, with a few rocking chairs swaying gently in the breeze. Flower beds lined the base of the porch, filled with a mix of late-summer blooms and overgrown greenery that gave the house a lived-in, comfortable feel. There were three other cars in the circular driveway, another sign that I was in the right place.

My anti-potluck sentiments played a game of Ping-Pong in my head against my need for friends. Companionship. Elijah was gone. Gabriella had her own twentysomething life. Terri still hadn't returned my call since she had her father take our grandson away from me, which meant she was colder than I'd imagined. And if I were being honest with myself, I thought my best friend was a little upset with me for divorcing a normal man, when she had been single and hoping for a normal man most of her life.

I pitied myself for not having any friends, no one in my age-group—a peer—to process life with.

Who starts over at sixty years old? How did I end up like this? I'd divorced Eric, not my life. Not my friends. Yet somehow, when we split up, all my other relationships suffered. Is that a thing? Why hadn't anyone told me that divorcing my husband would mean isolation? Retiring and moving to Robin Creek hadn't helped, but I needed affordable housing. I couldn't turn down mortgage-free, rent-free shelter.

I felt like an outsider in my own life, trying to navigate new relationships while holding on to the remnants of the old.

The knock on my window startled me. It was Sonia, with a smile. "You all right in there?"

"Yes," I said, reaching over to grab the container with my friendly offering.

Sonia stepped back and allowed me to open the door. Managing my purse, the food, and the door proved quite the feat, and I nearly dropped the food. Were it not for Sonia's free hand, I would have been eating taquitos with a dusting of dirt, because those weren't going to waste, period.

"Thank you," I said to her as she helped me straighten up.

"You're welcome. Smells good."

"Oh, it is," I assured her.

She teased, "Okay, I see you, Joyce! No need to be humble when you can back it up."

Sonia knocked on the door, and a woman who looked like Eileen's twin answered. "Hi, Sonia, thanks so much for coming."

"Of course, Liz. Anything for Eileen." The women exchanged a solid hug.

Liz asked as she offered me a smile, "Who'd you bring with you?"

"This is Joyce," Sonia explained. "She's new to the Chapter Chatters, but she recently moved back to Robin Creek. Her family has roots here."

Without further explanation, Liz hugged me like an old friend. Warm and tight. "Welcome home, Joyce."

Funny how being from the same place makes you family. "Thank you."

Liz took my dish toward the dining room. Sonia and I joined everyone else in the living room, gathered around Eileen, who looked like she'd lost a few pounds. Otherwise, she was herself.

As soon as I entered the room, the women stood to greet me, their smiles warm and welcoming. One by one, I exchanged hugs with each of them, feeling the genuine affection in their embraces. Each hug was different—some tight and reassuring, others gentle and comforting—but all of them were sincere. When I finally took my seat on a well-worn love seat, the cushions sagged just enough to make me feel like I was sinking into the embrace of an old friend.

If you want to make friends in a small town, you need to be friend-ly. Gabriella knew how to advise me well.

The talk naturally drifted toward Eileen's health, with everyone chiming in to check on her recovery. Eileen waved off their concerns with a lighthearted chuckle, thanking them profusely for coming and reassuring us all that she was on the mend, even if it was a slow process. The conversation was easy, flowing with the comfort that comes from shared history and mutual care.

As I sat listening, I glanced around the room at everyone's feet. Three of the ladies had manicured toes, the rest—the majority of us—had come to Eileen's house with real, lived-in feet. By that, I mean, no polish, calloused spots, dry spots, lopsided toenail lengths. Natural. In sandals, too, because it was still summer.

When I lived in the city, I always had my nails and toes done. Refused to wear sandals or open-toed shoes if my feet didn't look presentable. Now here I was, sitting in a room full of women who didn't give one iota about the condition of my feet. We were here for Eileen. For each other. This felt right, and I was grateful to be a part of it.

Around the dinner table, the atmosphere filled with the gentle hum of conversation and the occasional burst of laughter. The table itself was a patchwork of mismatched dishes and well-worn utensils, a testament to the many meals shared and the memories made. I didn't worry about who made what, or whose cat might have curled up in a serving bowl the night before. I just blessed my food and ate.

Of course, Gabriella's dish stole the spotlight. "What's in this?" Eileen crooned with wonder as she nearly choked from eating so fast.

"Sweet potatoes, black beans, and cinnamon, is all I know. I was too busy taste-testing to ask for details," I confessed.

"I would ask for the recipe," Valerie said between bites, "but there's a consistency to the tortilla and the filling that I'd never be able to reproduce without watching her, and years' worth of practice."

"Does she sell them?" Lupita asked.

"I'm sure she would, for the right price," I said, volunteering my jobless tenant. "Sometimes it takes her hours—days—to prepare the ingredients perfectly for her recipes. Room-temperature this, marinated that. She plans, she shops… It's amazing to watch."

"Clearly," Christine said with another chomp of her third taquito. "She's a master chef. Like the people on TV. You think she'd ever open her own place? I'd eat there every night, I swear."

"Well…" I approached the topic cautiously. "She has agreed to make a meal for anyone who's willing to help me fix up the house so it'll pass inspection. And I'm pretty desperate for help."

A soft silence fell.

This was not what I had planned to do. Well, yes, it was. But not so forthrightly. I'd hoped it would happen after I casually shared that I had "a little work" that needed to be done, and then they would offer to help me, and at first I'd say "Oh, no, I can't ask you all to help," and then they'd say "We insist," until I finally accepted their offer. Then I'd throw in Gabriella's cooking as a reward. That way it all looked more authentic, in a fake way. That was how I was taught to ask for help—the roundabout way.

But the route I had taken was a direct ask. Not something I was used to. It made me feel vulnerable to rejection.

"So, let me get this right," Althea said. "She'll cook us a whole meal if we help you fix up a few things around the house?"

"What kinds of things?" Sonia asked. "If I can't do it, I'll help."

"And Wardell will help, too, whether he wants to or not," Christine volunteered him. "I'll be there to make sure of it."

Lupita offered, "I have a cousin who owes me some favors. He can get supplies cheap, whatever we need."

Valerie shook her head. "I can't do no house-construction work; that would mess up my back and my disability case. But if you need some heavy lifting, I'll send my grandson over. Just say the word."

Their generosity set off my waterworks. "Thank you," I replied tearfully. I clasped my hands tightly in my lap, trying to steady myself against the wave of gratitude and embarrassment washing over me. "I—I didn't know how I was going to get it all finished before APS came back."

"APS?" Liz remarked, giving voice to the shocked looks on everyone's faces.

I hadn't meant to put *all* my business out there. And tonight was supposed to be about Eileen, not me. "Oh, don't worry about it." I dried my eyes. "It was a misunderstanding."

"You definitely don't want to be on their radar," Liz said. "Our cousin fell, broke her hip. Her husband was going to take care of her, but then he had a heart attack. Their daughter was trying to get back home from her job in Europe, but in the meantime, the officials got involved. Their daughter almost had to get FBI clearance to get her parents back in her care."

Eileen chimed in, "I think they mean well."

Liz shot back, "I think people show little to no respect for the elderly these days. It's like, you get one little wrinkle and your IQ automatically drops 15 percent."

Sentiments ranged somewhere between Liz's and Eileen's for the rest of the group. We might have disagreed on the motives, but one thing was for sure: These ladies were not going to let me fight this alone. I had an army now, and I couldn't have been more grateful.

CHAPTER 24

You don't know how much a person has influenced you until you take a step away from them. As I sat there absorbing the generosity of my newfound friends of Robin Creek, I heard negative whisperings in the back of my mind. *They're going to fail you. You can't depend on them. They only want you for Gabriella's cooking.*

Yet despite my second-guessing, my soul had witnessed and felt a genuine care coming from those women that couldn't be denied. Their laughter, the way they hugged me like I belonged, the softness in their voices as they asked about my well-being—it was real. So as I strapped myself back into the seat belt to leave Eileen's house, I deliberately shushed those negative voices.

"Be quiet," I ordered them as I gripped the steering wheel a little tighter. And all of a sudden, the voices didn't sound like me anymore. They sounded like Eric. Like Terri. Like my mother. All this time, these thoughts about how no one would be there for me hadn't been coming from me; they'd been coming from the people who'd surrounded me in the past.

But Gabriella wouldn't have said those things. Eileen or the group, either. Their laughter, the way they hugged me—it was real.

It was up to me to pick and choose whose voices I would allow to guide me.

What does *my* voice say?

My thoughts drifted to the day of my wedding shower. It had been thirty-one years ago, and my mother's house was packed with some family and mostly her friends, all gathered to celebrate my upcoming marriage to Eric. The living room was filled with the sounds of laughter and clinking glasses, gifts wrapped in pastel colors, and the unmistakable aroma of rose-scented candles my mother had insisted on burning. I'd been sitting in the middle of it all, surrounded by a mountain of gifts and smiling faces.

I remember opening each present with care, revealing toasters, dish sets, and towels with the initials of our soon-to-be-shared last name embroidered on them. I had laughed and giggled with my bridesmaids, feeling like I was stepping into a new chapter of life—one filled with hope and promise.

One of the church mothers—Sister Emma, in fact—had given me a book titled *Praying Up a Good Husband*. I thanked her the same as I had thanked everyone else for their gift, then handed it to my mother, who was recording the gift and giver in a notebook for thank-you cards later.

"You're going to need it," Sister Emma admonished as she chomped down on a chicken salad sandwich.

I remember thinking, *Eric is already good; that's why I'm marrying him.*

Nonetheless, I nodded and thanked her again.

But it was my mother's words that would stick with me, like a splinter buried deep beneath the skin. She said under her breath, "She's right. People will disappoint you in ways you can't even imagine once you really get to know them."

Her words landed like a stone in my chest, heavy and cold. I'd tried to brush them off, telling myself she didn't mean it—that she was just being cynical. But her tone, the certainty in her voice, had lingered. And though I didn't realize it then, it was the seed of doubt that took root in my mind, shaping my expectations for marriage. It was supposed to be tough and rough, full of disappointment. And I was supposed to carry the weight—even spiritually—so we could succeed, per the gift from Sister Emma.

In some strange way, my mother knew. Sister Emma knew. They both knew the bitterness of their own marriages, and the patterns handed down from generation to generation, where men work and women work plus do everything else needed to make a marriage work. Thanklessly. Love-lessly. It was the unspoken rule of survival. My mother's words weren't prophetic so much as they were typical. And I didn't resent her words; I'd received them.

Her words, not mine.

I blinked, snapping back to the present as the warm evening air filled the car. The memory faded, but its effects lingered. The divorce had been the first real step I'd taken in shedding that mindset, the belief that love and marriage had to come with disappointment. But the truth was, the divorce was only the beginning of the transformation. I had allowed myself to settle for so much less than I deserved, not just because of Eric, but because of the voices—my mother's, Terri's, even Eric's—that had shaped the way I saw myself. It was like I'd been wrapped in layers of expectations that weren't my own, and now, piece by piece, I was pulling it off.

Now, as I left Eileen's house, something shifted. A shedding of old skin. The way those women had shown up for me, the way they cared—there was no disappointment in sight. And it was up to me to decide whether I'd allow myself to accept that kind of goodness. And I knew just where I wanted to make my next move.

I spotted Richard just as he was locking up the door to his shop. My heart pounded a little harder than I expected as I hurried across the street, trying to catch him before he left.

"Richard!" I called out, waving.

He looked up, surprised, and gave me a slow smile. "Well, if it isn't Ms. Joyce Hicks. To what do I owe the pleasure?"

"I was hoping to catch you before you left," I said, feeling a flutter of awkwardness rise in my chest. This wasn't easy. I hadn't asked for help from anyone in years, and especially not a man other than my husband. I swallowed, trying to keep my voice steady. "I was wondering if you had time for some ice cream...and maybe... something else."

Richard's eyebrows lifted in curiosity as he turned the key in the lock. "Ice cream, huh? Haven't heard that one in a while. What's the catch?"

I fidgeted with my hands. "I need some help," I admitted, my voice softer than I intended. "With the house. The renovations are just...more than I thought they'd be. I don't have anyone else to ask, and I know you're a problem-solver."

He stared at me for a moment, clearly taken aback. "You want me to help you with your house?" His confusion was evident. "As a practice friend, still? Or is this more like...we're...in each other's lives now?"

"I—" I stumbled over my words, not sure how to navigate this conversation. "Friends are in each other's lives, aren't they?"

He turned away from the door and motioned toward the shop. "How about we close up here and go grab that ice cream? You can tell me what needs to be done with the house, and we'll figure it out."

I smiled, feeling a sense of relief wash over me. The fear of rejection had been louder in my head than the reality ever was. "That sounds good," I said, falling into step beside him.

As we walked, I noticed how easy it felt to be next to him. There was a quiet comfort in the steady rhythm of our footsteps, side by side. I hadn't felt this kind of ease with anyone in a long time, and it surprised me how natural this seemed with Richard.

He must have sensed my shift in mood, because he glanced over and smiled. "It's nice not having to put on an act around you," he said, his voice low and sincere. "I don't feel like I have to be someone I'm not."

His words mirrored exactly what I had been feeling. Maybe this was the start of something more than just asking for help. Maybe this was the beginning of a real friendship.

We continued walking, and I told him about the oven that still needed to be replaced, the half-done kitchen, and the other repairs that were piling up. Richard listened intently, asking questions here and there but mostly just letting me talk. It felt nice to share the load, even if just for a little while.

When we arrived at the ice cream shop, I glanced over at Richard, who was leaning on the counter, waiting for our cones. Instead of flashing one of his typical playful grins, he offered a small, genuine smile. It wasn't the look of a man trying to impress or conquer. No, there was no game in his eyes, no mask. He was simply Richard, looking at me like I was someone worth knowing—not as a prize, not as someone to win over. Just Joyce.

And that, I thought, was enough.

"I'm happy to help, Joyce."

"Thank you."

CHAPTER 25

Anxiety tightened my chest. Eight days. That was all we had left to get this place in shape before Anya's deadline. Eight days to fix leaky pipes, deal with the water heater, and caulk or seal bathrooms and windows. The electrician was scheduled to come in the next day to deal with the stove. It amazed me that I had spent so much on the upgrades, and yet there was more to do. Just like life, reconfiguring the layout doesn't fix everything. Sometimes you must tackle other issues along the way, especially when you're under scrutiny.

The house was my life, basically.

I glanced around as the ladies of the Chapter Chatters, along with, Liz, Wardell, and Gabriella, sat around the living room on my side of the house. Even Valerie had come. "For support," she said. "But nobody takes any pictures of me, understood?"

We all agreed.

This was the planning meeting. I'd called it so in the text message group I'd formed. It was a hot Thursday evening, 6:30 p.m. I'd turned up the air-conditioning so my guests would be comfortable. I picked up some cookies from the grocer as a form of thanks.

The only person missing was Richard, but he'd texted me that he was running a few minutes behind, so I wasn't worried.

There was a strange mix of anticipation and uncertainty in the air. I could see it in their faces. This wasn't going to be a quick fix, and we all knew it. Yet they'd all shown up for me. Even Wardell, though I suspect Christine had drug him by his ear.

"Thank you all for coming," I said, trying to keep my voice steady. "We've only got eight days—really six, if you take away the time for the electrician—to get everything done. APS will be back to inspect everything, and if we don't meet their requirements... Well, let's just say I don't want to find out what happens if we don't. We're going to handle everything on her list, major and minor. I want her to know that I'm okay. And I am, so long as I have you all with me."

There were nods and murmurs of understanding. Minus Wardell, of course. The frown on his face persisted, even as he availed himself of another cookie.

Just then, the door creaked open, and Richard stepped in, slightly out of breath but smiling. The sight of him brought ease to my body. I hadn't realized how much I'd been looking forward to him showing up until he'd entered the living room.

"Hey there," he said, walking straight toward me and pulling me into a brief but warm hug. I hadn't expected the hug, either, but I found myself leaning in to it just enough to feel the comfort in his arms. "Sorry I'm late." He turned to the rest of the group, offering a smile and a wave. "Hello, everyone. Name's Richard."

"Who doesn't know you? Your business has been donating to the library's programs for years," Christine said.

"Glad to help. What'd I miss?"

"The cookies," Wardell said as he swiped the last one out of the box.

Richard chuckled as he de-escalated Wardell's jab. "No worries. Don't need 'em anyway."

"What we do need is a plan," Christine said. "And I think my husband is the perfect person to help us with that. Right, Wardell?"

"Why does it always feel like I end up leadin' these things?" he muttered under his breath.

Christine shot him a sharp look, her lips pressing together in that way that told him he better straighten up fast. "Because you're good at it, Wardell. And because you love helping people, whether you admit it or not," she said, her voice firm but affectionate. She gave his arm a light nudge. "So, go ahead and show these fine folks why I married you in the first place."

Wardell grumbled under his breath again, but this time there was less resistance in his tone. He shifted in his seat, looking around at everyone, his frown softening slightly under the weight of Christine's expectations.

I sighed, knowing I had to address him, too. I tried to remember exactly what went wrong with our first meeting. "Wardell, I know you and I didn't have the best initial meeting. But we need you. We've got a lot of ground to cover. And you've got the most experience when it comes to construction."

Wardell's eyes flickered over to me, a hint of that old stubbornness still there, but I could see him digesting my words. His lips loosened when I mentioned his expertise. The compliment worked like a charm. He reminded me of a lady at the church where I grew up who sang like a lark. She wanted to sing, but she would always make the congregation beg for it. She sat in her seat, shaking her head for at least a minute while people yelled out, "Let the Lord use you," or "He will give you strength."

And then she got up there and belted it out like she'd been practicing at home for weeks.

Like Wardell, she just needed a little encouragement. Also known as *ego stroking*.

With a deep sigh, he leaned forward, elbows on his knees, and looked at me more directly. "APS is strict. We gotta go by the book if we want them to approve the work. You got a certified electrician for the oven?"

"Yes." I nodded.

Wardell stood up, stretching his arms out as if shaking off the reluctance. He rolled his shoulders back, planted his feet firmly on the ground, and looked around the room like he was surveying his new domain. He let out a grunt as though inspecting possible NFL draft picks.

Gabriella covered her mouth, apparently stifling a giggle. I shushed her.

"All right," he said, clapping his hands together once, the sound sharp enough to get everyone's attention. He hooked his thumbs in his belt and gave a slight nod toward me. "Joyce, tell me specifically what's on the list of stuff we need to fix."

I handed him a printout of the paper Anya had emailed me, and he scanned it. His eyes narrowed as he scrutinized the paper. After a moment, he exhaled, clearly taking stock of the situation.

"Okay, here's how we're gonna do this." He began pacing a little, back and forth across the room, his eyes flicking from one person to the next, as though mentally assigning tasks. "We'll break this down into teams. Plumbing's gonna need at least two people; the water heater team needs strength. That'll be me and Richard.

Caulking and sealing—that's anybody's game. And of course, we'll leave the kitchen wiring to the pros."

Lupita asked, "What materials do we need? I have a hookup at the hardware store."

"If you give me your number, I'll send a list."

Christine intervened, "I will handle the communication." The woman knew her husband had no business adding women's phone numbers to his phone.

Gabriella said, "And I'll work on a menu for the celebratory dinner, when we've finished the work and this is all behind us."

Valerie raised her hand. "May I request more of the black bean and sweet potato taquitos? I swear, I can't even sleep through the night without thinking about them."

"Sure thing," Gabriella said.

Wardell's stern face took center stage again. He crossed his arms and glanced around the group. "Y'all better go home tonight and watch some of my YouTube videos, because I'm not explainin' every little thing again."

A few more chuckles rippled through the room, and Wardell nodded, seeming satisfied that he'd empowered his teams. His tone had softened, but his direction was clear. He was stepping into the leadership role. He was the boss, and we were his underlings. Gladly.

I couldn't help but smile at that. Even though Wardell grumbled, there was a part of him that enjoyed this—leading, organizing, showing people what to do.

So be it.

"Young lady"—he pointed at Gabriella—"can you go on the internet and send my videos on caulking to everyone? My wife will give you my website name."

"I'm on it."

Valerie announced, "I'm out. Looks like y'all are about to start moving around. I've got a bad back; can't risk injuries. My prayers are with you all."

Wardell nodded. "Sounds like a good idea. Don't want you getting hurt."

Valerie tipped out, throwing kisses and hope at us.

The door had barely shut behind her when Wardell barked, "The rest of y'all start watching. Joyce, show me and Richard to the water heater." He gestured for Richard to follow along. With a third party present, I felt safe leading Wardell to the tiny closet closest just beside the laundry room.

The water heater was slightly off-kilter, leaning a bit to one side. It wasn't drastic, but enough to catch the eye. There was some wear and tear, rust around the edges, and the pipes were older, though nothing seemed immediately dangerous.

Wardell knelt down, inspecting the base and pipes. "It's tilted, but it's nothing we can't handle. The base might just need leveling. We can fix that with some cinder blocks and shims, no problem. And these pipes"—he pointed—"we'll swap them out with flexible copper ones. That should hold it steady, rectify the problem, and pass the APS inspection easily."

I nodded, feeling a bit of relief. "So we don't need to replace it?"

"Nah, not yet. This thing's still got some life in it. If we stabilize it and update the connections, we'll be fine."

I nodded, trying to absorb the technical details. "I don't know half of what you said, but the half I do comprehend sounded good," I said. "Thank you."

"We should take before-and-after pictures," Richard said. He tapped his pocket. "Shoot, I left my phone in the car. I'll be right back." He dashed off, leaving me alone with Wardell.

Before I could even process what had happened, Wardell said quietly, "Joyce, I just want to say… I'm sorry. For comin' on too strong when we first met. I know it wasn't right."

I blinked, taken aback by his confession but grateful for it all the same. Part of me had expected another offhand remark, but I saw something different in his eyes—earnestness. I breathed easier. "Thank you, Wardell. That means a lot. But let me tell you something—you've got a treasure in Christine. Not every woman would put up with you."

Wardell chuckled, scratching the back of his neck. "Yeah… I realize that every day of my life. She's made it real clear I need to straighten up if I want people to respect me—or even like me." He cleared his throat. "Now, let's get to work. Write down these materials I tell you we need so you can give the list to Lupita."

Dutifully, I typed the list of parts and tools into my cell phone. Richard returned and listened to the more detailed plan that Wardell suggested the second time around. I left the two of them alone, since I wasn't technically on the water heater "team."

I supposed I was just on the material-buying team, because when I got back to the living room, Gabriella had two sets of videos playing. One about caulking on the television, another about fixing leaky pipes on her large iPad. The girls had a classroom in full session.

About half an hour later, Lupita's list had grown to an estimated six hundred dollars' worth of materials we needed, but she assured us that she'd be able to get a few hundred knocked off with her contact at the store. Wardell shrieked, "Well, alrighty then! I need to be hooked up with your connections!"

Here again, Christine intervened. "She's my friend. That's enough."

Wardell charged us all to be back at the house tomorrow morning. "I need everyone here in the morning. Nine a.m. sharp to start on your assignment."

"I have to go to work," I blurted out as the others began to mumble their objections.

Wardell huffed like this was something we'd all been planning for months, knowing full well he just got this position less than an hour ago.

I gave him the don't-go-all-dramatic eye.

Richard smoothed things over with, "Why don't we all decide on a good time that works for everyone?"

"Saturday morning," Althea suggested. "That way we can all rest our bones and apply our ointment on Sunday. And that'll give me time to meet you all at the hardware store. I'm definitely going to need some help with this list," she thumb-scrolled her phone.

I shook my head. "Saturday won't work. I've got the electrician coming by. He may need to shut off the power for a while, and that'll make it too hot in here for us to work."

No one argued my point there.

"And I have a cooking contest Saturday," Gabriella said to my surprise.

My eyes flicked over to her immediately, searching her face. *A cooking contest this weekend?* I'd known she planned to compete again, but it wasn't like her to keep the details of her culinary plans quiet. If nothing else, I thought I was a shoo-in for head taste-tester.

But now, she was avoiding my gaze, looking at everyone else in the room except me. "Sunday?" she continued her quest.

"Sunday morning is for church," Christine said incredulously.

"After church?" Gabriella suggested.

Wardell mumbled, "I don't like to work on the Sabbath."

Christine stared him. "You don't even attend church on the Sabbath."

He shrugged.

Christine said, "Service ends at eleven. We can be here by eleven thirty."

"My church ends at noon. I can grab a bite to eat and be here by one," Richard said.

Gabriella echoed him as she threw out the suggestion, "One, then?"

Heads nodded.

"One, it is," I said, solidifying the plan, still distracted by Gabriella's unexpected declaration about the contest.

What's going on? I wondered again.

But Wardell had the last word, of course. "Okay. If we're gonna start that late on Sunday, we probably won't get finished in one day. Caulk and things need time to dry. So everybody plan to be here Sunday afternoon and Monday evening. Will that work?"

I was prepared to hop in and ask if maybe we could have some come Sunday and others come Monday because I didn't want to be too much of a bother. But the sight of all those eager heads bouncing up and down literally shut my mouth. They were all willing to sacrifice their time in order to help me. The good news sank in.

Wardell barked more orders. "Come dressed to work. Tennis shoes, hair pulled back, ready to put in some work. Take all your pain pills before you get here. Stretch. Eat a good breakfast, but not too much. It's hard to work over a bulging stomach."

Valeria gave him an "Amen."

Christine rubbed her husband's arm and whispered, "Okay, honey. That's enough. This isn't boot camp."

"Yes, it is!" Liz countered. "Because it could have been any one of us. Except you." She pointed at Gabriella. "Anybody could see one of us having a senior moment—locked out of our car, slip and fall at a park—and overreact. Start questioning our minds, our ability. Threaten our freedom. We gotta take the wheel!" She thrust a fist in the air.

"Take the wheel!" Gabriella, her lone soldier, yelled while pretending to hold a car's steering wheel.

Richard took a moment, glancing around the room as if drawing inspiration from the faces in front of him. "We can do better than that," he muttered. He straightened up, arms crossed, thinking hard for a second. Then his face lit up as an idea sparked.

"How about this," he started, his voice steady. "We're not just helping Joyce. We're helping all of us, right? So how about something that captures that—keeping our independence and watching out for each other." He paused for effect, then added, "How about, 'Stand strong, help along!'"

He thrust his fist into the air, and this time there was a different energy behind it.

"Stand strong, help along!" he repeated, louder.

The room seemed to wake up, and one by one, people began nodding, catching on to the spirit of it.

"Stand strong, help along!" Gabriella chimed in enthusiastically, raising her fist.

Sonia, looking a bit more convinced, followed suit. "Stand strong, help along!"

The others echoed it, and soon the room was filled with voices, stronger now, carrying the chant: "Stand strong, help along!"

Gabriella, ever the firecracker, couldn't just chant. She started dancing, moving her arms in a little shimmy that got everyone's attention. "Stand strong, help along!" she sang, hips swaying. Just dancing away like she hadn't thrown me for a loop with that cooking-contest announcement.

Why didn't she tell me? This wasn't the time for questions, though.

Not to be outdone, Eileen, usually so composed, grinned wide and jumped in with a jig of her own, bouncing from side to side. The sight of her doing an impromptu Irish dance had everyone in stitches. Laughter filled the room as we all gave in to the goofiness of the moment.

Sonia, with a wink, threw her hands up and spun around while Liz started clapping in rhythm. Even Wardell, who had been the grumpiest of the bunch, cracked a smile and joined in with a playful fist pump to the beat. "Stand strong, help along!"

It was contagious. Before long, everyone was moving, swaying, and chanting. Richard added a little twirl to his step, then threw his arm around my shoulder. "Stand strong, help along!" he called out, his voice full of laughter.

I gave in, laughing and raising my fist with the rest of them. My Robin Creek family. In this moment, with the chant echoing around me and the joy in everyone's faces, the house didn't feel like a burden. It felt like a project we'd all taken on together—proof that I wasn't alone.

Gabriella twirled into Richard, nearly knocking over a chair, which sent the room into fits of giggles again. Wardell shook his head, but the smile was unmistakable now.

"All right, all right!" Wardell hollered over the noise, half serious, half amused. "We gotta save some of that energy for fixin' this place up!"

The room erupted in cheers, but the chant had done its work. We were ready to face the task ahead—together, with laughter and plenty of support.

My friends grabbed their bags and began walking toward the door. Conserving our energy was probably a good idea, given Warden Wardell.

Just as I was getting ready to say goodbye to everyone, my phone buzzed in my pocket. It was Elijah.

"Thanks, everyone. I'll see you all Saturday. I have to take this call." I waved and stepped away from the group, leaving the lockup to Gabriella. "Hey, EJ. How are you?"

"I'm okay, Grandma," Elijah said, his voice quieter than usual. "Sounds like a bunch of people are with you. Who's there?"

"Oh, just Gabriella and the ladies from the library and some other people who are going to help with the final repairs around the house."

"How's Miss Gabriella?"

"Oh, she's fine. She's just seeing our guests to the door."

He sighed. "I wish I was there."

He wasn't the only one with that wish.

"You having a good time with your grandfather?"

"He's not too bad, but he's kinda strict. Like today, I wanted to go to the park with my friend, but Grandpa said no because… He said there are too many strangers around. And he said some of the kids in this neighborhood are questionable. He didn't even want to talk about it. Just said no."

I released the tension with a drawn-out breath, feeling like I wanted to rescue him but knowing I couldn't change the situation. Only his mother could do that. "I'm proud of you for sticking it out, Elijah. It's not easy, but you're doing great. Just keep being respectful, and before you know it, the summer will be over and you'll be back in a familiar neighborhood. I'm sure your mom and dad will let you play with your friends."

"I miss you, Grandma," he said, his voice unsteady.

"I miss you, too, EJ. I'm glad we had all those weeks together earlier this summer."

"Me, too."

After we said our goodbyes, I stared at the phone for a moment, a heaviness settling over me. Elijah was doing his best, but I could tell this arrangement wasn't ideal for him.

Richard walked up beside me, breaking me from my thoughts. "Everything okay? You looked a little worried when you took the call."

"Yeah. That was my grandson. He's...bored."

"Only child?" he asked.

"Yes." I left it at that, not wanting to go into all the drama with me and Eric and Terri—who still had not engaged in a grown-up conversation with me since she'd sent her father to pick up my grandson. The two times she'd called me back, I was in the car with EJ, so Terri and I couldn't really talk freely.

"I'm an only child, too," Richard said. "Teaches you how to be creative. Make up your own fun. Your own friends."

"Mmmm," I said, nodding at my phone.

"But you've got some real friends here."

I gave my full attention to him now. "Yes, I do. And I'm grateful. Friends are exactly what I needed."

He nodded. "Glad to be in the number."

His words lingered between us for a moment, and I felt a quiet gratitude growing stronger. This wasn't just about fixing a house anymore—it was about rebuilding something inside me.

I hadn't realized how much I'd missed being part of a circle like this until I found myself in the middle of it. And Richard, with all his teasing and quiet support, was becoming someone I could count on.

CHAPTER 26

Richard stepped back, nodding toward me as he made his way to the door. "I'll be back bright and early," he said with that same warm grin I was starting to get used to. His hand lingered on the door for a moment before he glanced back. "Take care, Joyce."

"You, too," I replied, and as the door closed behind him, I felt a calm settle in the room. It wasn't a bad feeling, just a reminder of the small connections we were building with each other.

Just as I exhaled and turned, Gabriella stepped back inside, looking a bit distracted. I could tell she had a lot on her mind—more than just the repairs and more than the contest. I kept my voice even as I asked, "You want to talk about the cooking contest?"

"I've been practicing my dishes at my cousin's house, using her oven. Between job interviews, of course," she said.

"I thought you didn't like your cousin much."

"I don't. But what else could I do? I needed an oven."

Guilt clutched my insides at the thought of Gabriella having to endure her cousin's bad attitude because I couldn't afford to provide an oven for my tenant.

"See?" Gabriella held out her hand. "This is why I didn't

tell you. I didn't want you to feel guilty, Joyce. I know we were both bummed about Celestia. Plus, we were both already upset about Elijah. I guess I just didn't want to add any more pressure on you."

"Pressure?"

"Yeah."

I blinked, taking in her words. Pressure? I was raised on pressure. In fact, I was so used to shouldering the pressures and burdens for everyone else, her declaration nearly offended me. She had no business carrying her problems alone! *This child is basically my mini-me.*

She stuffed her hands in her pockets. Fidgeting. "Annnnnd..."

I knew there was more to the story.

"This contest is citywide, sponsored by Robin Creek. I didn't want any speculation from Mrs. Maine or anyone else that I had special favors because I'm associated with someone who works for the city. I think it would be better if you didn't come at all."

I frowned, my heart sinking a little. "That's silly. Who would think something like that?"

"Ummm...Mrs. Maine," Gabriella said. "She's been talking to people about me. She asked at my job—well, my old job—to see if I'm undocumented. She's looking for a way to disqualify me from entry. Totally desperate."

A hot wave of anger surged through me. *How dare she?* The thought of someone like Mrs. Maine prying into Gabriella's life like that made my fists clench involuntarily. "That's because she knows you're gonna beat her one day," I hissed.

Gabriella shrugged. "Anyway, I didn't want you to get caught up in all of that, especially after everything you've already done for me. You have enough troubles of your own to—"

I held up a hand to stop her. "Gabriella, enough. My troubles are your troubles, and your troubles are my troubles. We're family now."

Gabriella smiled weakly. "I know. I just don't want Mrs. Maine or anyone else thinking I'm where I am because of anything other than my cooking."

Her words hit me hard, and I nodded, understanding more than I wanted to. "I get that. But you don't have to hide things from me to protect me. Come. Sit down."

We settled next to each other on the couch. As I looked at her, something stirred inside me. I wasn't just seeing Gabriella as my tenant anymore; I was seeing her as someone I truly cared for, someone I wanted to protect and guide—not unlike my own daughter, but with a different kind of bond. This young woman, with all her talents and dreams, had somehow slipped into my life and found a place in my heart, not as a responsibility, but as family.

As I formulated thoughts, I realized the speech I was about to give Gabriella was one that I also needed to hear. We were so similar in how we interacted with others, it was almost scary. And I could see that people-pleasing spirit in her, the same as it had been in me. I never liked Lorenzo, but the truth of the matter was that he broke up with her when it should have been the opposite, a long time ago.

"Listen, Gabriella. I know we've had some conversations about my ex-husband. About my daughter. And Lorenzo." I paused, carefully measuring my words. "You know, all of us—me, you—we've been so busy protecting everyone else's feelings that we've forgotten our own. I see it in you, that same urge to shield everyone from discomfort, to keep the peace."

Gabriella looked down, picking at her nails. "I don't want to hurt people. And I don't want to be a burden."

"I get that. But trying to protect everyone else's feelings at the expense of your own... It's not fair to you. I spent years doing that. Years trying to keep everything together—trying to make Eric happy, Terri happy, all the people we needed to impress. I thought it was my job to keep the family afloat, but all it did was drown me." I sighed. "And you? You deserve better than that, Gabriella."

She glanced at me, her eyes glistening. "But I feel like if I don't, I'll lose people."

I leaned forward, turning toward her. "The best, strongest relationships are the ones where people can be honest—where they can share what they really feel and know that the other person will still stand with them, no matter what. That's what I'm learning, and that's what you're teaching me, Gabriella."

Her eyes widened slightly. "Me? Teaching you?"

I nodded. "Yes. You've been showing me what it looks like to stand up for yourself, to follow your dreams even when it's hard."

Gabriella's lip trembled for a second, but she quickly composed herself.

I reached for her hand. "You're stronger than you think. And if we're going to be in each other's lives, we need to be able to tell each other the truth. That's how we build the kind of relationships—friendships—that last."

She wiped a tear from her eyes. "I've moved around so much in my life. The last time I had a semi-friend was in high school. Marcia. We were best friends from ninth grade until our junior year."

"What happened?"

"Her boyfriend tried to kiss me. And I told her. But instead of getting mad at him, she got mad at me," Gabriella said with a tiny whimper. "I texted her, inboxed her, but she just... It's like she didn't want to lose what she thought she had with him. They stayed together. Went to homecoming and prom together. The whole time I was thinking I should have kept it to myself. Then I'd have a friend."

"Oh, Gabriella. I'm so sorry Marcia chose him over you."

"I saw them on the 'gram. They're married now," she said. "So they were destined to be together, I guess."

I laughed. "Honey, just 'cause they're married don't mean the drama has ended."

Gabriella tilted her head onto my shoulder. "I hope she's happy, though. I really do."

"I do, too. Who knows? Maybe they both matured. But you did the right thing, Gabriella. You're honest. You told her what happened. Maybe she was embarrassed, or she wasn't secure enough to walk away. The choice Marcia made was hers; it's not a reflection of whether you were a good friend. I happen to think you're an amazing friend. I mean, you've talked me into making more friends. How about that?"

She laughed.

"I'm proud of you and proud to know you. And you are going to beat Mrs. Maine and everybody else in this town!" I told her.

Gabriella wrapped her arms around me in a tight hug. "Thank you, Joyce. That means the world to me."

I hugged her back, feeling the bond between us tighten in that moment. "You've got this, Gabriella. You always have."

"But promise me you won't come to the contest tomorrow."

"I couldn't if I wanted to. The electrician's coming. And if I did show up, I'd get kicked out, because I've got some choice words for Mrs. Maine!"

Gabriella sat up straight and looked at me down the bridge of her nose. "Hey, I will settle this once and for all. In the test kitchen. Not the streets."

"Not the streets," I repeated. "Kick her behind with your Blaxican boots!"

Gabriella's face crinkled. "What the heck?"

We both fell over in laughter at my ridiculous joke.

Saturday came faster than I expected. Gabriella stood by the door, ready to head to the contest, her excitement barely contained behind her nervous smile.

I walked over, handing her a small lunch bag with some snacks. "In case you need something between rounds," I said with a wink. "You're going to knock their socks off today."

She laughed softly, taking the bag. "I hope so. Thanks, Ms. Joyce."

I reached out, gently squeezing her hand. "Remember, you've worked hard for this."

Gabriella's eyes gleamed. "I'll try to remember that."

With one final hug, I watched as she walked out the door, my heart swelling with pride.

A few minutes later, the electrician pulled up in his van. Right on time. I greeted him and his assistant at the door and led them straight to the kitchen. "I've been waiting for this moment," I muttered to myself, watching as they unpacked tools and got to work.

Throughout the morning, I couldn't help but peek in from time to time. The sound of clinking tools and the hum of work gave me a sense of reassurance. This was progress. Real, tangible progress. But there was also a knot of worry building in my chest. What if something went wrong? What if the oven still wasn't compatible? What if there was a nest of termites behind the wall that swarmed through the house when he tried to replace the panel? I tried to push the doom-and-gloom thoughts aside, but they kept creeping back.

At one point, the electricians shut off the power. The house went quiet, still, but inside, I felt the buzz of anticipation. I paced the living room while the power was out, thinking of the bills and how it seemed like every time I turned around, this house found a new way to demand more from me. But it wasn't just the money—it was the fear that maybe I wasn't handling things as well as I thought. The oven was just one part of it. Could I keep everything together?

After what felt like an eternity, the power came back on. I rushed to the kitchen just in time to see the electrician testing the oven. He flipped the switch, and a low buzz filled the room as the oven sprang to life. Relief washed over me, and I realized I had been holding my breath. Soon, the oven would be back in working order, and I could see Gabriella using it again. I imagined her whipping up one of her Blaxican masterpieces, the smell of spices filling the house, the sound of her singing as she worked.

As usual, I'd gotten myself all worked up for nothing. *When will I learn?*

I smiled, peeking into the kitchen once more. They were close to finishing now. They checked the wiring, testing and retesting, while I stood at a distance, arms crossed, nodding to myself.

Finally, the boss called me over to inspect the work. I ran my hand along the sleek edge of the oven, no longer just a useless hunk of metal in the corner. It was ready. "This is going to make things so much easier," I said softly, mostly to myself.

I signed the paperwork, but not without a little wince at the bill. It was steep, but necessary. Staying independent and comfortable in my own home came with a price, but it was a price I was willing to pay.

After they left, I sat down at the table with a deep breath. The sight of the bill still lingered in my mind, but I focused instead on the satisfaction of what it meant. This house, this life, was still mine.

For a moment, I let that feeling settle in: a well-deserved pride in being able to stay in my home, to handle the repairs, and to keep things moving forward on my own terms.

CHAPTER 27
Gabriella

It's funny how something you've dreamed about for years can make you feel like you're on the verge of throwing up the moment you're about to step into it. I should've known this would happen. Even when I was a kid, when I finally got to do the thing I wanted most, that was when the panic would hit. Like, why do I even want this?

But here I was, standing at the back entrance of the Robin Creek Civic Center, holding my kitchen knives like a lifeline, about to enter the biggest cooking contest of my life so far. The civic center loomed over me, all steel and glass, making me feel smaller than I already did. I could see the banners inside with the names of past winners, their smiling faces reminding me how big a deal this was. People around me walked in confidently, like they were born for this moment. Was I really one of them?

I wiped my sweaty palms on my apron and checked my reflection in the glass door one more time. Part of me wondered what the hell I was doing here. The other part, though, whispered that I had a shot. It reminded me of the day I'd tried out for cheerleading. Ninth grade. Most of the girls had been cheering since pre-K, it seemed. They had gone to dance classes, gymnastics, weight training—all the things. I was only a *Dance Dance Revolution* champion at my local arcade, but I had heart. And rhythm. And nerve. Did I make the cheer squad? No. But I came close enough for the head coach to tell me that I should try out for the basketball dance team. It was a step down, but I wasn't daunted. I made that team and made the best of things.

My grandmother told me later that year, "Everything happens for a reason. You needed to work hard, gain the confidence. That's why you didn't make the main team… It was for you to grow."

Well, as much as I wanted to be grateful for just being here at this cooking contest, I didn't want to just grow. I wanted to freakin' win this thing! No junior team for me.

Hair pulled back tight, no frizz. My apron didn't have any mysterious spots—yet. *Deep breath. I got this.*

Still, a knot tightened in my stomach. It wasn't the cooking that scared me. Even though every meal is the tiniest bit different, I could cook blindfolded if I had to. It was *them*. The judges. The other contestants. Mrs. Maine. Being in competition always made me feel like I was back in middle school, trying to prove myself.

And then there was Lorenzo. We were done. But I felt like I was carrying around his words in my head. He'd always told me I was a great cook—like that's all I was. *A cook*. But never a business partner. Never someone with my own dreams, or depth. Was that it? Was this all I was—a cook to the world? Everybody's servant? What was I doing here? I forced myself to push the thoughts away, even though they pulled at me fiercely. How could someone feel so conflicted in just sixty seconds? It was like my mind was playing tug-of-war with itself, and I wasn't even sure which side I was rooting for. *Can I even concentrate in this state of mind?* I wished Joyce was here. Elijah, too.

I stepped through the door, and immediately, the energy inside hit me like a wall. Busy, buzzing, alive with clanking pots, chopping knives, and the low hum of nerves in the air. People were setting up their stations, arranging their ingredients like they were some kind of magic potions. I scanned the room, sizing up the competition. Some of them looked young like me, fresh-faced but determined. Others were older, seasoned chefs with that "I know what I'm doing" vibe.

And then there she was. Mrs. Maine. Standing near the front, flipping through a cookbook that was for sale. As soon as she spotted me, her lips twisted into a smirk.

Great.

I turned my back to her, trying not to let it get to me. Joyce's words echoed in my mind from last night: "Kick her behind with your Blaxican boots!" I'd laughed, but now? I wasn't so sure.

"Gabriella Santos, is it?" The voice startled me. I turned to see one of the contest coordinators smiling at me, clipboard in hand.

"That's me," I answered, trying to sound way more confident than I felt.

"Great. You're at station five. Judges will start in thirty minutes. Good luck!" She gave me a nod and moved on to the next contestant.

Thirty minutes. I had thirty minutes to get everything ready. I made my way over to my station, setting down my knives and taking in the ingredients laid out in front of me. Black beans, sweet potatoes, peppers, spices...everything I needed for my Blaxican taquitos, which I had tweaked a little more even after Joyce had taken them to Eileen's house. I also had my fusion street corn. This was it. This was what I'd been working on for months.

I spread out my ingredients and checked that everything was

in place. This was my battlefield, and I needed to get settled. But even as I started prepping, chopping the onions with quick, precise movements, my mind wouldn't shut up. *What if they think I'm not good enough?*

I could practically feel Mrs. Maine's eyes on my back, and it made me grit my teeth. The way she'd been going around asking about me at my old job, like I was on someone's "Most Wanted" list.

I focused on the food. Chop, chop, slice. My hands knew what to do, even if my brain was going haywire. The sweet potatoes hit the pan with a satisfying sizzle, and I felt a tiny bit of calm settle over me. Cooking always did that—pulled me back to center. The way the ingredients came together, the smells that filled the air... It was like home, no matter where I was.

The tension in my shoulders eased a little as the spices started to bloom in the heat. The familiar, smoky aroma of cumin and the brightness of lime zest pushed out some of the nerves. The rhythm of it, the way the knife glided through the onions and peppers, felt like muscle memory taking over. It was instinct. No room for doubt.

But there was still that edge in my chest, the part of me that wouldn't stop thinking. The part that kept whispering that maybe I didn't belong here, that I was just playing at being a chef. What would the judges think? Would they recognize what I was trying to do or just see some mashup of cultures on a plate?

I stirred the pan, the sweet potatoes softening just the way I wanted them to. And that's when the calm cracked again. What if these judges leaned toward traditional dishes? What if they couldn't see the story behind the food?

I let the thoughts drift away as quickly as they had come,

focusing on the smells filling the air. The flavors had begun to speak to each other. Everything was falling into place.

I glanced over at the other stations, some of them perfectly arranged, everything in neat little rows. And then there was me, with a flurry of ingredients scattered around like a whirlwind had passed through. It should have made me feel out of place. But in a weird way, it didn't. I thrived in this mess, this organized chaos.

I took a deep breath, stirring the mixture and letting the tension seep out of me. The food was where I found my balance.

"Five minutes!" someone called from the front.

My heart kicked up a notch, but I didn't let it show. I was almost done. Taquitos were assembled, the corn was grilled and seasoned. All that was left was the presentation. I plated everything carefully, making sure the colors popped, the edges were clean. Presentation mattered. They always said people eat with their eyes first.

I stepped back from the station, giving my dishes one last look. Okay, this was it. This was what I came for.

"Time's up!"

The judges started making their rounds, and I wiped my hands on my apron again, trying to shake off the nerves. I caught Mrs. Maine giving me another look, this one dripping with condescension.

Whatever. I'm not here for her.

The first judge approached my station, a tall guy with salt-and-pepper hair and an air of importance. He studied my dishes for a moment, then glanced at me. "Tell me about these," he said, his voice neutral.

I swallowed, forcing myself to speak clearly. "These are Blaxican taquitos—black beans, sweet potatoes, and spices, wrapped in a tortilla and fried. It's a fusion of Black soul food and Mexican flavors. And this"—I pointed to the second dish—"is street corn, grilled and topped with a blend of cotija cheese, hot sauce, and lime."

The judge nodded, picking up a fork. He took a bite of the taquitos first, chewing slowly, his face giving away nothing. I held my breath. Then he moved on to the corn, taking a small, deliberate bite. More chewing, more poker face.

I was about to lose it when he finally looked up, a small smile tugging at his lips. "Interesting combination. I like the blend of flavors. It's different."

Different. That could go either way, right?

He nodded once, then moved on to the next station, leaving me standing there, my heart pounding out of my chest. I exhaled slowly, watching as the rest of the judges made their way through the room, tasting dish after dish. It felt like hours before they were finally done, but in reality, it was probably less than fifteen minutes.

The judges retreated to the far side of the room, huddled in quiet discussion. The room vibrated with restless excitement. The other contestants began whispering among themselves, shifting from foot to foot. My pulse refused to settle as I tried not to glance at the clock. Minutes dragged on like hours, until one of the judges cleared his throat and called us to the front.

We contestants all gathered at the front, the air thick with anticipation. I spotted Mrs. Maine a few feet away, her arms crossed, looking smug. Like she already knew she'd won. Well, I wasn't so sure.

The head judge, a woman with sharp features and a no-nonsense attitude, stepped up to the mic. "Thank you all for participating in today's competition," she began, her voice echoing through the room. "We've tasted some incredible dishes, and the decision was not easy."

I could feel my heart in my throat. *Come on, come on, just say it.*

"And the winner of the Robin Creek Citywide Cooking Contest is..."

CHAPTER 28
Joyce

It was dark by the time Gabriella returned. The door burst open, and she stood there, breathless and wide-eyed. "Joyce!" she shouted, practically vibrating with excitement. "I won!"

Before I could respond, she rushed toward me, enveloping me in the tightest hug I think she'd ever given me. "I won! And... and there's more! I got a cash prize and a meeting with one of the biggest restaurant owners in Houston!"

I laughed, pulling back just enough to look at her face, tears brimming in both of our eyes. "You did it! I knew you would!"

Gabriella's eyes were shining as she clutched my hands. "I couldn't have done this without you, Joyce. You've been there every step of the way. You, this house, the ideas in the Green Book to make foods that travel well. I swear, God brought us together!"

We hugged again, both crying and laughing at the same time, feeling the joy of her success ripple through the room.

"I'm so proud of you, Gabriella," I said, my voice thick with emotion. "This is just the beginning for you."

And as we stood there, wrapped in each other's arms, I couldn't help but think about how far we'd both come—together. Gabriella and I finally pulled apart from our hug. The excitement still buzzed in the air, but now it was a silent kind of joy, one that didn't need words. I watched as she wiped the tears from her eyes, grinning like a kid on Christmas morning.

"I still can't believe it," she whispered, more to herself than to me.

"You better believe it," I said, nudging her gently toward the kitchen. "Come on, let's sit down for a minute. I want to hear everything."

Gabriella laughed, the sound full of relief and pride, and followed me to the table. She was practically bouncing in her chair as she recounted the details—the intensity of the competition, how she stayed calm under pressure, and that final, glorious moment when they called her name.

"And Mrs. Maine?" I asked, raising an eyebrow.

"Oh, she performed this tiny little fake clap, like the people on the Miss America stage who didn't win the crown," Gabriella said, her eyes twinkling with mischief. She imitated the fake clap with exaggerated, dainty movements, her lips pressed together in a tight, forced smile. "She gave me that look—you know the one, like she couldn't believe I beat her."

I chuckled, shaking my head. "What I wouldn't give to see it! I told you, you were going to beat her one day."

She nodded, her face softening. "You were right. And it felt good. But not in the way I thought it would. It wasn't about proving her wrong, because, really, I think she's just a mean girl who never grew up. Did you see that movie *Mean Girls*?"

"I did."

"Good. I thought I was gonna have to explain it to you," she said with a fake wipe of her brow.

I elbowed her softly in return.

She laughed. "Just kidding. Really, this contest was about proving to myself that I could do it." She paused, biting her lip as if weighing her next words. "It's not just about winning today. It's about knowing I can make a real career out of this. For so long, cooking has been my passion, but now it feels possible. I can finally see myself running a restaurant or maybe opening my own food truck. This is my future, Joyce." She looked up at me, her eyes bright with the possibilities ahead. "Can I call you Auntie Joyce, by the way?"

My heart sang so loudly, I'm surprised Gabriella didn't hear it. "I'm honored to be your Auntie Joyce."

"Cool. Auntie Joyce, I'm glad to know that I don't have to spend my life performing for an imaginary audience."

Her words hit me deep, stirring something inside that I hadn't realized was still there. We weren't just talking about cooking anymore. This was about life—both hers and mine.

"I'm glad you know that now," I said quietly, squeezing her hand. "Because it's true. You are enough, Gabriella. Always have been."

Her smile faltered for a moment, but then it returned, brighter and stronger. "I just hope I keep remembering that."

"You will," I said firmly. "You've got the whole world ahead of you, and nothing can stop you now."

We sat there for a while, talking and laughing. The peace was short-lived, though, when my phone buzzed on the table. I glanced down, seeing Terri's name flash across the screen. My stomach tightened. I stared at it for a moment, my heart sinking as the buzz seemed to vibrate through me. My daughter and I hadn't talked properly in weeks—not since she'd sent Eric to pick up Elijah without so much as a conversation. Now, seeing her name flash up felt like a reminder of all the things we hadn't said.

"Terri," I said as I answered, trying to keep my voice steady.

"Hey, Momma," she said, her voice a little softer than usual. "I wanted to talk to you about Elijah."

I sighed, feeling that familiar tension creep back in. "How's he doing?"

There was a pause on the other end of the line before she answered. "He's okay. But... There's been some trouble with Dad."

I stiffened. "What kind of trouble?"

"He's just... You know how Dad is," she said, her words slow and careful, like she was choosing them deliberately. "He's strict. And Elijah... Well, he's not used to it. They've been butting heads."

I bit my lip, trying to hold back the sharp retort I felt bubbling up. It would've been easy to say something like *What did you expect? I've been trying to tell you about your daddy for years.* But I wasn't that person, and I didn't want to be. Not with my daughter.

"I can't say I'm surprised," I said gently instead. "Your father and Elijah are two different people."

"Yeah, I know," she said, her voice quiet. "I just... I'm not sure Dad's house is the best place for Elijah right now."

Her admission caught me off guard. It was the first time she'd ever openly questioned Eric, the man she had defended for so long. I could hear the uncertainty in her voice, the doubt she was trying to sort through.

"You know," I said carefully, "your father is a good man in a lot of ways. But he's not perfect. No one is."

There was a long pause, and I could almost hear the gears turning in her head. "Yeah," she said finally, almost to herself. "I guess I'm starting to see that."

I wanted to tell her more, to talk about how we'd both grown up seeing our parents through a certain lens and later learned that we were all just people doing the best we can. But I didn't push it. This was her journey, just like it had been mine.

"How much longer do you have to be in Tennessee?"

"Well, I might have to stay a few weeks longer since I took this break to come home and rescue Elijah from Dad."

If I'd had time, I would have gone to get Elijah, but the repair schedule wouldn't allow for any promises. If Anya didn't give the house 100 percent clearance, I might have to quickly perform follow-up repairs.

"I know you're only thinking about what's best for Elijah," I said. "That's all I've ever wanted for him, too. To be happy and safe."

"I know, Momma," she said, her voice soft again. "I just need to figure out what that looks like."

"And you will," I assured her. "You'll figure it out, Terri. And whatever you decide, I'm here. I am capable of taking care of him, no matter what that APS lady said to you."

Terri drew in a breath, like she had a big message she needed to exhale, but I could hear she'd stopped herself. I could only trust that whatever she had to say would come out at the right time and place. It wasn't for me to pull it out of her, as much as I wanted to.

We ended the call without any real resolution, but for the first time in a long time, I felt like Terri was starting to see her father for who he really was—a human being, flawed like the rest of us. Maybe with that revelation, she could begin to understand the woman I was becoming, too.

CHAPTER 29

The early-morning sun filtered through the windows as I looked around at the gathering crew. We'd made it this far—four hours on Sunday and already an hour of repairs Monday. My little community had come together in ways I never imagined possible.

Sunday had been a whirlwind. We'd managed to reseal half the windows, fix one of the more problematic bathroom pipes, and caulk every crack we could find near the doors and fixtures. Anya hadn't mentioned all these things, but Wardell didn't want to leave anything to chance.

Or maybe he was power-trippin', I don't know. Either way, there was plenty left to tackle on Monday. Now all that stood between me and APS's final approval was this last round of work.

Wardell, ever the leader, clapped his hands and ended our second break by reiterating our assignments. His voice rang out with authority as he pointed to different tasks. "All right, people! We've got caulking to finish in the old bathrooms and sealing the windows around the house. Lupita, you and Christine handle the last of the window seals. Liz, Althea, you're on the bathroom team.

Richard and I will wrap up the plumbing now that it's had some time to settle."

I watched as they each went off to their stations, a sense of urgency and determination filling the room.

Gabriella winked at me as she slipped into the kitchen, preparing to whip up something delicious for that after-work meal I'd promised everyone. "It'll be amazing," she whispered. I could hear the excitement in her voice. She was still floating from her victory on Saturday. This meal would be her first chance to cook as the champion she had always been inside.

An hour or so passed. I walked from room to room, checking in with everyone. Wardell and Richard were hunched over the water heater, working on tightening some pipes, while Liz and Althea chatted in the living room as they sealed the windows so tight not even an ant could find a way in.

I stood back, watching them all work, feeling that deep sense of change within myself. For so long, I'd been used to doing everything on my own. Independence had been my shield, more so after the divorce. The thought of needing anyone else had felt like weakness, something I couldn't afford. But here, watching my friends—no, my chosen family—working so hard to help me, I realized that independence doesn't mean doing everything alone. It means being strong enough to ask for help and to let people in.

A loud thud sounded from the living room, followed by Wardell's voice: "We got a problem here!"

I rushed in, my stomach tightening. "What's wrong?"

"The water heater pipe's loose again," Wardell said, frustration creeping into his tone. "I thought we had it fixed, but it's not holding the way it should. It's gonna need a new fitting."

A wave of anxiety washed over me. This was supposed to be

the last day. The final push before the APS inspection tomorrow. What if this one problem derailed everything?

Richard caught my eye. "We'll fix it, Joyce. It's just a small setback. Don't worry."

I nodded, trusting him even though my nerves were frayed. "All right. What do we need?"

"I'll head to the hardware store," Richard said, wiping his hands on his jeans. "You want to come with me, Joyce?"

I hesitated for a moment, torn between going with him and staying to keep an eye on the work, but something in Richard's eyes said I needed to get away. "Sure," I said, grabbing my purse. "Let's go."

"Just ask for Jessie," Lupita reminded us as we headed out the door. "He knows the discount."

As Richard and I cruised down the road, I couldn't help but think about how different this moment would have been if it had been Eric sitting beside me. We were both the panic type, always convinced that disaster lurked around every corner. Every little thing felt like a crisis. I guess that was part of what made us work—our shared fear of the sky falling, of losing control. Over time, though, that kind of living drains you. It leaves you exhausted, empty. And maybe, I realized now, I was just as much to blame for feeding into it as he was. I'd been caught in that cycle of thinking the worst, seeing the worst, expecting the worst.

But sitting here with Richard, with his quiet calm. It felt like a release. Like I didn't have to be on guard all the time because, truth be told, almost none of the things I'd feared ever happened in my life.

I sat with that truth for a moment and allowed myself to get a different picture about tomorrow. Anya would come, inspect the house, and check off every box. She'd leave me alone after that, and my life would go back to normal. Gabriella's, too.

This was the mental picture I painted for myself, and the picture was so much brighter. So much healthier.

I could get used to this.

As we walked down the aisles, scanning for the right part, Richard finally spoke. "You know, Joyce, watching you with all these people… It's like you've created something here. A family."

I stopped in my tracks, surprised by his observation, though I had to agree it was true. "I was just thinking the same. Isn't it beautiful?"

He smiled softly, his hand brushing against mine as we continued walking. "You're not the only one who's changed, you know. These past few weeks, being here with you, it's made me realize something."

I looked up at him, suddenly aware of the warmth in his eyes.

"I've been falling for you, Joyce," he said quietly, his voice steady but full of emotion. "And I know it's probably the worst timing with everything going on. And I know you're not looking for a hero to sweep you off your feet, but I needed to tell you."

My heart skipped a beat. I wasn't expecting this, not today. But deep down, I knew. I'd felt it, too—the way we'd been growing closer, the way he'd been there for me without asking for anything in return.

"Richard, I…" I hesitated, the words caught in my throat. After the divorce, I'd promised myself I'd never let anyone in again. I'd been so sure that I was done with love, done with men, done with all the work it takes to bring two minds and backgrounds and experiences into agreement.

But standing here, in this hardware store of all places, I realized something. Richard wasn't asking me to shrink. He wasn't offering to swoop in and fix my life. He just wanted to be there—by my side.

"I feel the same way," I admitted, my voice barely above a whisper. "But I've been scared of getting hurt again. Scared of falling into a pattern."

Richard nodded, his hand reaching for mine and holding it gently. "I get it. And I'm not asking you to rush into anything. I just... I want you to know that I'm here. For whatever you need."

We stood there for a moment. It wasn't a grand declaration, but it didn't need to be. It was simple, honest, and exactly what I needed.

"Thank you," I whispered, squeezing his hand.

He smiled. "Come on. Let's get this part and head back. We've got a water heater to fix."

By the time we returned, the smell of Gabriella's cooking had filled the house. The aroma of spices and fresh-chopped garnishes wrapped around me like a warm hug, reminding me that this was my new home.

Wardell had everything back under control, and the repairs were moving along smoothly again. "You got it?" he asked as Richard and I walked in.

"Got it," Richard said, holding up the fitting.

As they worked on the final repairs, I wandered into the kitchen, where Gabriella was busy stirring a pot on the stove. "Smells like Mary and Martha and Jesus and all the disciples are cooking in here," I said, leaning against the counter.

She grinned at me. "You're going to love it. I'm making a little somethin' new I've been working on."

"You spoil us," I teased, but the truth was, I didn't mind one bit.

Just then, I heard the front door swing open, and Althea greeted someone whose voice I didn't catch right away.

I left Gabriella for the living room, where Miss Mary had poked her head inside. "Oh, hey, Li'l Joy," she said with a mischievous smile. "Thought I'd see if you needed a taste-tester."

We all laughed, and Lupita waved her in. "Come on in, Mary."

"Mighty fine. I need to get you to sign for receipt of this letter, Li'l Joy," Mary told me as I approached her, seeing as it was my home.

I wasn't expecting any packages, so this came as a surprise. My eyes scanned the envelope—plain, except for the certified mail sticker in the top corner. My heart skipped a beat as I took it from her and signed the receipt. Miss Mary lingered by the door, watching me with her usual curiosity.

"What is it?" Gabriella asked, peering over my shoulder.

I shrugged, sliding a finger under the flap to open it. The paper inside was thick and official looking, not like the junk mail I'd been getting since I moved in.

"Looks fancy," Wardell said from across the room. He was fiddling with a wrench, but his attention was clearly on me now. In fact, it seemed like Miss Mary and everyone in the house was now vested in my certified parcel.

I unfolded the letter, my eyes catching on the bold header: *Notice of Property Title Transfer—Finalized*. There was no one to contest the transfer, so this was only a technicality. But still... It was done.

For a moment, I just stared at it. The words blurred, and I had to blink a few times to focus. This was it. The official transfer of my grandmother's house. My house. A symbol of the independence I had fought so hard for, the freedom I'd always craved. And now, I was standing in it, fully owning the space and everything it represented. But instead of retreating into this house all by myself, I'd opened it up to people who cared about me.

I looked around at everyone: Eileen, Liz, Sonia, Christine, Wardell, Lupita, Althea, Richard, and Gabriella—and now Miss Mary. This was home now.

Gabriella touched my arm gently. "Are you okay?"

I nodded. I swallowed the lump in my throat. "Yeah. It's just... This is the final paperwork. The house is officially mine now."

"Oh, Auntie Joyce, that's amazing!" Gabriella grinned, wrapping me in a hug. The others caught on quickly, and soon I was surrounded by congratulations and pats on the back.

"About time you got this place in your name," Miss Mary said, wagging her finger at me. "Should've done that years ago, but I understand. Some things take time."

"I didn't realize how much I was holding on to," I said softly, more to myself than anyone else.

"Well, it's yours now, honey," Miss Mary said, her voice gentle. "And you've done a beautiful job bringing it back to life. I'm proud of you." Then she sniffed the air. "What is that smellin' so good?"

"My surprise," Gabriella sassed. "You want me to save you some?"

"Absolutely," Miss Mary chirped. "Soon as I make it around these last few blocks, I'll be right back here!"

Wardell commanded us to get back to work, and we finished the jobs just as Miss Mary returned and Gabriella's cousin dropped by with the main course, which my little friend had basically hidden from us until it was time for the big reveal. Gabriella had outdone herself this time. She presented us with enchiladas filled with tender, slow-cooked brisket, topped with a creamy chipotle sauce. On the side were her famous elote cups—sweet corn with cotija cheese, chili powder, and a hint of lime—and a watermelon salad with a tangy Tajín drizzle that balanced the heat of the enchiladas perfectly. The colors on the table were as vibrant as the flavors promised to be, and everyone let out a collective "ooh" as she set it down.

They all gathered around, plates clattering as everyone served themselves. Wardell was the first to dive in, and after a few bites, he nodded in appreciation. "This is it, y'all. The food's too good. Feels like we're havin' the Last Supper before Joyce faces APS tomorrow."

The group chuckled, though the joke was a little morbid. Still, I took it in stride, feeling strangely at ease. As I looked around the table at my friends, all laughing and enjoying the meal, I knew deep down that no matter what happened, I was going to be okay.

That night, I lay in bed, scrolling through the group text messages on my phone. Everyone was saying they'd had a wonderful time, commenting on Gabriella's food, joking about how sore they'd be in the morning.

I laughed to myself, feeling my own bones creak as I shifted under the covers. For the first time in a long time, I felt...content. At peace. When I tell you it was priceless, I mean just that.

I sent up a silent prayer, thanking God for bringing these people into my life and asking for strength and peace for Elijah and for myself.

Tomorrow's visit from APS would come with its own challenges, but for tonight, I was grateful. Grateful for the journey, the people, and the hope that had been restored in this little house that had become my home—every nail, every floorboard, and even my shiny new oven.

CHAPTER 30

I stood by the front window, peeking through the curtains for the umpteenth time. Anya was due any minute. Gabriella, bless her heart, was busy in the kitchen, making enough coffee to jazz up an entire army. But as for me? I couldn't sit still.

"You okay, Auntie Joyce?" Gabriella called from the kitchen. Her voice had that sweet lilt of care, like she knew how nervous I was but was trying not to make a big deal about it.

"I'm fine," I muttered, though I wasn't sure if I believed it. "I just wish she'd get here already."

Just then, the faint sound of tires slowing, then rolling across the rocks in my driveway, caused a pounding in my chest. It was Anya. For a second, I thought about pretending like I wasn't home. Or maybe Gabriella could tell her I'd gotten sick.

But I knew that wouldn't solve anything. All the people who had helped me deserved to know that their work wasn't in vain. We did this together.

Gabriella poked her head out from the kitchen, an eyebrow raised. "That better be Anya, or this coffee's going to waste."

I smirked despite my nerves and took a deep breath before

pulling the door open. Sure enough, Anya stood on the porch, tablet in hand, her expression as unreadable as ever. She looked exactly as she had the last time—right down to the same black kitten heels. It was like she had a uniform, one of those ten-item wardrobes everyone claims makes life easier.

It occurred to me for the first time that while I was stressed out today, Anya must have a stressful job every day. She'd probably made some hard recommendations, taken away keys, removed children from guardianship due to true elder abuse.

Surprisingly, compassion for her showed up in the midst of my fears. Miss Mary had been right about Anya's plight. She wasn't the enemy here—she was just thoroughly doing her job, and a tough one at that.

"Ms. Hicks," she said, nodding in greeting. "Ready for the inspection?"

"As ready as I'll ever be," I replied, trying to keep my voice steady.

Before I could invite her in, the sound of footsteps behind me caught my attention. Gabriella came out of the kitchen, wiping her hands on a towel. "Hey, Anya!" she said brightly. "We've got coffee if you want any. Auntie Joyce made sure we were ready for you."

Anya's eyes flickered between the two of us, her stoic expression softening slightly. "Coffee sounds good, but first let's get this inspection started."

"Sure. Right this way." I pointed toward Gabriella's hallway again.

As I turned to lead the way, Gabriella gave me a quick, silent nod. I could feel her reassurance, like she was telling me without words: *You've got this. We've got this.* I took a breath and nodded back, my heart calming ever so slightly.

I guided Anya through the house, trying not to hover but failing miserably. Every creak of the floorboards, every tiny imperfection, felt magnified in that moment. Anya inspected everything with the precision of a surgeon, jotting down notes on her tablet, taking pictures, running her hand along the edges of the windows, checking the caulking, and testing the plumbing.

I followed her silently, every step filled with anticipation. My mind raced through everything Wardell, Richard, and the others had worked on. Surely we hadn't missed anything…right?

Just as Anya was bending down to check the baseboards, there was a knock at the door.

I froze, shooting Gabriella a look that screamed *Who's that?*

Gabriella shrugged, heading toward the door. "Probably just a friendly face," she said with a wink, swinging the door open.

Sure enough, Richard stood there, a casual smile on his face. "Hey, I was in the neighborhood and thought I'd stop by. How's the inspection going?"

I raised an eyebrow, but before I could say anything, Eileen showed up right behind him, holding a tin. "I brought a little something for after the inspection," she said, beaming. "Thought you could use the sugar boost." She lifted the lid slightly, revealing a few dozen cookies. "Chocolate chip."

I couldn't help but chuckle at the timing. "Y'all just 'happened' to stop by, huh?"

Richard rubbed the back of his neck sheepishly. "Moral support, Joyce. You know we've got your back."

Anya watched the scene unfold, her clipboard lowered now and a hint of a smile tugging at the corner of her mouth. "You've got quite the team here, Ms. Hicks," she said.

I nodded, glancing around at Gabriella, Richard, and Eileen.

"Thank you both for coming," I said softly, realizing just how much that meant.

The three of them followed Anya and me toward the kitchen, and that's when the real show began. Richard, Eileen, and Gabriella were practically breathing down Anya's neck, making comments as she moved from room to room.

"Look at that caulking job!" Richard said, a little too enthusiastically, pointing to the kitchen windows. "Sealed tighter than a drum."

Eileen chimed in, leaning over to inspect the same window. "And don't you just love how smooth the plumbing work is now? That's craftsmanship!"

Gabriella gave a knowing smile but didn't say a word, just watched the show unfold.

I caught Anya's eyes for a split second, and there it was—the tiniest smirk tugging at her lips. She knew exactly what was going on but wasn't about to ruin it. Her professional demeanor stayed intact, but I could tell she was amused. *All right, all right,* I thought. *Maybe we're overdoing it just a bit.*

Anya finished her inspection of the last room and straightened up, her pen hovering over her clipboard as she prepared to give her final assessment.

Just as she opened her mouth to speak, there was another knock at the door.

"Oh, Lord," I muttered under my breath. "Who now?"

It was Wardell and Christine, stepping inside like they'd been invited to a cookout. "Hey there!" Wardell boomed, his eyes immediately taking in the scene. "Saw all the cars in the lot and figured there must be a party goin' on!"

Anya raised an eyebrow but stayed silent, watching as Wardell surveyed the room like he didn't know exactly what was happening. "Well, don't this place look mighty fine!" he said, nodding approvingly. "Who's this?" he asked, gesturing toward Anya like he hadn't a clue.

Anya, keeping her composure, said, "My name is Anya. And I agree with you. It looks like several construction pros came through here for these repairs, great and small."

Wardell puffed out his chest and couldn't help but grin. "Well, you know… We do what we can," he said, obviously pleased with himself.

Christine rolled her eyes and gave him a playful slap on the arm.

"Christine, Wardell," I interjected, trying to steer the moment back to the main event, "Anya was just about to let us know her final thoughts."

"Well," Anya began, glancing over her notes, her eyes scanning the room one last time. "Everything seems to be in order. The repairs are solid, the plumbing is fixed, and the windows are sealed properly. I'm happy to say that your house has passed inspection, Ms. Hicks."

A wave of relief washed over me, my knees nearly buckling from the release of tension. I'd been holding my breath for so long, I wasn't even sure I remembered how to exhale. Applause and a few hoots ensued right there in my living room.

"Thank you, Anya," I managed to say, my voice clogged with emotion.

"Take the wheel!" Eileen hollered to the ceiling. Clearly, she was fully healed from all sickness and disease.

She quickly covered her lips and told Anya, "It's an inside thing."

Anya nodded, her eyes softening. "You all have done a great job here." She faced me now. "And it's clear you've got people around you who care. That's just as important as the repairs." She took a bite of her cookie.

Gabriella let out a cheer, rushing over to hug me tightly. "I told you we had this!"

Richard clapped me on the back, grinning from ear to ear. "And I told you not to worry, Joyce."

Even Eileen looked like she was about to tear up, and I couldn't help but feel overwhelmed by the love and support that filled the room.

Anya gathered her things and made her way to the door. "Good luck with everything, Ms. Hicks. You've earned it. I'll send confirmation of the closed case in an email later today." She turned to Christine. "And thanks for the cookie. It's delicious."

"Any time, sweetheart. But not at my house, you hear?" Christine warned.

Wardell jumped in with "It'd be all right either way. She already knows the quality of my work."

Anya smile politely. "I'll let myself out, if that's okay."

"Sure thing," I said. "And you take care of yourself, young lady. Do more of what makes you smile, you hear?"

"Yes, ma'am." My house-worries walked out the door with her.

"Looks like you're not going anywhere, Auntie Joyce," Gabriella said, grabbing a cookie for herself.

I laughed, feeling lighter than I had in years. "Looks like it."

But before I could say anything else, Richard stepped closer, his eyes meeting mine in a way that made my heart skip a beat. He leaned in and pressed a soft kiss to my cheek, and for a moment, everything went still.

I blinked, caught off guard by the tenderness of it. Without thinking, I turned and kissed him back—on the lips.

The room went silent, and when I pulled away, I could see the surprise in everyone's eyes, and I felt my own eyes bugging out. But instead of feeling awkward or embarrassed, I felt…joy.

"I see you, Auntie Joyce!" Gabriella teased, her eyes wide with playful shock. "Going for it, huh?"

I grinned, shaking my head at her antics, but inside, I knew she was right. I wasn't just surviving—I was living.

Joyce Hicks was back and better than ever…even if I was a little late to my own life's show.

CHAPTER 31

Wednesday morning, I walked into the office with a newfound sense of peace, feeling like a different person. The fiasco of the house, the repairs, the APS drama—it was all behind me. My coworkers must have noticed the change, because more than one of them commented on my smile, asking what had me so happy. "Just life," I responded, and I meant it.

The week flew by in a blur of good news and smiles that I couldn't seem to wipe off my face. Anya's inspection had gone better than I could have hoped for, and it felt like crossing the finish line after a long race.

Richard and I had been texting back and forth all week, making plans for a Friday-night date. It felt strange but exciting to be planning a date again after all these years.

Gabriella was equally thrilled—she was preparing to head out to Houston for her meeting with the chef she'd met after winning the contest.

Friday came faster than expected. I dropped Gabriella off at the airport early that morning. When we finally pulled up to the Departures curb, Gabriella hopped out and yanked her suitcase from the back seat. She was so full of nerves!

I parked and put on my emergency lights to give her a hug that would hopefully calm her down.

"This is it, huh?" she said, her voice shaking slightly. "I still can't believe I'm doing this."

"You're more than ready," I said, standing back to look her square in the eye. "You've earned this, Gabriella. And when you come back, you'll be better than ever. They're lucky to have you this week in Houston, and that little bed-and-breakfast downtown is lucky to have you as head chef when you return. Not sure how long you'll be there, though, at the rate you're learning."

She gave me a wide smile. "I wouldn't have made it this far without you. You've been...everything. I don't know how to thank you."

"You already have," I said. "You've been such a light in the house, Gabriella. You're going to do great things, and I'm so proud of you."

We hugged tightly, and for a moment, neither of us moved. When we finally let go, Gabriella wiped her eyes and gave me one last, determined nod.

"When I get back, we're going to celebrate," she said, grinning through the tears.

"I wouldn't miss it for the world," I said, feeling the pride thrum through my heart. Gabriella's success might mean I'd need to work full-time for the next two years, of course. But I'd always been a hard worker; what else was new?

She grabbed the handle of her bag and headed inside the airport, glancing back one more time to wave. And just like that, she was off. The next chapter of her life had officially begun, and I knew that whatever happened, Gabriella's future was bright. I was glad to bask in the light with her.

I headed off to work. By the time I got home from working a full shift that day—I was granted some extra hours on our busy Fridays—I was ready to settle into the evening and get ready for my date with Richard. I opened the door to my house, already thinking about what I'd wear and whether I should text him to confirm the time. But before I could even set down my things good, the doorbell rang.

I frowned, glancing at the clock. Richard couldn't be here this early—he had said he'd pick me up at six, an hour from now. I opened the door, expecting maybe a neighbor or someone selling something. But instead, there they were—Terri and Elijah, standing on my doorstep like a blast from the past.

"Grandma!" Elijah shouted, running straight into my arms, hugging me so tightly I could barely breathe. The warmth of his little body against mine made my heart burst with joy, and for a moment, I didn't care about the surprise visit.

"Hey, EJ!" I said, bending down to hug him back. "What are you doing here?"

Elijah pulled away just enough to look up at me with his wide, innocent eyes. "Momma said we could come surprise you. Is that okay?"

I smiled, running a hand over his hair. "Of course it's okay. I'm always happy to see you."

Terri stood behind him, looking both exasperated and unsure. She wore her locs pulled up in a ponytail, her khaki jumpsuit had an uncharacteristic dirty spot on it, and the dark circles under her eyes said she was here on her last bit of energy. "Hey, Momma," she said, stepping forward to give me a short hug.

"Terri. Good to see you as well," I said sincerely, concerned for my daughter. The stitch of strife dissolved away. Terri was a workhorse; it takes one to know one. "What brings y'all all the way to Robin Creek?" I stepped aside and opened the door wider, welcoming them inside.

I wasn't sure how I expected her to answer my question. Surely she wouldn't lie and say she was checking on me. Even as I stood there watching my daughter collapse onto the couch, I made up a story in my mind. EJ and Eric had a falling-out. Terri left her training to get back home and resolve things, standing in the gap between her husband, her child, and her father.

God knows I know that role.

Terri sighed. "The APS lady reached out to let me know everything was all right with the house."

I blinked, caught off guard. *Anya?* I hadn't expected her to follow up with Terri about the inspection, but maybe it was her way of showing Terri that I had things under control.

"Well, yeah. Everything's fine," I said, trying to process the situation. I sat next to her, but immediately another knock came at the door. I hoisted myself up to answer it for a second time. When I opened it, there stood one of Elijah's little neighborhood friends, holding his bike with one hand and looking hopeful. "Can Elijah come out and play?"

I glanced at Terri, who gave me a slight nod, and then back at Elijah. "Sure, but stay close to the house, okay?"

"Okay!" Elijah bolted out the door, the boy following close behind.

With Elijah safely outside, I turned to Terri and motioned for her to follow me to the kitchen. "Come on, let's sit for a minute. I've got some of Gabriella's food left over. You're going to love it."

The kitchen was filled with the lingering aromas of the Blaxican fusion Gabriella had made before heading to Lubbock.

It was like the smells had soaked into the walls, making the whole house feel warm and inviting. I pulled out a couple of plates and started warming up the leftovers, aware of Terri's eyes on me the entire time.

"So," she began, leaning against the counter, "you're really okay, huh?"

I glanced at her, trying to read the tone behind her question. Was she worried? Skeptical? "I am," I replied simply, setting the plates down on the counter. "Better than I've been in a long time, actually."

Terri's brows furrowed, and she crossed her arms over her chest. "It's just… I guess I've always thought of you as…well, you know…reliable. Predictable. You were always the one who kept everything together no matter what."

I nodded, taking a deep breath before I answered. "I know. I still am reliable. But that doesn't mean I don't have a life of my own. I love you and Elijah, but I'm more than just someone you can call to handle things at the drop of a hat."

Terri blinked, her expression softening. "I didn't mean it like that. It's just… You've always been the one who sacrificed for everyone. I guess I never thought about you having your own life outside of Daddy and me and Eric Jr."

I smiled, feeling a strange mix of pride and sadness. "That's the thing, Terri. I still love you, but I also deserve to live my life the way I want. I've spent so many years taking care of everyone else, and now I'm finally taking care of myself."

Terri's eyes widened slightly as she processed my words, and for the first time, I saw a flicker of understanding cross her face.

I cut to the truth. "So, what happened with your father and Elijah?"

Her shoulders fell. She shifted uncomfortably in her seat. Then she covered her eyes with one hand. "Sheeesh. I mean, Elijah is kind and smart, and he's also a child who speaks his mind."

"And?"

"And Dad classifies a child telling you they'd rather take a shower than a bath as talking back. They clashed. Dad tried to spank him. Elijah ran next door to the Woodsons' house. Thank God they called me instead the police, or there'd be *another* investigation in the family. With one phone call, you know."

"Yes, I absolutely *do* know," I emphatically agreed. I went so far as to raise my hand like I was about to testify on a witness stand. "One phone call, one person's interpretation of events, and—poof—you're on the wrong side an inquiry. Suspect number one."

Her head lolled up and down. "I know, I know."

"No, you *don't* know," I continued, not coming from a place of anger, but a place of hurt. It was time to speak my truth to her, to name my feelings so we could deal with them together. "You didn't call me when you got faulty information from APS. Instead, you called your father. Sent him here to get Elijah without so much as an opportunity for me to let you know what was really happening. That hurt, Terri," I said, not even trying to keep my voice steady.

She stared down at her lap. "I'm sorry. I just… I'm so angry about you and Dad breaking up," she gushed, and tears sprang from her eyes. "My parents… You two are my rock. Together. It feels like my whole foundation has crumbled way because *you* decided Daddy wasn't good enough for you anymore."

It bit my lip to keep from defending myself. I was past that now.

Terri sniffled, wiped her nose, and continued, "But then… When EJ called me crying, begging me to get him from Paw-Paw's house, I knew..." She shook her head. "Dad's always been a hard-nose, but he's so much harsher without you. I knew you'd been kind of a buffer all this time. But I just now realized that the person who is the buffer has to absorb all the sharp edges. And there's only so much one person can take."

For a brief moment, I felt vindicated. All the years I'd spent trying to shield Terri and EJ from Eric's worst tendencies were finally being seen for what they were. But the satisfaction was short-lived. My heart broke as I watched the realization settle over my daughter's face, the slow unraveling of her image of her father. Every child deserves to hold on to their heroes for as long as they can, and now Terri had to let go. And poor EJ—so desperate, so shaken, that he'd begged her to come get him. It was almost too much to bear, but I kept my face steady. I couldn't apologize for the choices I'd made to protect myself, and I certainly wasn't going to gloat over what felt like a bittersweet victory. This wasn't a triumph; it was a reckoning, and no one was walking away unscathed.

"You don't have to be the buffer," I told her. "You're EJ's mom. You do what's best for him. And set some healthy boundaries with your father, for your own sanity."

"I guess... I guess I never thought moms have a limit. That sounds terrible, doesn't it?"

I paused for a moment, considering her words. It didn't sound terrible to me—it sounded like the truth. The truth that so many mothers live with, carrying the burden of their children's expectations, their husbands' expectations, society's expectations, without ever stopping to consider what's helpful to themselves.

"No, Terri. It doesn't sound terrible. It sounds like the way a lot of people see their moms," I said, sliding her plate across the table.

"But I'm not a rock. I'm human. I have feelings, needs, dreams... just like you do."

Terri looked down at the plate in front of her, her fingers tracing the edges of the napkin. She didn't say anything for a long moment, and I could see the wheels turning in her head.

"I'm sorry, Momma," she finally said. "I didn't mean to assume that the divorce was all your fault..."

She trailed off, and I saw the tension in her shoulders, the way she tried to hold herself together. It was the same way I used to hold myself together—strong, composed, but always on the edge of breaking. It hurt to see her like that, but I knew this was her journey. Sometimes the hardest truths are the ones that set us free.

I squeezed her hand, my heart breaking for her. "I know it's complicated, baby. But you're not alone. We'll figure it out together, but you must let go of this notion that you have to manage your father. You've got a son and a whole husband, child."

Terri nodded, wiping her eyes. "I just... I don't want to lose Dad, too."

"No, no, nooooo!" I drew her in for a hug. "You haven't lost me, Terri. I'm right here for you, for EJ, for your husband, your brother. Just because I'm not married to your father doesn't mean I've abandoned you."

Terri sniffled again, and her body relaxed in my embrace.

I stopped talking, giving my words the silence they needed to sink in. This was growth—this was her realizing that she didn't have to carry the weight of the world on her shoulders.

Terri sat up and glanced at the clock on the wall and her eyes widened. "Oh no. I didn't realize it was getting so late! I have to get back on the road soon. I have a ton of work to catch up on before Monday. Is it okay for Elijah to stay here for the last week of summer?"

I set my fork down and looked her square in the eye. "Terri, I love Elijah, and I love spending time with him. But Gabriella's gone, and I'm about to go on a date. You can't just drop him off and expect me to rearrange my plans tonight."

Terri's eyes widened in surprise. "A date? You're going on a date?"

"Yes," I said firmly, not allowing her tone to shake me. "I'm going on a date. And while I'm happy to watch Elijah for this last week, you're going to have to stay with him until later tonight. I have plans, and I'm not canceling them."

Shock painted her face as she tried to process this new version of me—the version who didn't drop everything for her, the version who had boundaries.

"But, Momma—"

"Terri," I said, interrupting her before she could finish, "would you ever go to anyone else's house, drop your child off unannounced, and expect them to drop everything for you?"

She blinked, caught off guard by the question. "No, of course not. But this is different. Elijah's your grandson."

"And I love him more than anything in the world," I replied. "But I'm also a person, Terri. A person with a life of my own. And tonight, I'm asking you to make adjustments for *me*, just like I've made them for you all these years."

"I never thought about it that way," she admitted.

"Well, now's a good time to start," I replied, smiling gently. "You've got a life to live, and so do I. But we can still love each other and be there for each other without losing ourselves in the process."

Terri sat there, her fingers toying with the edge of the table, absorbing everything I'd said. I could see the mental gymnastics happening right before my eyes. Part of me felt a little guilty for pushing this realization on her so suddenly. But the other part of me—the part that had been exhausted by the constant self-sacrifice—knew that it was necessary. Besides, she was the one who'd suddenly popped up on my doorstep.

"I get it, Terri. This is new for both of us."

She gave me a small, hesitant smile in return. There was still a lot left unsaid between us, but this moment felt like a turning point. For once, we weren't playing the same roles we'd been stuck in for so long. We were beginning to meet each other as equals—as two women, navigating life and motherhood, trying to find balance without losing ourselves in the process.

Just then, the doorbell rang again. I smiled, knowing exactly who it was.

Terri looked at me, her eyebrows raised in question. "Is that…?"

"Yes," I said with a grin. "That's my date."

Terri blinked, clearly still trying to wrap her head around this development. But she didn't say anything, just nodded as I made my way to the door.

When I opened it, there stood Richard, looking as handsome as ever in his casual button-up shirt and jeans. His smile was warm, and just seeing him there eased the last bit of nervousness that had been lingering in the pit of my stomach since Terri had walked in.

"You look beautiful." His lips pressed against my cheek. "You ready for our night out?"

"Almost," I replied, stepping aside to let him in. "First, I want you to meet someone."

Richard's eyes followed me to where Terri was sitting at the kitchen table. For a moment, she didn't move, her eyes darting between me and Richard as if trying to piece together a puzzle she hadn't known existed. Then, just as quickly, her expression shifted. She squared her shoulders, her lips pressing into a thin line, like she was ready to go into full-on protective mode.

"Terri, this is my friend, Richard," I said, my voice calm and steady. "Richard, this is my daughter, Terri."

Richard extended his hand, his smile as easy and genuine as always. "It's nice to meet you, Terri."

Terri took his hand, shaking it slowly, her eyes sizing him up. "Nice to meet you, too."

There was a brief silence, the kind that usually happens when two important parts of your life finally collide. But Richard, being the easygoing person he was, didn't seem fazed by it at all. He just stood there, his hand resting lightly at his side, waiting for whatever was going to happen next.

Terri looked from Richard to me and then back again. "So… you two are…?"

"We're dating," I said simply, deciding there was no point in dancing around it. "And tonight we're going out."

"Okay," she said slowly, her eyes narrowing just slightly as she studied me. "I guess I wasn't expecting all this."

I chuckled, crossing my arms over my chest. "Well, neither was I, but here we are."

Another pause, and then something shifted in Terri's expression. It wasn't judgment, exactly—more like acceptance and realization of facts.

"Well, I hope you have a good time," she finally said, her voice softening just a little.

"We will," I said with a nod, glancing at Richard, who gave me a reassuring smile.

I motioned toward the table. "Go on and sit down. Have some

more of Gabriella's food. There's more than enough for you and Elijah to eat tonight. You know you want to."

"Okay, Momma," she said, walking back to the table.

Before I left, I placed a gentle hand on Terri's shoulder. "I love you, Terri. You're doing the best you can, and that's enough. But tonight is for me."

"What time will you be back?"

"When I get back."

Terri looked up at me, her expression one of surprise and maybe even admiration. "Have a good time, Momma."

With that, I left the house with Richard, ready for the first night of my new life—one where I was finally learning how to make myself one of the top priorities, without guilt, without hesitation.

I wasn't just stepping out into the unknown. I was stepping into my own, with open arms and a full heart.

READ ON FOR MORE HEARTWARMING FICTION FROM MICHELLE STIMPSON IN *SISTERS WITH A SIDE OF GREENS.*

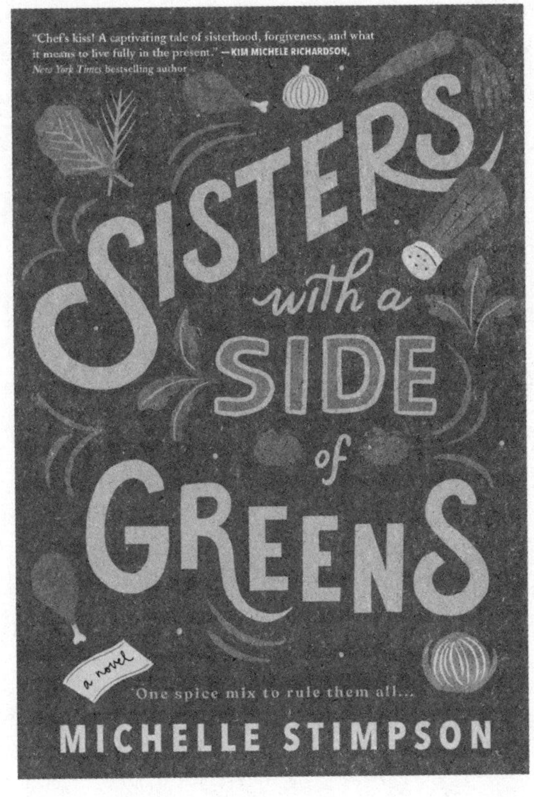

Available now from
Sourcebooks Landmark

CHAPTER 1
Rose

Some days, you wake up, and you're supposed to feel different, but you don't. Take, for example, your birthday, your anniversary, the first day of the year. You want to be excited, but it's just another day, like all the days before it. I mean, it's definitely a blessing that most of the days in my fifty-nine years of life were just normal. No big, huge, breath-snatching tragedies, unless you count the day my husband left me for another woman, which I do *not* count as a tragedy because the truth is: my husband wanted a wife, but he didn't want to be a husband. Kind of like when you want to be fit, but you don't actually want to be one of those exercise-y people. And you want to eat dessert every night.

Dessert is good. So are wives. Really, who *wouldn't* want a wife? Somebody tending to hearth and home, somebody society says should be loyal, faithful, and respectful to you? Shoot, I want a wife, myself.

I know the ideal is for men to reciprocate for women. But that's not the everyday reality—especially not the faithful part, because we have an actual dictionary-word for a husband's other woman. Right there between "mistreat" and "mistrial" lies the word "mistress."

Wives, however, don't have a word for our "other" man in the entire English language. I'm not advocating for us to have a cheat-word. I'm just saying us not having one declares, "It's so unacceptable for a woman to do this, we ain't makin' a word for it, ma'am."

Maybe our word could be misteress?

Anyway. David leaving me was not tragic, nor was it unexpected.

Neither was my retirement day. Except it actually was a pivotal day, marking a line in my life's sand.

That morning, I got up, washed with my winter vanilla bean–scented scrub, whipped the bonnet off my head, moisturized my platinum-blond kinks, and let them point wherever they pleased. I pulled, zipped, buttoned, and buckled my uniform into place. The light-blue short-sleeve knit shirt bore the United States Postal Service logo, a white eagle on a darker blue square. How many times had I caught sight of this patch out of the corner of my eye and thought, "Is that a spot? No, it's the eagle."

I took one last look in my bathroom mirror and, mentally blocking out the bottles of beautifying potions strewn across my countertop, gave myself a once-over.

Not bad for fifty-nine and retired. Not bad at all.

I had beat the system a little by dyeing my short Afro blond before the gray could claim victory. My waistline was still present, aided by a standard-issue leather belt. Okay, the waist got exaggerated by the belt, but I was still glad to own one. That belt was the only "sexy" thing in my wardrobe, if one could count a black garrison belt as "sexy." My fashion preferences and penchant for jewelry died soon after I started working for the government. What hadn't suffered was my smooth, barely wrinkled skin. It brought plenty of speculation from strangers. I could tell by their age-related questioning. "Do you have kids? Or grand—"

I'd shake my head before they could finish, not offering an explanation. In my thirties and forties, the question about children gut-punched me every time. David and I never had children. We couldn't. Actually, *I* couldn't.

People need to mind their own business.

I slid balm across my full lips and gave them a solid smack. I smiled at myself. My dimples winked back. It was time to go to work one last time.

After warming up a frozen frittata and pouring coffee into a thermos, I breezed past the refrigerator and headed toward the garage door. I'm not sure exactly what happened, but somehow my knee caught the corner of the wall, and I swear it felt like an ax whomped my left kneecap. Glass broke. Time collapsed. I dropped the thermos and grabbed my knee, as though holding it would relieve the pain that became my entire existence in an instant.

Somehow—I must have hopped?—I made it to a chair in my dinette and sat, rocking back and forth, as I rubbed the throbbing knee with both hands. That's when I saw the picture of Momma on the floor. The glass protecting her airbrushed photo had split in three places, but her dark, beautiful face wasn't scratched. I'd get another frame. A better one, which was something I'd been meaning to do, anyway. Momma deserved to be remembered in something more than a cheap certificate holder moonlighting as a frame.

The thought that I'd be late to work tried to enter my consciousness. I was too busy rocking my knee and thinking about my mother. Besides, I'd been late to work before. What could they do to me today?

Ten minutes later, I'd recovered enough to free Momma from the broken glass and attempt to reset her picture in the frame.

That's when I saw the words written on back of her photo. *My Rose, Keep God first, family second, and you will bloom into all your dreams coming true.* If memory served correctly, my sister had given me the picture, already mounted inside the frame. So I had never seen these words before. It was a good thing I'd never seen Momma's handwriting, her demands, the promise she didn't have the authority to make, on the back of her picture.

For the thousandth time, I disagreed with my mother. I laid the picture and the frame on the dining table, unassembled. No time to ponder her presumptuous words.

I hobbled into my car and drove the seven miles from my home to the post office, something I had done for the previous fifteen years. Before then, I had driven twelve miles, back when I lived in the Oak Cliff area of Dallas. After the divorce, I moved into a smaller place and prayed I wouldn't get relocated due to all the cutbacks.

My prayers were answered. I'd remained at the closest post office most of my thirty-one-year career with the United States Postal Service.

Traveling the familiar—dare I say mundane—route to work, I wondered for the first time if I should have prayed that prayer to stay at the post office. Not just the location, the job itself. What if I'd gotten laid off, fired, or forced into early retirement? Would my desperation have driven me toward a different destiny?

Bloom into all your dreams coming true.

There's no way to change the past. I let the idea flitter out of my brain again as I pressed my badge against the sensor and entered the employee parking lot for the last time. I settled back into the heated seat of my five-year-old Honda SUV and watched the gate slide to the right.

Hmph. Appropriate. Been waiting all my life for an open gate.

The gate seemed more rickety, slower than it had ever been. *Why hasn't somebody fixed or upgraded it in all these years?* Surely the technology existed.

Yet I idled as I had done countless times, sitting in this identical spot behind the steering wheel of four different cars over the years. My knee still aching. Waiting for the gate to open. Wondering about the past and the future. What could have been if I hadn't spent the previous thirty years playing it safe with this good government job? What lay ahead of me without it? I hadn't envisioned myself after employment until that very morning. I had put off thinking about my future, fearful that I might find more of what I'd accomplished lay in the past. Nothing significant. Nothing worth filling a book, a diary, or even an interesting conversation.

A burst of heat reminiscent of perimenopause flashed over me. Anxiety wormed through my veins. I couldn't delay this internal conversation any longer. Today was my retirement day. The beginning or the end—or both.

Acknowledgments

First and always, I thank my Abba Father, my Babba, my God for the talent and gift to write. Over these years, You have given me so many stories to tell, so much love to infuse in the characters and plots. I'm grateful to partner with You!

For my family—thanks for checking in on me to ask how things are going and giving me the freedom to step away from all those traditional obligations to fulfill my dream of "writing a book" many times over.

To my writing friends turned personal friends: CaSandra McLaughlin, Rhonda McKnight, Tia McCollors, Pat Simmons, Michelle Lindo-Rice, Vanessa Miller, Vanessa Riley. Thank you all for the encouragement and the prayers that gave me the "umph" to finish this work.

Thank you to my agent, Emily Sylvan Kim, for pushing me back up on the saddle. To the Sourcebooks team—Deb, for challenging me when I needed it and believing I could pull through. Jocelyn, for your marketing genius and always friendly, always open attitude. That means so much!

And to my readers: Thank you so much for walking through life with me for all this time. It's such a pleasure to meet new readers and keep in contact with those who go way back! I appreciate you!

About the Author

Michelle Stimpson has had a distinguished publishing career writing Christian and inspirational contemporary romance fiction. She has won an Emma Award, two Christian Literary awards, and Best Feature Film at Capital City Black Film Festival. She lives in Dallas, Texas.

Visit Michelle online at www.michellestimpson.com.